To the men and women of the

United States Naval Special Warfare

Praise for Ron McManus and The Drone Enigma

"Once I started it, I couldn't put it down.
Most novels are to be tasted,
The Drone Enigma is to be devoured."

—Captain Jack Lieberman, USNR (Ret.)

"Superbly written nail biter...Tied together masterfully...
Great military authenticity...Grabs you and won't let go...
The breathtaking threat of armed drones in the hands
of terrorists brought to reality...What a ride."

—Colonel Stephen D. Cork, USA (Ret.)
Author of the military thriller, *Sir I Can Explain*

"This novel has the plot and enough
real-life technology to place it squarely in
a group with the legends of the genre."

Bob Armfield, Agent (Ret.), Raleigh-Wake CCBI

"A harrowing adventure in the high tech world
of unmanned aircraft. A fast-paced thriller
you simply can't put down."

—Darin Gibby, author of *The Vintage Club*
and *Why Has America Stopped Inventing?*

The Drone Enigma

by Ron McManus

Published by

 Bay Beach Books

Virginia Beach, Virginia

The
DRONE
ENIGMA

Ron McManus

VIRGINIA BEACH

Prologue

SOMETHING HAD CHANGED. Hassan Abdul-Bari Aswad surveyed U.S. forward operating base Camp Hammerbeck, northeastern Afghanistan, through his night vision binoculars, observing the heightened activity his men had reported. The Marines were creatures of discipline and routine—nothing happened without a purpose. Routine, however, spawned predictability. Aswad concentrated his attention on a small group of men who had arrived at the Kunar Province camp the day before. His men said they were replacement soldiers, but he noted they wore different uniforms, body armor, and helmets, and they stayed together rather than fraternize with the Marines. Something else caught his eye. One was smaller and had a different gait. He zoomed in on the subject of his curiosity and watched until the soldier glanced in his direction. A woman.

^ ^ ^ ^

Aswad awoke before sunrise and returned to his observation point. He stood alone and scanned the base through his binoculars as the winter sun rose. With his hands on his hips, he came to terms with what he saw, and smiled. The Americans were gone. After months of fighting, he was the victor. Or was he? Could this be a clever deception to lure them into the open?

Before sending his men into the compound, Aswad positioned observers in the hills. They would alert him if the Americans were waiting there or circling back. Then he sent his team leader, Abdul-Wajid Shadid, and a few men to search for mines and booby traps while he waited outside the perimeter of the base with the others. After almost two hours, Shadid returned. "Our search is complete. We located and disarmed several mines and booby traps. We found a mine in front of the munitions bunker and disarmed it. Allah has rewarded us. Inside is a treasure of ammunition, grenades, and mortar rounds."

Aswad frowned. "Check everything. It's probably a trap."

Booby trapping ammunition was nothing new. During Vietnam, U.S. Special Forces and the CIA replaced the gunpowder in ammunition with high explosives and left it behind for the Viet Cong. Aswad always ordered his men to destroy any they found. This large cache was different; it was one they could not ignore. They needed it for themselves and for the other insurgent groups.

An hour later, Shadid reported they found no traps. "We examined several cases and magazines. The munitions are ours for the taking."

Aswad was silent as he considered Shadid's report. He knew of only one way to ensure the ammunition was safe. "Have Ameer fire a few rounds. Everyone stand clear."

Ameer Antar was fresh from training and eager to prove himself. If someone were to die today, it would be him. Tragic as his death would be, the impact on the team's effectiveness would be less than that of any of his experienced men.

Aswad watched as Ameer, his hands shaking, inserted a magazine into an American rifle. Ameer closed his eyes and took a deep breath, then turned his head away and fired several shots into the air. The sound of the last shot was still echoing off the hillsides when Ameer opened his eyes and twisted his head back and forth, looking at the others as if surprised to be alive. Now smiling, he reloaded and fired again, using magazines selected at random from the bunker.

By midafternoon, the American munitions were on the

way to a large cave in western Pakistan, a central supply and distribution point for operations near the border. News was spreading throughout the region that the Marines had been defeated and the strategic infiltration route to and from Pakistan was once again open.

∧∧∧∧

A few days later, Hassan Aswad and a few of his men squatted on the ground near the opening of a cave in the early evening sun. The ammunition from the American outpost was enough to supply Taliban operations for months to come. Aswad had sent Abdul-Wajid Shadid to deliver the first shipment of ammunition to the insurgent teams operating nearby. The bulk of it, however, was in the small cave. He listened to the men boast about their victory and debate which factor was most paramount in achieving it.

"The isolation of the outpost," said Abdul Zahir, the most senior of the men who remained at the cave.

"Yes, but our sustained attack was more important. We wore down the American cowards. We outlasted them," said Jamal Baz, a fearless fighter who had been wounded twice during the long months of battle against the Marines.

"They retreated like a bunch of old women," said Ameer Antar, the man who had test fired the ammunition from the bunker.

Aswad understood their excitement, although he remained unconvinced by their arguments. Marines do not abandon a position without defeat. The outpost was an integral component of the American strategy to close the routes into and out of Pakistan, yet the final victory was a bloodless gift, contrary to everything he knew about them.

Aswad walked toward the sun, now low in the sky. He would rejoin his men for Maghrib, the Islamic prayer at sunset, but now he needed a moment of solitude to think.

∧∧∧∧

In a secure bunker at Creech Air Force Base, thirty-five miles north of Las Vegas, Nevada, Air Force Major Doug

Shepherd stared at the image on the video display. The image was transmitted from the camera of a land-based MQ-9 Reaper drone circling thousands of feet over eastern Afghanistan, near the Pakistan border. To Shepherd's right, his tech sergeant operated the drone's cameras and sensors. Both men wore flight suits and were settled into what they called their "Naugahyde Barcaloungers." It was Friday, near the end of their sixty-hour week.

The heads-up display, showing the drone's speed, altitude, and other data, overlaid the video image. Four other screens displayed satellite images and data. A digital gauge on the bottom left corner maxed out, indicating the area under surveillance was the source of the homing signal. On the screen, Major Shepherd zoomed in on the small group of men sitting in a circle.

Shepherd went through his firing checklist, including target confirmation by the field team, before taking the final step.

"Request permission to fire, sir. We have visual and electronic confirmation of the target," Shepherd said to Lieutenant Colonel William Byrne, who was standing behind him, watching the screen over his shoulder.

"Granted. Blow them to hell, Major."

"Yes, sir. Three, two, one." Shepherd pushed the button on the drone's throttle and squeezed a gray trigger on the joystick.

The AGM-114 Hellfire air-to-surface missile, guided by the signal, flew at Mach 1.3, approximately nine hundred and fifty miles per hour. Instead of traveling in a straight line from the drone to the cave entrance, the missile zigzagged between the mountain peaks.

^ ^ ^ ^

As the shadows grew longer, the temperature dropped. The color of the earth and sky would soon blend into one. To some, the landscape was rugged, barren, and monotonous. To Hassan Aswad, his homeland was an awe-inspiring sight of which he never tired. A faint buzzing noise, like a wasp, caught Aswad's attention. He looked toward the cave. "Drone!"

The men sprung up and sprinted toward the entrance of the cave. Searching the sky for the unmanned aerial vehicle,

Aswad saw something streaking toward the cave from low in the heavens, as if sent by God. In an instant, he knew what it was, but before he could even process that thought, the missile struck. The explosion shook the earth under his feet before the shock wave from the blast lifted him off the ground and threw him backwards. He covered his head with his arms to protect himself from the rocks that pelted him.

∧∧∧∧

Major Shepherd saw the flash of the explosion on his monitor, as did the others who had gathered around for the test of the Navy's new targeting system. They shouted in unison. A couple of them punched their fists in the air. When the smoke and dust began to clear, he zoomed out for a wider view of the damage. A man was running away from the impact zone.

"We have a squirter, sir," said Shepherd.

"Don't waste a Hellfire on one man. Locate the signals for the other ammunition locations," ordered Lieutenant Colonel Byrne. "I'll be back to give you authorization to fire after I notify Lieutenant Commander Hamilton with Naval Special Warfare. She will be pleased."

Shepherd stretched out his arms and moved his head from side to side, forward and back, trying to relax his stiff neck. He glanced at his watch. In two hours, give or take thirty minutes, he would be home having dinner with his wife and children.

1

JACOB "JAKE" PALMER, investigative consultant, pressed his forehead against the small window of the regional jet as it descended below the cumulus clouds that hung over the Chesapeake Bay. The V-shaped wakes streaming behind the fishing and pleasure boats were the only blemishes on the tranquil water below. His early afternoon flight from Philadelphia was on final approach to Norfolk International Airport. Ahead and to the left of the flight path, he spotted the gray ships of the U.S. Navy docked at the amphibious base. Using them as a reference point, he located an area isolated from the rest of the base by a black iron fence—the Naval Special Warfare facility. Palmer felt a surge of belonging and pride. He envied the men there, members of one of the world's most elite special operations units, all at the peak of their mental and physical capabilities. However, distanced by over a thousand feet and ten years, he was relieved he was no longer an active part of it.

Palmer was on the way to see Wade Cody Jansen, his friend and former Navy SEAL teammate who had saved his life, and in doing so, forever changed his own. Jansen was now the vice president of risk management for Lynnhaven Technology Group, a Virginia Beach-based defense contractor. Over the years, Palmer had lost contact with everyone from his military past except for Jansen. While not his intention, he found that after leaving the service, his priorities had changed. His e-mails and phone conversations with Jansen were neither regular nor frequent, but they made the point that he wanted to stay in touch. The opportunities for Palmer to return to Virginia Beach and visit him had come and gone, each with a seemingly valid reason why it was not convenient. The days became months; the months became years.

The previous week, Palmer had called him to catch up. He thought about their conversation.

"I need a break. I've been running myself ragged," Palmer had said. "I've made four trips to London for legal proceedings related to that case I worked last year. So I killed that murdering scumbag with my bare hands. *Big deal.* The world's better off without him. He was about to rape and kill Fiona."

"You're not charged, are you?" Jansen asked.

"No," Palmer said. "But I witnessed one of the murders his partner in crime committed, the same asshole who shot me in the shoulder. Can you believe that?"

"I'm not impressed. You've been shot before."

"Not by a random bullet from some civilian I was chasing."

Jansen laughed. "The nerve of that guy. Did they convict him?"

"I testified at his trial during my last trip. He was sentenced to life in prison."

"For the murder or for shooting you?"

"I'll never understand why they don't have the death penalty in the U.K."

"I'm not really feeling your pain, Jake. You've been to Afghanistan, Somalia, Iraq, and several other hellholes. London? The Brits make the world's best beer, except maybe for the Germans and Belgians. Something else is bugging you. It's that woman, isn't it? Fiona."

"Maybe."

"Hell yeah, that's it."

"I just need a nice simple case to take my mind off of things, one that doesn't require a lot of energy, thought—or require me to work with a woman," Palmer said, emphasizing the last requirement with a laugh.

"I may have just what you need, if you're interested."

Jansen would say nothing more over the phone, other than the assignment would reconnect him to his past. As the plane's tires screeched on the runway, Palmer reached for his shoulder, rubbing the scar from his recent bullet wound.

He collected his luggage at baggage claim, including a locked metal case the size of a briefcase. Before he closed the trunk of his rental car, he rotated the tumblers on the case's combination lock and opened it, confirming his Sig Sauer 9mm pistol and ammunition were there and undamaged. He couldn't imagine he would need the gun, but he never traveled without it, except for his trips to the U.K., where with few exceptions, handguns were prohibited.

2

DRIVING FROM THE airport to Lynnhaven Technology Group, Palmer felt comfortable and at home. He recalled the good times: fishing with friends on the Chesapeake Bay, crab cakes in the local seafood restaurants, concerts on the beach during the summer, and the songs played over and over on the radio and in clubs, like U2's "Beautiful Day," House of Pain's "Jump Around," REM's "Losing My Religion," and anything by Jimmy Buffett. Some of the songs still evoked memories of his emotional highs and lows. If he had time before he left, he might drive by the small 84th Street cottage near the oceanfront that he had shared with three of his teammates.

Lynnhaven Technology Group, known by most as LTG, was located on a hundred-acre site in a rural area of southeastern Virginia Beach and comprised several modern, characterless buildings with adjoining parking lots. He followed the signs directing visitors to the administrative building, parked, and went inside. A security guard, who doubled as a receptionist, gave him a clip-on visitor's badge and told him to wait in the lobby until Jansen's secretary, Nikki Cusworth, came to escort him.

Palmer was reading a glossy LTG promotional brochure

when Cusworth arrived. She pulled her blond hair back from her face and introduced herself, her eyes discreetly moving up and down as she talked.

"He's so excited," she said on the way to Jansen's office. "He's told me all about you, and his war stories are epic. Well, not actually stories about the war, because he doesn't talk about that. Stories about your off-duty escapades."

"Wade's stories get better with each telling—a kernel of truth to remind you they happened but with enough BS to make you question if you were actually there."

When they arrived at Jansen's office, she motioned for Palmer to enter and then she left, closing the door behind her. Jansen's back was to the door. When it closed, he swiveled his chair and saw Palmer. In a booming voice loud enough to be heard through the office walls, he said, "Son of a bitch! Jake Palmer." Jansen limped toward him from behind his desk.

They shook hands and embraced, pounding each other on the back. Jansen's starched white shirt fit snugly around his chest, and his large belly hung over his belt. Palmer estimated his six-foot-two frame now carried something north of two seventy-five, about fifty pounds more than when he last saw him.

"Nice secretary," Palmer said.

"Nikki keeps me organized. I don't know what I'd do without her. I spend more of my waking hours with her than with Carol," he said, referring to his wife.

"And she's easy on the eyes." Palmer looked around the large office. "Corporate America is treating you well."

"Not bad, is it? Good pay, decent hours, and I sleep in my own bed most nights."

"You're a better man than I," Palmer said. "After I left my corporate job, I spent a couple of months diving in the Caymans, pondering what to do with my life. On one of those dives, the answer became as clear as the water around me. I wasn't cut out for a desk job, and I wasn't going to be happy working for anyone. I had to be my own boss."

"Believe me, I've had plenty of days when I've walked out that door at night with no intention of returning. After dinner with the family and a good night's sleep, I decided, as bad as it is sometimes, opportunities at this pay grade don't come along every day, not for a one-legged man with a big mortgage, a wife, two kids, and a dog." Jansen patted his right leg that had been amputated above the knee and fitted with a prosthesis. "The only easy day was yesterday, right?"

"Damn straight." Palmer paused. It was a conversation he wasn't ready to have. "Tell me about this case. I'm here mostly on blind faith."

Jansen told him that Angela Huntington, a thirty-eight-year-old project engineer, had been working in her lab when she became violently ill with nausea and vomiting. One of her coworkers called the company's emergency number. Within minutes, the first responders arrived and administered basic first aid. They made her as comfortable as possible until the ambulance arrived. She was taken to the hospital, where over the next couple of days her condition worsened. She died three days after being admitted. After the medical examiner concluded she died from a massive dose of the chemical element thallium, the police became involved, suspecting she was poisoned. LTG used the colorless, odorless substance in high-temperature superconducting material research and manufacturing, although Huntington would not have come in contact with it during the normal course of her job.

"What do you want me to do?"

"Work with our occupational health and safety team reviewing the circumstances surrounding her death. They need some hands-on guidance."

Palmer paused a moment. "Do you want me to investigate her death?"

"Only to understand whether LTG is in any way responsible. Is there anything we did that contributed to her death or didn't do to prevent it? For example, were our internal controls for the storage and management of thallium sufficient?"

"Why me? Anyone could babysit some corporate admin types."

"You said you wanted a simple case, and I think you'll find it more interesting than it sounds. With your military and legal experience, combined with your investigative skills, you're ideal. You'd also be our independent liaison with the police."

Jansen told Palmer that the police, suspecting someone at

work poisoned her, obtained warrants and searched Huntington's lab and home, confiscating her work and personal computers and cell phones. Rumors were circulating before she died that she was having an affair with a married senior executive.

"Huntington was working on our contract with the Naval Special Warfare Support Activity Two," Jansen said.

"What are you doing for them?" Palmer asked. Naval Special Warfare Support Activity Two provided intelligence support for Naval Special Warfare Group Two, which included SEAL Teams Two, Four, Eight, and Ten, all based in Virginia Beach. Palmer and Jansen had served on SEAL Team Two.

"Until you accept and sign the confidentiality forms, I can't say. Before you do, there's something I didn't tell you on the phone. I was afraid it would put you off. The project lead for Naval Special Warfare Support Activity Two is Lieutenant Commander Lara Hamilton." Jansen flashed a sly grin.

Palmer crossed his arms as he sifted through his conflicting emotions related to Lara Hamilton's association with the case.

"I can see why you withheld that piece of news." Palmer hadn't seen or heard from Lara Hamilton since they broke up the month before he graduated from the University of North Carolina at Chapel Hill. She was in the Naval Reserve Officer Training Corps, NROTC, and would have been commissioned when she graduated the following year. Of the many women he had known, she was one of the few who warranted more than a passing thought.

"We were introduced at a project team meeting several months ago. Her name rang a bell. You used to talk about her on occasion after you had too much to drink. I asked if she knew you. She said you were friends when you were at UNC. That's all she said, so I let it drop. She's their information operations officer, working with SEAL teams to identify technologic solutions to tactical problems. After a solution is identified, the Navy contracts with private industry to develop it. We're one of those companies. Once developed, Hamilton field-tests the solution with the team."

"Does she know you contacted me to work on this?"

"Of course. I had to tell her about Huntington's death. Her only concern is the impact the death and police investigation will have on the project timeline and upcoming field test. She didn't have a problem with your involvement. Don't worry. You'll work with the internal team and the police, not the Navy. I'll keep her informed about the progress of the investigation."

"It's probably best that way," Palmer said.

"What's it been, about twenty years? Get over it. You know she never married, and you're not getting any younger, my man. The two of you should resolve whatever unfinished business you have, unless that English lass of yours has you on a short leash."

"I'm not settling down anytime soon, if ever. I'm too set in my ways."

"Have it your way. Well, are you going to take the assignment or not?"

"Of course. Why else would I be here?"

Jansen handed him a business card with Virginia Beach Police Lieutenant Mike Hawkins's contact information. "I'll let Hawkins know you're our point man."

Jansen's desk phone rang. "I told Nikki to hold my calls," he said, more to himself than to Palmer.

"I'll step out."

"No need. I'll only be a minute."

While Jansen was on the phone, Palmer got up from his seat and looked at the bookcase behind Jansen's desk. There were numerous photographs and certificates, including his Bronze Star and Purple Heart. On the center shelf of the bookcase was a photograph of Jansen, his wife, and two children, posed in front of the huge King Neptune statue on the Virginia Beach Boardwalk. On the adjacent wall, there was an old paddle with a plaque below it. Palmer thought of his home. If there was any decorating style at all, it was minimalist bachelor pad. His certificates, awards, and photographs, including the few pictures he had of his family, were packed away. He wondered if perhaps he should put some on display. *No. I travel a lot, and they would only collect dust.*

Jansen was still on the phone, his brow furrowed and his lips pressed tightly together. When he hung up, he said, "Sorry to cut this short. I have to go. One of our shit-for-brains employees claims his laptop was stolen. I met with him about it this morning. Now he has a fire under his ass to see me again. Can you join Carol and me for dinner? We've a lot to catch up on."

"I'd love to see her. Sure she wouldn't mind?"

"I'm certain. It'll just be the three of us, nothing formal. The kids are both away this week. They're on summer break and would rather be off with their friends than at home with us. You're staying at the Hilton, right? I'll pick you up at eighteen hundred on my way home. Take this with you." Jansen slid some papers across the desk.

"What is it?"

"Your contract. Look it over and bring it to dinner tonight."

Palmer took a pen from his jacket pocket, signed the document without reading it, and pushed it back across the desk.

Jansen's face lit up. "I'm excited about working together again."

"Just like old times."

Nikki made a copy of the contract and escorted Palmer to the reception desk. He signed out and handed the guard his temporary visitor's badge. Once outside, he felt the warm afternoon sun on his face. Lara Hamilton told Jansen they had been friends at UNC. Maybe after all these years, if he were asked, that's also how he would describe their relationship. He wondered what she looked like today but could only imagine the slender, young college co-ed with a sparkle in her eyes, a wide smile, and a faint smell of perfume on her neck.

3

ALONA GREEN TRIED to relax, reading a book on the tattered, musty-smelling sofa in a house in Conshohocken, just fifteen miles from the center of Philadelphia. The locals called it *Conshy*.

Thunder rumbled and Alona looked up to see the first raindrops of the late afternoon shower splash against the window. In the overgrown yard beyond, weeds crept halfway up the empty birdbath. The long narrow yard received the bare minimum of care, enough to prevent drawing unwanted attention to the house. It was the type of neighborhood where everyone tended to his own business and no one else's.

Across from her, Shaun and Graham—she only knew their first names—were seated in front of two desktop computers with twenty-seven-inch screens on a table that ran the length of the room. A laptop sat between them, connected to both their computers. Only the clicking of the keyboards and the hum of the printer interrupted the silence. The stack of printouts on the table next to the printer was several inches thick.

The men appeared to be in their mid- to late twenties. Their demeanor was one hundred percent geek. Green had been around the type enough to recognize them—skilled computer programmers with introverted personalities who felt more comfortable interacting online or via text message than face-to-face.

Graham had unkempt brown hair, wore faded blue jeans and a T-shirt adorned by the name of some one-hit-wonder heavy metal band. Shaun's long, wiry hair protruded from the Philadelphia Phillies baseball cap that he wore backwards. He had worn the same tattered jeans and dark blue T-shirt for the past two days. Green shook her head ever so slightly. *Doesn't Graham care that he's beginning to smell like a crowded subway car in the summer?*

The two of them worked without interruption, taking breaks only long enough to eat or go to the bathroom. Soon, either Owen Fuller would report his laptop missing, or Lynnhaven Technology Group, the company where he worked, would discover what they were doing and shut down access. Green suspected Shaun and Graham had established a self-imposed time limit with the laptop because of the real possibility of their intrusion being discovered and LTG pinpointing their physical location. Because LTG was a defense contractor, the FBI could become involved.

Green walked to the window and stared out. It was raining harder now, and the wind had picked up.

"Getting restless, blondie?" Graham asked.

"As a matter of fact, yes. I'm going to the hotel and work out."

"Sit down. You're not going anywhere. We're almost finished."

"This is ridiculous," she said. "When am I going to get my final payment? You owe me twenty-five thousand dollars. I was due the money when you accessed their network."

"We're almost done. They denied network access with Fuller's ID and password yesterday, but we were prepared for that. We're shutting it down tonight regardless of whether we're finished or not. Our boss will send the money over then. Better save your receipts. The IRS might audit you." Graham punched Shaun in the shoulder, and they laughed.

"Assholes," Green said, returning to the couch.

She picked up her book and set it in her lap. Although everything had gone according to plan since switching laptops with Fuller, she had an uneasy feeling. *Why didn't they pay me the rest of the money after they confirmed access to the secure LTG network? Why do they want me to stay?*

She was not afraid of Shaun and Graham, but she had three basic rules to which she always adhered: Stay safe, work alone, and trust no one. She knew the house well and its ingress and egress points. When Shaun and Graham were not watching, she had unlocked a window in each room and made sure it was not stuck.

"What the hell is that?" Graham exclaimed, jarring Green from her thoughts.

"None of your or my business. That's what the hell it is," Shaun snapped.

"Look what they're up to. This is insane. We're going to have the feds on us like white on rice."

"What did you expect? LTG's a defense contractor."

Green stood and walked toward them. "What is it?"

"None of your business either." Shaun stepped between her and the screen and pointed toward the couch. "Get away."

She was inches from his face and glared into his eyes before returning to the couch. Shaun and Graham stared at the laptop and whispered excitedly to each other.

Shaun shut down the application on the screen and closed the laptop. "Do not touch this, or you'll not get your money."

They left and went into the room they used for private teleconferences, slamming the door behind them. Green was tempted to open the laptop and search for whatever Graham had seen that distressed him but decided it was not worth the risk of being caught.

A short while later, after she had resumed reading, she thought she heard the front door creak open and shut. The door was always locked; Shaun insisted on it. She closed the book and listened. She could hear Shaun and Graham's muffled voices in the other room and soft footsteps in the entry foyer. She stepped out of her shoes, walked to the doorway, and peeked around the doorjamb. Two men, wet from the rain, were leaning against the wall on each side of the door to the room where Shaun and Graham were working. They had on light jackets and caps pulled down so the bills partially covered their faces. From what she could tell, they both had short black hair and olive skin. One of the men held a pistol by his side.

Screw the final payment. She had thirty-one thousand dollars in her account. Rule number one: Stay safe. Game over. She put on her shoes, grabbed her purse, and stepped quietly to the laptop. She jerked out the power and USB cables and tucked them under her arm. As she was crawling out the window, she heard shouting from the other room, then four gunshots in rapid succession.

Green dropped to the ground and ran to her car in the driveway. A car she had not seen before was parked on the street in front of the house. She was parked behind Shaun and Graham's clunker because she made frequent trips out for food and other necessities. She got into her car and backed to the end of the long driveway, where she waited for an opening in rush hour traffic. *Come on, come on,* she said to herself, urging the cars to hurry so she could get out.

She glanced toward the house. The two men were sprinting toward her. She had a clear view of their faces: Middle Easterners in their early to mid-thirties.

One of the men grabbed the passenger-side door handle and tried to open it. The doors had locked when she put the car in gear.

"Stop!" he shouted, banging on the car door window with his fist.

Green hit the gas and backed into the lane of traffic, almost hitting the side of a car that swerved past her and kept going. She screeched to a halt. Another driver slammed on brakes and skidded sideways on the wet road, stopping a few feet before colliding with her. She heard the driver lay down on the horn. She jammed the gearshift into drive and floored the accelerator. In the rearview mirror, she saw the driver's angry face. He was shouting and flipping her off. The rear tires spun on the pavement before gaining traction. She looked toward the house. The two men were running inside. She sped out of the neighborhood and drove to the Blue Route, I-476, heading for I-95.

Green's hands were shaking. She had escaped almost certain death. She wondered why they had not chased her in their car. *Did they go back to confirm Shaun and Graham were dead?*

Or was it to get the laptop? When they discover the laptop is missing, they'll know I have it. Whatever the reason, they could not catch her. She had too big of a head start.

4

PALMER WAS WAITING outside the Hilton when Wade Jansen pulled up to the entrance in a white SUV. "You're late," Palmer said, tapping the face of his watch. "It's six-o-five."

"Screw you. Your watch is fast."

Palmer laughed and got in.

Jansen used his left foot for both the accelerator and brake. There was neither a Virginia handicap license tag on the front of the vehicle nor a handicap tag hanging from the rearview mirror. *Jansen would never admit a weakness,* Palmer thought as he watched his friend drive.

The four-lane road curved west away from the oceanfront, becoming Shore Drive, a tree-lined, divided road separating First Landing State Park and Joint Expeditionary Base East, known by most as Fort Story. The drive to Jansen's home in an upper-middle-class neighborhood took about twenty minutes.

Carol Jansen met them at the door with a big smile, wiping her hands on a dishtowel. A small white dog ran up to them when they entered the foyer and jumped up and down on Palmer's legs, begging for attention. He reached down and petted the excited ball of white fluff. After talking to Palmer for a few minutes, Carol excused herself and returned to the kitchen. Jansen and Palmer went into the family room, the dog trotting along behind them.

Jansen mixed a couple of gin and tonics at the wet bar and handed Palmer one. When they sat, the dog jumped in the chair and snuggled in beside Jansen, who rested his arm on him and scratched him behind the ears.

"So what's with the frou-frou dog?"

"He's Carol's dog, Snowflake."

"Carol's dog, huh?" Palmer said with a chuckle.

Jansen laughed with him. "After that last mission, I was laid up for quite a while, recovering from the surgery and adjusting to the new leg. This old boy stayed by my side night and day, as if he knew I needed his company."

Palmer looked at the dog and took into account what Jansen had said. He raised his head slowly, his eyes meeting his friend's. "Wish I could have visited. I was deployed for another month after we were medevaced out. When I returned home, I was discharged and went straight off to law school at Duke."

"I don't remember much about that chopper ride. But before whatever was in the medic's needle kicked in, I remember you hollering that I shouldn't have come back for you, that it was your turn to die. In my drug-induced state, I recall thinking, 'His turn? Why didn't someone tell me we were taking turns?' "

"One of us had to hold them off or none of us would have survived. You saved my life. I've never forgotten that, and I never will."

"And I've never regretted coming back for you. Not for one second."

Palmer reached out and clinked glasses with Jansen, then downed the rest of his drink. He held his empty glass up and looked at it.

Jansen glanced at his watch. "Let me check with Carol on dinner and see if we have time for another."

Palmer was glad they'd waited to revisit that day. Relaxing in Jansen's family room, with their hands wrapped around a stiff drink, made it less difficult. Perhaps he should have said more, but what had been communicated between them was greater than the spoken words. Jansen had not allowed his injury to define him. He had a good life, in many ways better than Palmer's.

"Carol says we have time for one or two more. I'll call a taxi to take you back to the hotel, so I won't have to worry about driving. Ready for another?"

"Why not? In the words of Mac McKiernan, 'moderation is vastly overrated.'"

Thomas "Mac" McKiernan was a six-foot-five redhead with the gift of gab. He had joined the SEAL Team Two a year before Jansen and Palmer left the Navy. "The Three Musketeers," as they were soon tagged, quickly bonded.

"He's still with the team," Jansen said, mixing the drinks. Palmer watched him pour a double or maybe a triple; he didn't bother with a jigger.

"I'm not surprised. He was a young man then and had the body and chiseled-face look of a lifer. Before Carol rings the dinner bell, tell me what's on tap for tomorrow."

"First thing in the morning, we'll meet with Cora Donegan, the Human Resources rep on our team reviewing the death. She's a tough nut, the best HR rep I've ever worked with. I consulted with her about that stolen laptop case I mentioned to you this morning. I knew in my gut that bastard was lying. After you left today, I met with him again. He said he hadn't been completely honest before. Now he claims there was a mix-up at airport security."

"What kind of mix-up?" Palmer asked.

"A woman he met on the flight grabbed his laptop by mistake. He said their laptops were identical. When they went through security, she got his and he got hers. He gave me the one that's supposed to be hers. We checked it out this afternoon —clean as a whistle, too clean. Other than the operating system and pre-installed software, there's nothing on it. The only fingerprints we found were his. Whoever has his laptop used his ID and password to access our secure networks. When we disabled access by his ID and password, the hacking continued. It stopped suddenly this afternoon. They must have known we were onto them and would track their location."

"If he met her on a flight, why were they going back through security? What did they do, go to the airport hotel for a quickie between flights?"

"Good question. I'll find out tomorrow. I'm meeting with

him again."

"The crap you must have to deal with. Do the police have any leads on who poisoned Huntington?" Palmer asked, intent on getting the conversation back on track.

"None they told me about, although I believe they're going with the jilted-lover theory. Maybe Hawkins will tell you more than he's told us."

"You said Huntington was working on the LTG project with the Navy. Now that you have my signature on a contract, tell me about the project."

"If you want specifics, ask your former girlfriend, Lieutenant Commander Hamilton. I can only tell you that it involves systems development for UAVs, unmanned aerial vehicles."

Palmer shook his head. "Drones. Ever since a caveman picked up a rock and threw it, men have been searching for better ways to kill each other. Where does it stop?"

"God only knows," Jansen said, shaking his head. "Can you believe we flew three B-2 bombers, worth about two billion dollars each, twelve thousand miles from Whiteman Air Force Base in Missouri to bomb Libya in support of the Libyan rebels? We can't afford to fight wars that way. Drones reduce risk to our soldiers and increase high-value target deaths at a low cost. Think our drones are state of the art now? Wait a few years. You'll see entire air wings of drones launched from a carrier or remote base. Say hello to the future: war without warriors."

"How do you feel about that?" Palmer asked.

Jansen leaned forward and asked rhetorically, "How do I feel about that?"

Palmer answered his own question. "Makes *me* feel obsolete," he said, only half-joking.

"It's no different than dropping bombs from thirty thousand feet or launching missiles from submarines," Jansen responded. "You never emotionally connect with the target. If, through the use of these technologies, we avoid putting American lives at risk, I'm all for it."

"There's no question about it," Palmer agreed. "Drones are a technological leap for which the enemy has no response. The more drones we have in the air providing surveillance and launching missiles, the less of us there are in harm's way. But somehow the thought of fighting wars like a video game from halfway around the globe scares me shitless."

"You sound like one of those tree-hugging, global-warming liberals."

Palmer took another long drink from his glass. "No way. I'm just frustrated. We run al-Qaeda out of Afghanistan, and they set up shop in Iran or Yemen or some other hellhole. At best, we keep them at bay. They are an enemy that doesn't think twice about killing their fellow Muslims, calling them martyrs, like that somehow makes it OK."

"We have to keep up the fight and remain vigilant," said Jansen. "It's like weeding the garden. You can eradicate every weed, but come spring, they're back. But if you stop weeding, the weeds overtake everything. We can't afford to let that happen."

"Our enemy kills far more innocent civilians than soldiers, while in the eyes of the world we are held to a zero tolerance standard for civilian casualties," Palmer said. "They spend almost nothing while we are spending ourselves deeper into recession, fighting a war where ultimate victory is elusive, if at all achievable, and where the long-term solution must include a lasting and costly American military presence."

Jansen cocked his head, his brow furrowed. "Who are you, and where the hell is my friend Jake?"

Palmer took another drink. "Must have been that second drink on an empty stomach, plus the one I had at the bar before you picked me up."

Jansen laughed so hard that Snowflake cocked his head and looked at him before jumping out of the chair and scampering off to the kitchen. Jansen shook his head. "You're turning into a crusty old fart."

Carol came into the room and announced dinner was ready. "Have you men finished rehashing old times, past glories, and politics, so we can talk about more pleasant things while we eat?"

"We've only just started," Jansen said with a belly laugh.

5

ALONA GREEN DROVE south on I-95 for about three hours before exiting near Washington. Traffic, as usual for the Beltway at this hour, was crawling. She used the time to make a telephone call. Her contact needed to know what had happened, not that he would do anything to help her. He told her to stick with it. He would be in touch. *Stick with it? What's that supposed to mean?*

A fear had been growing inside her since she left Conshohocken. Had the men placed a tracking device on her car? She took the next exit and drove into the parking deck of a shopping mall she had seen from the highway. She watched the GPS until the "signal lost" message appeared. The signal from a tracking device, if there was one, would also be lost.

Green parked in a brightly lit space and began her search. She was on her knees with her head underneath the rear of the car when she heard footsteps. She sensed someone stop behind her.

"Can I help you, ma'am?"

She gasped, jerked her head around, and stood up. Her heart raced. The man appeared to be in his seventies. She looked past him without speaking, her eyes darting from side to side, searching for the two Middle Eastern men.

"Car trouble?"

Green took a deep breath and exhaled. "No, thank you. You're kind to ask. I heard a rattling noise. I was looking to see if anything was loose. Everything seems OK."

The old gentleman nodded. "That's good. If you hear it again, you should have it checked out. Sometimes what appears to be nothing turns out to be something serious."

"I will. Thank you."

After he entered the mall, she recommenced her search for a tracking device. She stepped to the front of the car and looked into the driver's side wheel well. There it was in the shadows near the top: a black box about two inches by two inches with a magnet that secured it to the car. She pulled it off and pried opened the box with a nail file she had in her purse. Inside was the GPS tracker. She had seen similar ones before, available on the Internet for a couple hundred dollars. Green examined the device in the palm of her hand and dropped it on the parking deck floor. She stomped on it with the heel of her shoe, ground it into the concrete deck, and kicked the pieces against the wall. If she were being followed, the men would come to the parking deck, where the tracking signal was lost, and look for her car. That would buy her some time.

On her way back to the interstate, she stopped at a fast food restaurant and ordered from the drive-through window. She needed to leave the area in case they spotted her car. She would eat while she drove.

6

"MORNING, JAKE," JANSEN said when Palmer entered his office for their nine o'clock meeting. "Meet Ed Taylor, my associate director of security operations."

Taylor appeared to be in his fifties, with short gray hair and a neatly trimmed goatee. "It's a pleasure to meet you at last. I've heard a lot about you," Taylor said as he gave Palmer a firm handshake.

"Are you working on the Angela Huntington case?" Palmer asked.

"No, thank God. That's all yours." A buzzing sound came from Taylor's cell phone in the pocket of his sports coat. Taylor extracted it and looked at the screen. "Sorry, that's my reminder alarm. I'd better get going, or I'll be late to my meeting." Before he left, he opened the portfolio he was carrying, took out one of his business cards, and handed it to Palmer. "Call me if you need me," he said as he left.

"Ready for Cora?" Cusworth, Jansen's secretary, asked after tapping on the open office door.

Jansen motioned with his hand to show her in. He introduced Cora Donegan to Palmer, giving her a summary of his background and experience, including his previous employment as a regulatory attorney for Blackwell & Anderson

Pharmaceuticals. As they sat, he told her that Palmer was now the lead on Angela Huntington's case and LTG's point of contact with Lieutenant Mike Hawkins of the Virginia Beach Police Department.

"Shouldn't Human Resources or Legal be the primary contact?" Donegan asked.

"We'll be in a better position if someone independent of LTG takes the lead. The boss already approved it."

Donegan nodded without comment.

"The police are treating Angela's death as a possible homicide, and it may be," Jansen continued. "However, we are not conducting a murder investigation. That's their job. Our job is to determine if her death was the result of work-related exposure to thallium and assess the strength of our internal controls on the storage and safe use of the chemical."

Donegan interrupted. "The police said the thallium level in her blood was too high for chronic low-level exposure."

"Educate me," Palmer said. "Didn't you say yesterday that in the normal course of Huntington's work as a project engineer, she would not have been exposed to thallium?"

"That's right. The thallium LTG uses in superconductor manufacturing is a powdery substance, which can be inhaled, ingested, or absorbed through the skin. Day to day, her time was spent in her office, in her lab, and in project meetings, all of which have zero risk of exposure. If she went into an area within the manufacturing facility where she might have been exposed, she would have worn a bunny suit."

"A clean room suit, like those used in sterile manufacturing in the pharmaceutical industry?" Palmer asked.

"Right. Legal wants data confirming that toxic levels can't be achieved by on-the-job exposure. They need documentation of the range of thallium levels in our work environment and a medical opinion that, if detectable, those levels have no adverse clinical implications. Testing has already begun. Of greater importance, our employees demand assurance that they are not at risk. They're understandably nervous about this."

"Can't say I blame them," Palmer replied.

"We also need to be absolutely certain our hazardous materials storage and handling procedures are right and tight.

That includes thallium. Jake, your team will need to review records of any previous hazardous material exposures and all government inspections, as well as internal audits of the process. Go back as far as when we first used thallium."

"I've scheduled a meeting for you this morning with Frank Waxman, our chief compliance officer," Donegan said to Palmer. "After Angela's death, his team audited our compliance with procedures for thallium handling and storage."

"During the course of the internal investigation, we may come across something pertinent to the criminal case. If that happens, what should we do?" Palmer saw the potential for overlap with the police investigation.

"We can't withhold information or evidence from the police, regardless of how trivial it may appear," Jansen said. "If you find something, inform our Legal representative on the team. He's one of our best. Depending on what's found, Legal will either inform the police or ask you to inform them. Bottom line—use your judgment. I'm delegating a lot to you. Make wise decisions."

"Tell me about Huntington," Palmer said. "What was she like? Did she have any run-ins with her co-workers?"

Jansen looked to Donegan to answer.

Donegan said the Ph.D. engineer had been with LTG for about five years. Huntington was concerned her career was floundering and met with her. With Huntington's approval, Donegan obtained some structured feedback from Huntington's managers and peers and reviewed the results with her. On the positive side, she was perceived as intelligent and hardworking. On the negative side, they said she often demonstrated self-serving behavior, putting her own interest over that of the team or project. Some even described her as intrusive and nosy. She fared somewhat better with management than with her peers, who described her as driven to succeed but a little too detailed-oriented, failing to see the big picture. Huntington was visibly upset with the feedback and wanted to know what to do. Donegan suggested some personal and business objectives for her, one of which was to be assigned to a high-profile project where she could prove her worth. A couple of months later, Huntington was designated the lead engineer on the Naval Special Warfare project.

"Owen Fuller is the leader of the NSW project," Jansen said to Palmer. "He's the employee I mentioned, the one who lost his laptop."

"That has nothing to do with Angela Huntington," Donegan snapped at Jansen before Palmer could comment. "That's an internal issue unrelated to our task and Mr. Palmer's assignment."

"Without mentioning any names, I told Jake about it to demonstrate how intelligent people sometimes do stupid things."

Donegan shook her head. "Can we please confine our discussion to Angela's death?"

"Did he or anyone else resent her for worming her way onto the team?"

"I'm not aware of any resentment," Donegan said. "The project team members are under a great deal of pressure. They were glad to get the help; however, they were surprised by her appointment. Office gossip was that she was having an affair with a senior executive, and he exerted his influence to get her the assignment."

"Any hints of an affair in her e-mail correspondence? E-mail and Internet searches are backed up and can be accessed even after the user has deleted them from their PC or laptop."

"The police have confiscated her work and home computers and phones. We've gone through our back-ups of her work e-mails and her phone call history for the past twenty-four months," Donegan said, referring to a document she had brought to the meeting. "That's how long we archive them. We found nothing out of the ordinary."

"I want to talk to Fuller," Palmer said.

"I'll try to arrange it for tomorrow morning, but I need to be present. Fuller was pretty unnerved by the whole interrogation thing about the laptop." Donegan gave Jansen a sideways glare.

"What's the problem?" Jansen said with a shrug of his shoulders. "He wasn't being truthful about what happened to the laptop, so I applied some gentle pressure."

Palmer laughed and looked at Jansen. "I'm sorry. I had this mental image of you interrogating him. Remember that Taliban mullah we captured? Thirty minutes with you, and he wouldn't stop talking."

Jansen laughed. "Poor soul. I finally had to tell him to shut up."

Donegan looked over the top of her glasses at Jansen and Palmer and shook her head.

7

FRANK WAXMAN, LYNNHAVEN Technology Group's compliance officer, was a bald, rotund man in his early fifties, with teeth that were too white. Palmer caught a whiff of stale cigar smoke. He imagined him leaning back in his chair with his feet on his desk after everyone had left, lighting up a cigar for a quick, forbidden smoke in the non-smoking building.

"I understand your team audited LTG's internal controls for the use of thallium in the workplace," Palmer said from his seat opposite Waxman.

"The audit has been completed, and the report is being prepared," Waxman said.

"When will it be issued?"

Waxman nodded his head. "I'm aware of the urgency. I've had senior management and OSHA people crawling up my ass ever since she died. It'll be issued to management when I've signed off on it, not before."

"Can you tell me what the auditors found?" Palmer asked.

"They audited our internal procedures, processes, and records related to the receipt, storage, use, monitoring, and hazardous waste disposal of thallium. On the surface, everything looked good. Employees with any possible risk of exposure had been trained on the safe handling and storage of thallium, as well as how to recognize symptoms of overexposure. Our—"

"They didn't recognize Huntington's."

Waxman leaned forward in his chair. "In their defense, neither did the emergency medical technicians or the doctors," he said, raising his voice. He paused, cleared his throat and composed himself. "Symptoms of acute thallium poisoning develop so fast that even the most knowledgeable employee wouldn't suspect it, least of all Angela, who appeared to be fine one minute and seriously ill the next."

Palmer could tell Waxman, who held a powerful position in the company, did not like being grilled; and like a skillful witness in court, Waxman would not lie and would not volunteer information.

"I can see why Angela Huntington's symptoms were overlooked, not how someone got the thallium to poison her," Palmer said.

"If you'll allow me to continue without interrupting, I'll tell you. Our internal controls, procedures, processes, and training are adequate for mitigation of the risk of chronic exposure to thallium or any of our hazardous chemicals, not for acute toxicity or poisoning."

"Why not?"

"Door and window locks are designed to prevent honest people from getting into a house. The most inept burglar, on the other hand, has no problem breaking in. Likewise, we operate on the premise that our employees want to do the right thing and do their best to comply with our internal policies and procedures. Our procedures are written from the perspective that everyone wants to avoid direct exposure to toxic substances and will comply. If, however, someone is determined to circumvent those controls, there's little that can be done to prevent it. Our controls certainly don't take into account that a whacko might want to administer a lethal dose of thallium to a fellow employee."

"Did your auditors determine how the murderer got it?" Palmer asked.

Waxman's ears were red, and his neck veins were bulging. He paused, took a deep breath, and exhaled slowly before answering. "The auditors verified that a small but lethal quantity of thallium was missing from inventory. To the casual observer, the accountability logs looked fine. However, an auditor discovered someone had altered several entries."

"Will you come to our health and safety team meeting and tell them what you've told me?"

"Wouldn't miss it. Don't forget, everything I've told you is confidential."

"Understood. And don't forget to send me a copy of the audit report. One more thing—did your auditors determine who stole the thallium?"

"No, and it's not possible with absolute certainty to determine whether or not the missing thallium was used to poison Angela Huntington."

"Where else would it have come from?"

"It is not my job to determine the origin of the thallium used to poison Angela."

"Whose job is it?"

"The police," Waxman said, raising his voice.

Palmer thanked him for his time and stood to leave.

"Before you go, let me offer some unsolicited advice. Everyone is on edge about Angela's death. We don't need some cowboy stirring things up any further than they already are."

Palmer grinned at Waxman and said, "Yippie-Kai-Yay."

ON HIS WAY to the Virginia Beach Municipal Center, Palmer phoned Lieutenant Hawkins to confirm their meeting. Hawkins was finishing up at a crime scene near Rudee Inlet at the oceanfront and asked if they could meet at the King Neptune statue on the boardwalk at 31st Street. Hawkins said he would be wearing a tie, and it would be the only description Palmer needed.

The three-mile long Virginia Beach Boardwalk runs between 3rd and 40th Streets. Like most days in the summer, this day it was filled with people wearing some combination of shorts, T-shirts, and bathing suits, and either barefooted or wearing flip-flops or sandals. The one exception was a man, leaning against the railing, wearing long pants, a short-sleeve shirt, and a paisley tie. Hawkins looked as if he had stepped straight out of a seventies television police drama. He had a neatly trimmed mustache, and his salt-and-pepper hair was combed back away from his face.

Palmer introduced himself to Hawkins, and they began walking south, keeping pace with the tourists, who clearly were in no hurry to get anywhere.

"Jansen told me you were SEALs and served together in Afghanistan and Iraq."

"That was a long time ago."

"I had a few run-ins with SEALs when I was a beat cop, usually to break up bar fights."

"Sorry to say, I've been in a few of those. Too young to know better and too drunk to care."

Hawkins smiled at Palmer's self-deprecating comment. "He said you're not an LTG employee. You're a lawyer turned private investigator?"

"That's right. I'm leading LTG's internal health and safety team reviewing Huntington's death and serving as LTG's liaison with the police. The company wanted an outsider for the job—someone independent of corporate politics and pressures. I have a law degree and have practiced law, both private and corporate. I'm not practicing now. I'm an independent investigator."

"Let's get one thing clear up front, Palmer. I'm investigating Huntington's death, plain and simple. That's my job. I don't need or want help from LTG or from you."

"You won't get any. We're evaluating the thallium levels in all rooms and labs where exposure might have occurred, to confirm our compliance with EPA and OSHA exposure limits. We believe LTG's safety procedures and internal controls mitigate the risk of overexposure. LTG needs to assure its employees that they are safe, and we need to provide you with that information for your investigation."

Hawkins stopped walking, loosened his tie, and faced Palmer. "The toxicology results confirmed the thallium levels in her system far exceeded what would be expected with chronic exposure. Do you believe in the normal course of her job, Huntington could have been exposed to enough thallium to poison her? Maybe she screwed up, spilled some on her, inhaled it—or whatever—and somehow received a lethal dose."

"LTG's position is that any job-related exposure would have been minute. She wasn't stupid. If she had spilled some on her or inhaled it, she would have let someone know."

"Do you believe she was murdered?" Hawkins asked.

"That's your call. Murder's a legal and criminal determination. The way I see it, since Huntington died from a lethal dose of thallium, you have three probable scenarios." Palmer counted them off with his fingers. "She committed suicide, a co-worker poisoned her, or someone outside LTG poisoned her. If her death were by her own hand or that of a co-worker, then it's of concern to LTG because their internal controls for handling and storage of thallium may be inadequate. And you can rule out suicide. She had better, faster, and more readily available ways to kill herself than by thallium poisoning, which causes a slow, painful death. People who commit suicide want to die in seconds, not days. And last, if someone outside of work poisoned her, where did the murderer get the thallium?" Based on what he had learned from Frank Waxman, Palmer knew a fellow employee probably poisoned her with the thallium missing from storage. He could not tell Hawkins because the audit report had not been issued to management. After it was, LTG's Legal department would review it and decide what to release to the police.

Hawkins took the pad of paper and pen from his pocket and scribbled some notes. "Mind if we stop and grab a bite?" He pointed to a Dairy Queen on the boardwalk at 17th Street. The top of the exterior of the rounded building, which appeared to have been around since the fifties, was covered with yellow, red, white, and blue tiles in no recognizable pattern. Hawkins ordered a turtle pecan cluster Blizzard, and Palmer ordered an ice cream sandwich. They ate as they walked north, back toward the Neptune statue.

"What type of attorney did you say you are?" Hawkins asked before taking a spoonful of his ice cream.

"I was with a private law firm for a while, practicing corporate law before becoming a regulatory attorney for a pharmaceutical company."

Hawkins told Palmer that the EMTs responded to a 911 call from LTG. The police were not notified because the call for medical assistance was routine: An employee had become ill and required urgent medical care. When Huntington died three days later, the medical examiner sent the police the death certificate, which cited thallium poisoning as the cause of death, and he was assigned to the case. He obtained a warrant to search her home and workplace. During the searches, the police confiscated her personal and work computers and mobile phones. The work computer and mobile phone failed to reveal anything of interest. However, her home computer and cell phone were another story. They found frequent personal e-mails, phone calls, and text communications between her and an LTG executive.

"Who's the exec?"

"You'll know soon enough."

"Was there anything in the communications to indicate a problem had arisen between them? Had there been a falling out?"

"Nothing, just the crap you'd expect to see between a man and a woman having an affair: darling this, honey that, saying what they wanted to do to each other—the kind of stuff married people never say."

Hawkins went on to say that he believed Huntington was murdered; and since it was unlikely that someone outside of LTG could obtain the thallium to kill her, he was working on the assumption that someone at work poisoned her. He had already interviewed some of her co-workers and planned to interview others, including her lover, during the next couple of days. He would be accompanied by a government toxicologist, who would go over anything and everything to do with LTG's use of thallium.

"Is there anyone who expected to benefit from her death?" Palmer asked. "Beneficiaries for her company and personal insurance policies, for example?"

"Huntington was unmarried and lived in a modest townhouse. She took the minimum life insurance policy option with the LTG medical benefit package. I expect there's enough to pay off her debts with a tad left over for funeral expenses."

In Palmer's mind, LTG was clear of any criminal liability, although if a civil suit were filed, LTG would still have to defend itself. Then there would be the question of whether procedures written from the perspective that, as Waxman had said, "employees want to avoid direct exposure to toxic substances" was sufficient or should the procedures have been written so tight as to also prevent an employee from circumventing controls and using thallium to murder someone? That would be an issue for a civil court to decide. Otherwise, Palmer was confident that Hawkins, who seemed competent and focused, would find the person responsible for Huntington's death. This assignment was going to be as easy as this walk along the boardwalk. Just what the doctor ordered. Palmer inhaled a deep breath of the ocean air.

"Lieutenant, I'll let you know if we find anything that would be of interest to you." Palmer handed him his business card. "My cell phone number is on the card. You can also reach me at the Hilton. I don't plan to be here long, a few days this time and then short, periodic trips until everything's wrapped up."

9

WADE JANSEN WAS at his desk when his phone rang.

"Are you the head of security at Lynnhaven Technology Group?"

"Who wants to know?"

"Alona Green. I have a laptop that belongs to one of your employees, Owen Fuller."

Jansen did not want to overreact and scare her off. Like a fish nibbling on the bait, if you try to set the hook too soon, you will lose it. "It's good to hear from you, Ms. Green. He told me he had inadvertently switched laptops with you in airport security. These things happen."

"That's right. I want to return it."

"And we'd like to have it back."

"Let's not play games. I know you're aware the laptop was used to access LTG's secure networks. You're trying to decide whether to call the police or handle it yourself. Think about it. Do you really want to get the authorities involved in your security breach? That would concern the government agencies that have contracts with you. They might question the security of your networks."

"I'm listening."

"I'll return the laptop and talk to you about what I think they were up to."

"They?"

"There are ... were others. Another option is for me to hang up and destroy the laptop or perhaps turn it over to the Navy along with an ID and password."

Jansen considered her offer. Even though the ID and password she had were now invalid, if she reported the incident, the Navy would initiate a thorough investigation. Things would get complicated.

"Fuller gave me your laptop. I have it here in my office." Jansen looked over his shoulder at Green's laptop on the bookcase behind his desk.

"You keep it. It's of no use to me. Besides, it was clean when the laptops were switched. I can't be sure it still is."

This woman was smart. LTG security techs had entered hidden codes and software that would have allowed them to track the laptop and access its data if it were returned to her. "I'm curious. Why didn't you call Fuller?"

"We had a little too much to drink on the plane and at dinner. He was coming on pretty strong. I guess I encouraged it by my behavior. In the light of day, I knew I had acted foolishly. Tell him I'm sorry."

Sorry my ass, Jansen thought. *Fuller was only a means to an end, accessing our secure data and information.*

"You make some valid points about how the authorities and our customers might perceive this. I'm willing to hear you out. Where are you?"

"I'm in Virginia Beach. I have to see you tonight."

Jansen was not sure with whom he was dealing or whether she was still working with others. He decided it would be safer to meet her at LTG, if she would agree. *Why did she want to see me tonight? What's the urgency?* "I usually work until six or seven o'clock. By then, most everyone's cleared out. Could you be here by six-thirty?"

"I'll see you then."

Jansen gave her directions to the company and told her he would inform the security guard at the desk that she was coming. He leaned back in his chair. He wanted to ask her more, but did not dare, not now. If he asked too many questions, she might not show. He would do that after he had Fuller's laptop—after he found out what really happened.

^^^^

On the way to his hotel room, Palmer called Jansen and briefed him on his meeting with Hawkins.

"That's more than he's told us," Jansen said. "Did he name Huntington's lover?"

"No, but whoever it is, I have a feeling Hawkins will be paying him a visit in the next day or two."

"I'll notify Cora. I'd love to be a party to that conversation."

"If you don't mind, I'll see you tomorrow. It's a beautiful day. I'm going for a run on the boardwalk."

"I'm afraid I'm stuck here for a while. I have a meeting this evening with Alona Green, the woman who has Owen Fuller's laptop."

"You found her," Palmer exclaimed.

"No. She found me."

10

BACK IN HIS room after his run, Palmer pulled off his sweat-soaked T-shirt and grabbed a towel from the bathroom and a bottle of water from the mini-bar. He opened the door to the balcony and was stepping outside when his phone rang. He gulped down some cold water and glanced at the screen—Patrick, his brother. He stared at the phone. They rarely saw each other and talked on the phone only when one or the other needed something or had something important to share. Palmer's bar of "important" was set much higher than his brother's. Even when he was shot in London, Palmer did not call his brother or his father. One more ring and the call would go into voicemail. He touched the screen and held the phone to his ear.

"What's up, Patrick?" Palmer asked, stepping on the balcony and wiping the sweat from his face with the towel.

"Are you sitting down?"

Palmer had little tolerance for family melodrama. "No, I'm not."

"You'd better find a chair."

"Patrick, I'm busy. Tell me why you called, or call me tonight when I'm not working."

"You really need to relax, bro."

"I am relaxed. What's up?"

"Dad is getting married."

Their father had raised Jake and Patrick after their mother and their pastor were discovered having an affair. The couple eventually moved to Florida, where they were married. To cope with the situation, their father threw himself into his job, working night and day. After Jake went to college, he and his brother, who was the older child and much closer to his father, grew apart. His brother worked for his father in the financial sector in New York. Every time the three of them got together, they tried to tempt Jake into joining the family business with the promise of making gobs of money. He always refused. Both thought Jake was wasting his life when he was in the military. They supported his decision to go to law school after leaving the Navy; but later, when he quit his job as a pharmaceutical regulatory attorney to become an investigative consultant, they told him he was making a huge mistake.

Palmer heard muffled voices and the rustling of paper. *Patrick must be in an office.*

"Really? Who's the lucky woman?" Palmer asked.

"Um," Patrick said, collecting his thoughts. "Michelle Petrochelli. You met her last Christmas when you were here."

"How could I forget? She's half his age." Palmer had gotten the distinct impression she was coming on to him. When, as a test, he told her he was between jobs and recovering from a gunshot wound, she quickly lost interest.

"I know—and young enough to be our sister," Patrick said.

"Younger sister."

"She's signing a prenup."

"How romantic. I wish them well. Why didn't he call me?"

"He said it would be better if you heard if from me and got used to the idea before he talked to you."

"Getting used to the idea might take awhile."

"He'll call you in the next couple of days."

"Have they set a date?"

"They want to get married as soon as possible. But it's going to be one of the year's biggest social events, so they'll need at least six months to plan and prepare. I'm guessing it'll be a Christmas wedding."

"A church wedding?"

"That's a sore subject with Dad. He hasn't been to church since ... well, you know."

"Thanks for the heads-up, Patrick. I promise I'll be appropriately excited when he calls. Does Mom know?"

Patrick did not answer, and again there were muffled voices. "I've got another call, Jake. Take care of yourself. Where are you, by the way?"

"Virginia Beach."

"That's nice. Talk to you soon."

Palmer took the phone from his ear and shook his head. His brother was at work and distracted. The call to him was just an item to be checked off his list today. Call Jake—Done. Next item: Screw someone out of his or her life savings.

He could see it now, a Christmas wedding with all the over-the-top dinners and parties with business associates and clients being the bulk of the guest list. His father would write the entire event off as a business expense. Could he tolerate three or four days of it? Maybe he would invite Fiona Collins, the woman in London he had been seeing, to be his plus one. He had told Jansen she was driving him crazy; and that was true, but only because their relationship was suffering, the result of the three thousand miles of ocean that separated them and the demands of their careers. If he were honest with himself, he felt closer to her than he ever had to anyone. The idea of spending a few days with Fiona in New York at Christmastime began to lift his spirits. Being with her would get him through the ordeal of his father's wedding.

11

HASSAN ASWAD WALKED through the tribal village north of Peshawar in northwest Pakistan, where he had been for six months. He was not concerned about being seen. They knew him only as a Taliban fighter who had been injured in a drone attack. The people of the small village supported the insurgency; and of greater importance, they feared the Taliban. In the tribal areas along Pakistan's border with Afghanistan, fear trumped Pakistani and American military compassion or influence.

That day, after the dust from the missile strike had cleared, Aswad had limped back to the cave and searched the area where, only moments before, his men had been laughing and rejoicing. Except for a few smoldering body parts, nothing remained of Zahir, Baz, Antar, and the others. He dropped to his knees and prayed, tears running down his cheeks through the dirt on his face onto his beard. Allah had guided him away from the others and spared him for a purpose. He prayed that Allah would make that purpose known to him.

Aswad had made his way to the tribal village where he recovered from his injuries. He had a broken collarbone, fractured left arm, multiple cuts and bruises, and a persistent ringing in his ears. He did nothing to refute reports that he had been killed in the attack, preferring to remain anonymous to everyone except to his second-in-command, Abdul-Wajid Shadid, and a handful of senior Taliban leaders, with whom Shadid communicated on his behalf. Shadid had been traveling between Taliban outposts at the time of the drone attacks and had narrowly missed death himself. Shadid had searched for him for weeks before finding him in the village.

During his recuperation in the weeks after he arrived at the village, and before Shadid found him, Aswad slipped into depression. His dreams of chasing the Americans from Afghanistan, as his mujahedeen father had done with the Soviets in the late seventies and eighties, seemed more distant than ever. He blamed himself for taking the ammunition from the abandoned U.S. Marine forward operating base. All his instincts told him to destroy it. Initially, he thought the subsequent attack was only on his team at the cave, but when he learned that drone-launched missiles killed other groups that had been sent ammunition from the base, he was convinced the ammunition contained some new form of tracking device that enabled the drone to lock onto their positions.

After Shadid arrived, he argued that he, not Aswad, was responsible for their deaths, pointing out that he was the one who convinced Aswad to take the ammunition instead of destroying it. Shadid challenged him to strike back at the Americans and recommended all-out attacks across Afghanistan, similar to those of the Viet Cong in the Tet Offensive against the Americans in 1968.

Aswad had dismissed Shadid's plan as impossible to coordinate across the diverse insurgent forces and impractical because of the drones that monitored movements of large numbers and struck without warning. The debate, however, motivated Aswad to think through other possibilities and arrive at his own plan to strike at the Americans in an attack so novel it would be totally unexpected, its impact equivalent to or greater than the attack on the World Trade Center. The fundamentals of the attack had germinated in the back of his mind years earlier, waiting for the precise time when all the elements necessary to pull it off were in place. Because of the improbability of that happening, he had almost forgotten about it. Now that conditions were favorable, he became singularly focused on developing and planning the complex steps required. He bounced ideas off Shadid, who took responsibility for communicating with other parties without divulging who was leading the mission.

By late spring, the pieces were in place, the timing was right, and the few people needed to implement the plan were available and on board. Aswad was a new man, healed from his injuries, inspired by his attack plan, motivated to move forward. The precise date of the attack was not yet set. It depended on factors out of their control; however, based on intelligence information from within the al-Qaeda and Taliban organizations, the window of opportunity would arise sometime during the summer.

Shadid, who had been away for two weeks, was beaming from ear to ear when he walked into Aswad's small, sparsely furnished room and told him of the news regarding the final preparations. The date had been agreed upon, and the men would arrive tomorrow. Shadid had spent time with them during their training.

"This is great news indeed," Aswad said. "None too soon, I might add. While you were away, there have been three more drone attacks in North Waziristan. Our causalities are mounting. We were wise to locate here. The vast majority of the CIA's drone attacks still occur in North and South Waziristan. Still, we must be cautious."

"Holding up here has not been pleasurable, but at least we can be confident that no one in the village is an American sympathizer."

Aswad paced the room. "The time to prepare has past, and the countdown to our attack has begun. At last, it is time for me to come out of hiding."

12

PALMER SAT AT one of the outdoor tables at the Hilton near the boardwalk where he could see the ocean and watch the people walking, biking, and running. The sun was low in the western sky, and the shadows of the hotels were stretching toward the pounding Atlantic surf. The evening sea breeze made for a pleasant night to eat outside. He ordered a bottle of Red Rock Merlot with his meal. The waiter returned with the bottle cradled in his hands like a nurse showing a mother her newborn baby. He rotated the bottle until the label was on top. Palmer nodded, affirming it was the one he had ordered. The waiter opened the bottle and poured a small amount in the glass for him to taste.

"I'm sure it's fine. Just pour."

The waiter stood up straight, apparently taken aback by Palmer's casual attitude toward the tasting ritual. He poured a few ounces into the large glass. "Excellent choice. This is one of my favorites. Give it a few minutes. The black cherry, plum, and earthy wood tones will burst from the glass."

"I'm not that patient." Palmer looked at the waiter and gulped down about a third of what he had poured.

The waiter set the bottle on the table and walked away.

By the time Palmer finished his entrée and pushed the clean

plate to the side, the sun had set. On the boardwalk, casually dressed people walked off their dinner; on the beach, people strolled barefoot at the water's edge. Near the horizon, he spotted the dim outline of a cargo ship on a course to some distant port. He poured the last of the Merlot into his glass. Maybe it was the setting or effect of the wine, but he felt good about the assignment and his return to the area where he had spent a good portion of his life. Most of all, he felt good about reconnecting with Wade Jansen. Maybe Thomas Wolfe was wrong: You *can* return home. He was about to take a sip of wine when his phone vibrated on the table.

"Jake, is Wade with you?" It was Carol Jansen.

"No. I saw him this morning at the office and talked to him midafternoon. He said he was going to work late."

"It's nine o'clock, and he hasn't come home. I've tried his office and his cell phone. He's not answering. I called Nikki, his secretary, at home. She said he was there when she left at six o'clock. She gave me your number and said he might be with you."

"Maybe he stopped somewhere for a beer."

"If he did, he would have called to let me know. He always does."

It was probably nothing, but Carol seemed frantic with worry. "How about I go to LTG and check."

"I don't want to put you to any trouble."

"No trouble at all. I'll phone you after I get there. If he turns up before I call you, let me know."

Palmer caught a taxi at the hotel entrance. On the way, he called Jansen's cell phone—no answer. When he arrived at LTG, the uniformed night guard, who looked to be well past retirement age—at least seventy by Jake's estimate—asked what he wanted. Jake told him about Carol Jansen's call.

"I've been here since four o'clock. I haven't seen him leave. He had a visitor earlier in the evening. I signed her in."

The woman with the laptop. What was her name? Alona Green.

"I'll call his office." The guard dialed Jansen's office number. "No answer."

"Let's go see," Palmer said.

"If he's there, he would have answered."

"He may have had a heart attack. I'm going with or without you." Palmer walked toward the elevator.

"Wait, you can't go—"

"Watch me."

The guard rushed to the elevator and stepped in after Jake. When they got to Jansen's office, his door was closed. The guard turned the handle.

"See? It's locked. He's not here. Senior managers are required to secure their paperwork—we have a clean desk policy—and lock their doors when they leave. Wherever he is, he's not here."

"Open it," Palmer demanded.

"No. It's a secure space."

"Open the door now, or I'm going to break it down."

"All right, all right. You'll have to wait outside while I check."

The guard fumbled with his keys, trying three or four before he found the right one. He unlocked the door and opened it enough to peer inside from where he stood. Palmer shoved by him into the dark office. He immediately sensed the ironlike smell of blood. He stepped further into the office, lit by only the dim ambient light from the windows and open door.

Palmer stood, unable to move. Carol Jansen's fears were justified.

13

"NO. PLEASE, GOD. No," Palmer said. Wade Jansen was slumped back in his chair with his arms hanging down on each side.

The guard took one step into the office and turned on the lights.

Without touching him, Palmer moved closer and saw that Jansen had been shot twice, once in the forehead and once in the center of the chest. The first was a kill shot, and the second was absolute confirmation there would be no miracle recovery. He was shot at his desk without any sign of a struggle. *Maybe Green surprised him, or maybe it was someone else, someone he knew. Who could have done this? How? Why?*

He walked around the desk, careful not to step in the pool of blood. The guard stayed near the door and called 911. Although Palmer was certain Jansen was dead, he felt his neck for a pulse. His skin was still warm. His heart sank, and a wave of nausea swept over him. He recalled that day in the Shahi-Kot Valley in eastern Afghanistan. Their mission had been to root out Taliban and al-Qaeda fighters believed to be wintering in the valley in advance of a spring offensive. During the course of their reconnaissance, the team was attacked. Exposed and outnumbered, if air support didn't arrive soon, they wouldn't survive the next few minutes. One option remained. Fall back. Buy some time. Hope for the best.

Palmer had provided covering fire while the team pulled back. He was reloading in preparation for his withdrawal when, in the blink of an eye, they had charged his position. He would fight to the last shot, but he would die, allowing his teammates to live. Before he could slam the magazine in his rifle, he heard the shots. Three of the insurgents fell. Wade Jansen had returned for him. Palmer, his rifle reloaded, fired, and two more went down.

He and Jansen backed out of that valley of death that day. Palmer was wounded in the side, a clean in-and-out wound, and kept fighting. One hundred yards from the fallback position, Jansen was hit in the right leg and went down. A high velocity round had shattered his knee. The lower part of his leg dangled from the rest, attached only by what little ligaments, muscle, and tissue remained. With their teammates providing covering fire, Palmer dragged Jansen the remainder of the way. The Taliban were within minutes of overrunning their position when Palmer heard the unmistakable sound of U-60 Black Hawk helicopters. The Taliban heard it too and fled. The helicopters saturated the area with a relentless barrage of gunfire. The few Taliban who weren't killed vanished into the mountains.

The helicopters lifted off with the SEAL team aboard and banked away from the gunfire coming from the mountainside. He and Jansen were on the medevac helicopter that flew in with the Black Hawks. The medics attended to Jansen first. Palmer's wound was less serious and could wait until Jansen was stabilized. He remembered, as if it were yesterday, looking at the worthless piece of sand and rock below them. He placed his rifle in his lap and held out his hands, palms up. They were steady, not a hint of a shake or tremor. He felt the pulse in his wrist and counted—sixty-five beats per minute, a few beats faster than his resting heart rate. He knew the time had come. If he did not leave, he would become someone he neither recognized nor wanted to be.

He had been good at what he did and was addicted to the adrenaline rush of a mission. Leaving the life he loved would be hard, but the killing had become too easy, too rote. Also, the short rotations home and back, with insufficient time between them to adjust to either place, had become increasingly difficult. Like a businessman who awakes in a hotel and has to take a moment to remember what city he is in, one mission had begun to meld into another; and more than once, Palmer had to remind himself whom he was fighting and for what purpose.

"The ambulance and police are on the way," the security guard said, jarring Palmer back to the present.

"Stay back," Palmer said. "We don't want to contaminate the scene any further than we already have."

Palmer looked at Jansen's desk. The flat-screen monitor for his computer was on the corner of the desk. The only other items on the desk were a desk lamp, telephone, pen, and a laptop in the center. He recalled seeing the laptop, or one like it, on the bookshelf. Jake knelt down and looked at the floor under the desk and around the chair. A small notepad lay on the floor beneath Jansen's right arm, as if it had fallen out of his hand when he had been shot. He picked it up and examined it. Printed at the top were "Lynnhaven Technology Group" and the company logo. Under that was Jansen's name and title. Palmer held the notepad by the edges and read the handwritten notations scribbled on the top page: *Alona Green—Pawn or Queen? Owen Fuller Shaun and Graham? Spooky.*

But it was the last notation that made him take notice. *Big problem. Call Jake.*

The guard had stepped into the hallway and was talking on the phone. Palmer slipped the notepad into his pocket.

The guard came back into the office. "I notified Ed Taylor, security operations second-in-command," the guard said, his voice trembling slightly. "He's on his way. I also called another security guard to cover the front desk."

"You OK, ol' timer?"

"I guess."

Palmer heard sirens. "Go to the entrance and bring them up. Before they get here, I need to phone his wife."

The guard nodded and left to meet the paramedics. Palmer called Carol Jansen and told her Wade had been shot and was dead. Palmer let her absorb the news. He heard her begin to cry. He felt awful about not telling her in person, but he didn't know how long he would be tied up with the police. Once she gathered herself, Carol told him it was news she always expected to receive when Wade was a SEAL, not now. After she called him, she feared the worst and asked one of her neighbors to sit with her while she waited for him to call back. She then sobbed uncontrollably. He could hear another woman's voice—the neighbor trying to comfort her. After Carol regained her composure, she said she would ask the neighbor to drive her to LTG to see Wade. Palmer advised against it, saying she wouldn't want to remember him like this. He would come by later, regardless of how late it was. He owed her that much.

Palmer looked at Wade Jansen and placed his hand on his shoulder. "I will find whoever did this and bring them to justice—my form of justice."

14

THE AMBULANCE ARRIVED, followed a few minutes later by two policemen, who were patrolling near the LTG site. The paramedics completed the required assessment procedure. Someone from the medical examiner's office would make the official pronouncement of death. The guard phoned another security guard, who stayed at the entrance to direct law enforcement officers to the scene and to keep out unauthorized personnel, including the press. The police secured the crime scene and made the security guard and Palmer move to the hallway. When the crime scene investigators and other law enforcement officers turned up, Palmer and the guard were moved to a conference room a few doors from Jansen's office. A policeman stayed with them.

Almost an hour after Palmer and the guard discovered Jansen's body, Lieutenant Hawkins walked into the conference room. He was in casual clothes and looked as if he had been at home relaxing when he got the call about the shooting. Palmer and the guard were seated at the table. Hawkins, without shaking Palmer's hand, introduced himself to the guard before sitting across the table from them.

Palmer told Hawkins about the phone call from Carol Jansen and finding Jansen's body. He said after he and Hawkins met at the boardwalk, he called Jansen to update him on their meeting and tell him he was headed to the hotel. Jansen told him he would be working late. He had a meeting with a woman who had inadvertently switched laptops with one of their employees when the two of them went through airport security.

"What was her name?" Hawkins asked, looking up from his notepad.

"I believe it was Green—Alona Green. She would have signed the visitor logbook when she arrived and left the building," Palmer said.

Hawkins glared at the security guard, who seemed to be nodding off. "Do you have anything to say? Did this Alona Green check in with you when she arrived?"

The guard opened his eyes wide and sat up straight in the chair. "She signed in, and I called Jansen. He came and got her. The logbook's at the front desk," the guard said.

Hawkins ordered the policeman who was standing by the conference room door to go to the front entrance and bring the logbook. The policeman left, closing the door behind him. Hawkins took a moment before he turned to the security guard.

"Do you remember what she looked like?"

The old man leaned back in his chair. A smile spread across his face. "She was real pretty. I remember she had long blond hair." The guard hesitated. "And a short skirt. She had a beautiful smile and a sweet voice."

As distraught as Jake was about Jansen's death, Palmer had to bite his lip to keep a straight face.

"That's kinda hard to put on an APB. Do you have security cameras in the building?"

"We have a security camera at the main entrance to the building and at the loading dock in the rear of the building."

"Is there access to the building other than through those entrances?"

"Yes, but those doors are only used by employees."

Hawkins looked up from his notepad. "Do they require an ID badge to enter and exit?"

"No, only to enter. We were going to implement a badge-activated entry and exit system, but Human Resources said that it was intrusive. The employees suspected management would use it to track their comings and goings."

"I'll need to see all the security video for today. What else do you know about this woman, Palmer?"

"Only what I told you. Her laptop was switched with an employee's when they went through screening at an airport. She was coming here to return the laptop and, I assume, get hers back. I remember seeing a laptop on Wade's bookshelf when I was with him yesterday. I was in his office again this morning, but couldn't say whether it was there or not. Wade said the employee initially reported it had been stolen, then changed his story."

"What's the employee's name?"

"Cora Donegan in Human Resources can fill you in on the laptop switch. I really don't know much about it." He had already said too much. Donegan could tell Hawkins the rest. Fuller might know how to find Alona Green, if that was her real name. The police would follow the same leads, but they had procedures and red tape. He could operate unencumbered by search warrants, subpoenas, and Miranda warnings. He needed to talk to Donegan and to Fuller before Hawkins did.

"I'll talk to Donegan tomorrow. Is the laptop on Jansen's desk the same one you saw earlier?"

"The one I saw before was the same color and approximate size as the one on his desk. I couldn't swear it was the same one."

Turning back to the guard, Hawkins asked, "Was Alona Green carrying a laptop when she arrived? Did Jansen bring her down after they finished meeting?"

"She had some sort of computer bag, as I recall. I didn't see her leave."

"So she's either still here, or she left when you were away from the desk. Which is it?"

"I can't say. After she arrived, I waited awhile, 'cause I wanted to see her again. But after about forty-five minutes, I decided to walk around, to check on things, you know. She could have left then."

Hawkins shook his head. "How long were you away from the desk on your walkabout?"

The guard put his hand to his face and bit at his thumbnail. "Can't really say. Maybe thirty minutes. I also went to the head to take a leak. Seems I can't go for more than an hour or so without having to piss. It's that dang diuretic my doctor has me on. My wife says I piss out more than I drink in."

The door to the conference room opened. The policeman had returned with the logbook. Hawkins took the book from him and flipped through the pages until he came to the last ones where there were entries. There were five columns on each page: Visitor Name, Party Being Visited, Arrival, Departure, and Comments. He ran his finger down the pages until he reached the last entry.

"Alona Green arrived at six-thirty-five p.m. to see Wade Jansen. There's no departure time."

The guard shrugged his shoulders.

"Could she still be in the building?"

The guard shrugged again.

This time the policeman did not wait to be told what to do. "We'll search the building, sir."

An hour passed before the policeman returned. It was eleven o'clock. Ed Taylor, Jansen's associate director of security operations, was with him.

"Except for some maintenance workers, the building is empty," said the policeman.

"Who are you?" Hawkins asked Taylor.

Taylor introduced himself to Hawkins. "I just arrived. I've been briefed on Jansen's death," said Taylor. "What can we do to help?"

"Do you know anything about this missing laptop? Jansen's last known contact was Alona Green, a woman Palmer says was returning an employee's laptop that was switched with hers at the airport recently. She logged in but didn't sign out, and your security guard didn't see her leave," Hawkins said, motioning with his thumb in the direction of the guard.

"Wade was handling the laptop situation himself. He mentioned it in passing, but didn't tell me the name of the employee involved or any of the details."

"Palmer says he remembered seeing a laptop on the bookshelf behind Jansen's desk, but can't say whether it is the same one that's on his desk. He suggested I talk to Cora Donegan in Human Resources. I'll be back tomorrow morning. I'd like to see her along with the employee who had the laptop switched."

"I'll schedule it. Just let me know when you'll be here. I'll also have our folks check out the laptop to see if it's one of ours, if you like."

"I may ask you to do that later, after we check it for fingerprints and have our tech team examine it." Hawkins glanced at his wristwatch. "It's getting late. I probably won't get out of here until after midnight. Schedule it for midmorning."

Hawkins told Palmer and the guard they could leave.

Before Palmer left the conference room, he stopped and spoke to Taylor. "With Wade dead, I assume you're acting head of security. I want to be involved in this investigation."

"You're too personally connected to be objective."

"Let me put it another way. I'm going to be involved with or without LTG's sanction. Add it to my existing contract. No extra charge. I'll be the point for Huntington and Wade's deaths, and Hawkins will have only one contact."

"I'm not sure," Taylor said.

"Unless you have a problem with it, that'll simplify my communication with LTG," Hawkins responded, overhearing them.

Taylor was reluctant, but said he would clear it with Legal and the CEO. If they approved it, Palmer would report to him.

15

PALMER TOOK A taxi to Jansen's home and told the driver to wait for him. Carol had called her children, who were on summer break and out of town. They were on their way home. She asked what had happened. Who shot him? Palmer told her that little was known and that the police were investigating.

"Why would anyone do this? I don't understand," Carol Jansen said, wiping tears. "Why?"

"I don't know, but I promise you, I'll find out. Is there anyone who would want to harm him? Had he argued with anyone?"

"No. Everyone liked Wade. He could be tough when the situation required it, but he was a good man. He never talked about work. That began when he joined the SEAL team, and I knew better than to ask. When he came home from those missions, he was distant and short-tempered. After a few weeks, he would return to his old self. Then he would leave for another mission, often with little or no notice. How did you men do it?"

"We did what we had to do. Wade was one of the best. He saved my life, Carol. I wouldn't be here today if he hadn't come back for me. I'm going to find his killer if it's the last thing I ever do. That I swear to you."

Palmer stayed with Carol a bit longer to comfort her. He too needed someone to comfort him, someone who understood the pain he felt and the emptiness in his heart. His girlfriend, Fiona, was the only person who came to mind. She had lost her parents in a car crash. She would know what to say to him and what not to say. More importantly, she would listen to him. He should have visited Wade sooner and maintained a closer relationship. Wade had wanted that more than he did. Phone calls and e-mails were not the same. He thought about the excuses he made when Wade invited him to visit, the things that, at the time, seemed much more important. There was law school, the law firm, the position at B&A Pharmaceuticals, and starting his healthcare investigations business.

When Palmer got to the hotel, it was one in the morning. Sleep came in sporadic intervals of ten or fifteen minutes. At six, he surrendered to his insomnia and got up. He drank coffee from the in-room coffee maker and watched the news. There was a report of a shooting death at Lynnhaven Technology Group, during which the reporter said the name of the victim was being withheld until the next of kin were notified. Palmer finished his coffee, showered, and dressed.

A front had moved in overnight. He ate breakfast by the window in the hotel restaurant, watching sheets of rain sweep over the rough Atlantic water. The weather matched his mood—somber and gray.

16

THE MEN ENTERED the house in the tribal village north of Peshawar in northwest Pakistan at random times during the morning. Hassan Aswad was the last to arrive. A group of elderly men standing near the house nodded to him as he passed by them and walked in.

Aswad looked at the twenty men seated in a circle on the floor of the twelve-by-twelve-foot room. Most continued to talk among themselves when he entered. His second-in-command, Abdul-Wajid Shadid, had warned him that the group was a mix of experienced men and new recruits who had completed the training program but were untested in battle. And while the new men were capable, they did not know Aswad and had little respect for him or the chain of command.

"Quiet!" Shadid said.

"My name is Hassan Abdul-Bari Aswad. In the next few days, we will execute one of the most important missions Islam has ever undertaken." As Aswad spoke, he turned his head and looked each man in the eyes before going to the next. He wanted to make a connection with each man when he spoke. "This mission, if successful, will draw the attention of the world. It will be more memorable than the 9/11 attacks on American soil by our al-Qaeda brothers. Have no doubt, we *will* succeed. Regardless of the strength or numbers of our enemy, we will prevail. To fail is to bring shame and disgrace upon Islam and upon yourself and your families."

"We are honored that Allah has blessed us with this opportunity. Can you tell the men about it?" Shadid asked.

"I can tell you what your roles will be. As for the mission, I will not risk our objective being compromised by a leak. Even now, there is a traitor among us, one who spies for the Americans and their Pakistani brothers."

The men looked at Aswad and then at each other. They began to whisper among themselves.

Aswad stood and walked behind the men, watching Shadid as he went around the circle. When he stepped behind one of the younger men, Shadid nodded. Aswad put his hand on the man's head.

"Hanif, it is you."

Hanif, who appeared to be in his early twenties, turned his head around and saw Aswad.

No one spoke on his behalf, even his friends who knew and trusted him.

Hanif stood, pleading his case. "No! I am not a traitor. I am here to serve Allah and to serve you. What have I done?"

"Seize him," Aswad shouted to Fariq Najjar, a veteran of several missions with Aswad.

Najjar grabbed the young man and held him. Aware of what was likely to happen, the man screamed his innocence. Aswad stepped behind a panel that was against the wall and came out with a scimitar, a curved sword.

"Hold him down on the table," Aswad said calmly.

Hanif was jerking and pulling to escape. Shadid joined Najjar, standing on the opposite side of the table, and pressed Hanif's arms and shoulders down so that his head was near the center. Grasping the scimitar with both hands and extending it out in front of him, Aswad calmly rested the blade of the scimitar on the back of Hanif's neck before he slowly raised it above his head. Hanif kicked his feet and cried for mercy. The other men were on their feet, in shock at what they were witnessing.

Aswad stepped back, planted his feet, and swung. Instead of coming down onto Hanif's neck, he swung the scimitar toward Najjar, who was looking at the others so as not to see the beheading. When the razor sharp scimitar sliced though Najjar's neck, his head flipped through the air, bounced twice, and rolled against the wall, his lifeless eyes still open. His body stood for an instant before it collapsed onto the floor. The men gasped, some turning their heads away.

Shadid released his grip on Hanif, who rose from the table and dropped to his knees, speaking to himself and thanking Aswad for sparing his life, although he was still unsure whether or not he was going to die.

Aswad dropped the scimitar on the floor and put his hands on Hanif's shoulders. "Forgive me, my brother. You were not the traitor." Speaking to everyone, he said, "Let you and the others see what happens to those who go against Allah and, in doing so, go against me. Now, clean up this mess. We will continue our meeting when you are finished."

The men scrambled to dispose of Najjar's body and head and clean up the blood.

Aswad walked outside and stood at the side of the house, listening to the sounds of the village. "Forgive me, Allah. It is for the greater good that Fariq Najjar was sacrificed. Take him into your fold, as you do all martyrs for the jihad."

Aswad regretted Najjar's death. He was a faithful Muslim. He was no traitor. Aswad did not, however, regret what his death would bring. By killing a man the others knew was close to him, the execution was forever seared into their minds. They were now terrified of Aswad and would follow his commands without question, and they would tell others, who would also fear him. Had he killed one of the new recruits, the impact would not have been as great.

In about thirty minutes, Shadid came outside and told Aswad the men were ready. When he entered, the nineteen men were seated in a circle in complete silence, their backs erect and their hands folded in their laps. Najjar's body had been removed and the blood mopped up. Aswad sat with them on the floor near the large red stain at which the men occasionally glanced. When Aswad started to speak, all eyes turned to him.

"Now we begin what will become Islam's greatest victory, not against unsuspecting and unarmed civilians, but against its military might. We will demonstrate the power and will of our people."

17

BY SEVEN-THIRTY Palmer was signing in at Lynnhaven Technology Group. He wanted to interview Owen Fuller before Lieutenant Hawkins did. If anything, all Fuller would know was that Palmer was working with LTG's internal team reviewing the death of Angela Huntington, one of Fuller's project engineers, and would be unaware of Palmer's interest in Alona Green, the laptop switch, and Green's connection to Wade Jansen's death.

Palmer waited in the lobby for the Human Resources director's secretary to escort him to her office. When she arrived, she told the security guard he required a contractor's badge and handed him the authorization signed by Cora Donegan. In less than a minute, Palmer had a photo ID badge that authorized him to come and go without signing in and out or having an employee escort while in the building. On the way to Donegan's office, her secretary told Palmer that Ed Taylor had called Donegan late the previous night to tell her about Jansen's death. Donegan, in turn, called to tell her the bad news and asked her to come in early for what would be a long and emotional day.

"I'm so sorry for your loss," Donegan said when he entered her office. "This has to be difficult for you. Are you OK?"

"I'm going to find his killer."

"Of course, we'll cooperate with the police to find whoever did this."

He could tell Donegan did not comprehend just how serious he was. Nothing else mattered to Palmer now. He was all in and would find the person or persons responsible. "Did you know that Wade met with Alona Green last night?"

"Laptop Alona Green? How did he find her?"

"She called him." Palmer gave Donegan a summary of what had transpired the night before. He told her he had to meet with Owen Fuller before Hawkins did, and he needed to know the details of the laptop incident.

"I'll tell you all I know. While Fuller was in California for a business meeting, Security discovered LTG's secure networks—ones Fuller was not authorized to use—were being accessed from his laptop. Security denied access by his ID and password, but the hacking continued. When Fuller returned to work on Monday, Security brought him to Jansen. Fuller told Jansen the laptop had been stolen while he was on a business trip. He hadn't reported it because he believed that without his ID and password, no one could boot up the laptop, much less access LTG's systems. Jansen didn't believe him and contacted me because he wanted Fuller suspended from the company until his investigation was completed. I told Jansen that his suspicions were not an adequate basis to suspend anyone, and that the CEO wouldn't support the suspension of the leader of LTG's most important project at such a critical stage. Jansen wasn't happy about it but authorized a new ID and password for Fuller. Later Monday morning, Fuller called Jansen and told him that he had not been completely truthful and needed to see him again. When they met, Fuller told Jansen that his laptop was switched at airport security with an almost identical one belonging to a woman named Alona Green, whom he had met on the flight from the U.K. Fuller said that later, when he and Green discovered what had happened, they tried to get together to exchange laptops but were unable to arrange it. Fuller seemed as surprised as anyone to learn that his laptop had been used to access our systems."

"Has Wade's death been communicated to employees?" Palmer asked.

"We sent out a brief statement from the CEO to all employees early this morning. It was all over the morning news shows. We had to send something out before they arrived." She handed him a copy of the communication.

The communication, drafted for the chief executive officer, expressed the great sense of loss of a valued senior manager, who had served his country in the Navy before coming to LTG. LTG would be cooperating with the police ... blah, blah, blah. The specifics, such as cause of his death, were omitted. Palmer slid the document back across the desk to Donegan.

"Can we meet with Fuller? Lieutenant Hawkins will be here soon."

Donegan picked up the phone and called Fuller. They spoke for a few minutes.

"He can meet with us now. I don't think he knows about Wade's meeting with Alona Green."

"That's what I gathered from hearing your side of the conversation. The police have withheld Green's name from the press. The television news reporter said the unnamed LTG executive was shot in his office yesterday evening after meeting with an unnamed person around the time of death. Hawkins will probably bring a police sketch artist with him. They use electronic tablets now with software that creates a composite based on the description from the witness. Once they have a good likeness of her, they'll give it to the television networks and ask for the public's help in finding her. We have to move fast."

18

ON THE WAY to Owen Fuller's office, Palmer asked Donegan, "What's your take on Fuller?"

"Super bright, intelligent, confident to the point of being cocky—"

"But?"

"He's somewhat of a loner and struggles with people management. The success of a project leader depends on the ability to get things done without direct line management of the individual project team members. You need to influence and motivate them."

"Fuller's approach?"

"He pushes them hard and threatens to throw them off the project if they don't do their job. We're fortunate because the importance of the project has meant that some very good and experienced people are assigned to it. They're self-motivated and tend to overlook his shortcomings. If Fuller gets this project to the finish line on time and on budget, and it looks like he will, it will be a huge feather in his cap."

When they entered his office, Fuller rose from his chair and introduced himself.

Palmer studied him. Fuller appeared to be in his late thirties, about five feet ten inches tall and slender, almost skinny. The last time he had any routine physical activity was probably high school gym class. The frames of his black designer glasses disappeared under his styled black hair. He wore a dark-blue golf shirt that was buttoned to the top, khaki pants, and scuffed brown loafers. Palmer had seen plenty like him—sixteen to twenty years of education and a couple of years behind a desk, struggling to make the transition from academia to the real world.

Fuller pulled out a chair at the table and motioned for Palmer and Donegan to join him. "I can't believe Wade's dead. Do you know anything more than was on the news this morning?" Fuller asked.

"Someone shot him," Donegan said. "The details haven't been released. Jake was a close friend. He has been contracted to work with our health and safety team reviewing Angela's death. He's an independent investigator—a former corporate attorney."

"Angela's death left a huge hole in our project team," Fuller said. "Although she had just joined us, her background and experience were ideal. She was a perfect fit."

Said Palmer, "I'll also be LTG's point of contact with the police on Wade Jansen's death. That will simplify communication. I have to say that these seemingly unrelated events occurring in such close proximity give me pause."

"It is odd, isn't it?" Fuller said.

"Let's begin with the death of Angela Huntington," said Palmer. "What was Huntington's role on the project, and what do you know about her death?"

"The project is classified. If you need to know about it, you'll have to talk to the Navy's project leader, Lieutenant Commander Hamilton."

"I will."

"When I put together the Perseus project team, I encountered two types of people: those who yearned to be on the project because it is challenging, exciting, stimulating and in the end, rewarding work, and those who wouldn't touch the project with a barge pole. The work's hard, the hours are long, and the stress is incredible. Angela was the former. She begged to join the project team and, from what I know, lobbied anyone and everyone who could possibly influence her assignment. Once she was on the team, I got to know her. She was a talented engineer and a hardworking woman. She was one of the most inquisitive people I've ever met."

"An inquisitive scientist is a positive attribute. On a personal level, would you say she was intrusive or nosy?"

"She wasn't out to win the project team's congeniality award, if that's what you're asking. That was fine with me. I'm running a project, not a popularity contest. I want people on the team with different personalities and perspectives—people who identify and solve problems in different ways."

"What do you know about her death?"

"Same as everyone. She became ill at work and was rushed to the hospital. Three days later, she was dead of what the police are calling thallium poisoning."

"How would she have been exposed to toxic levels of thallium?"

"How, when, and by whom she was poisoned remains a mystery. It's not like thallium is kept on the shelf in a glass bottle with a skull and crossbones on it. Only those trained and qualified in its use are authorized to obtain it; and when they do, stringent procedures dictate how it is used."

"Know anything about the affair Huntington was rumored to be having?"

"Don't care, not interested. What someone does with their personal time is of no concern to me, as long as it doesn't interfere with their work."

"Let's move on to Wade's death."

Fuller looked puzzled. "What could I possibly tell you about that?"

"I believe his death was related to your laptop and the person who took it from you—Alona Green."

Fuller's eyes widened, and he sat straight in his chair. "What?"

"Alona Green called Wade yesterday and arranged to meet with him alone last night. She wanted to return your laptop."

"That sorry bitch knew better than to call me."

"Why the anger? I thought it was an innocent switch at the airport," Palmer asked.

"That's what she wanted me to believe, so I wouldn't report it while she used it to access our networks. She was the last person to see him alive, wasn't she? I bet she killed him."

"The police want to talk to her and believe you may be able to help them find her. From what I understand, you've changed your story regarding the loss of your laptop two or three times. Now tell us the truth about what happened," Palmer said.

"You're right, and I'm sorry. Let me tell you how Alona ended up with my laptop."

19

"I MET ALONA on the British Airways flight from London to Philadelphia," Owen Fuller began. "I was in London to meet with one of the technical partners on the project and was traveling on to a related meeting in California."

Fuller said Alona Green had sat beside him in first class on the flight from London. He had not paid much attention to her until the plane hit some turbulence shortly after takeoff, and she grabbed his arm, saying she was a white-knuckle flyer. It was then he realized how attractive she was. She had long blond hair, a fantastic figure, and perfect teeth. Green told him she had been visiting a friend in London and was on her way to Seattle for a business meeting. She described herself as a self-employed consultant. During the flight, he took out his laptop a few times to do some work. The first time, Green commented she had one like it, although she never took it out of her computer bag stowed in the overhead compartment.

"Was her bag like yours?" Palmer said.

"No. We couldn't have switched bags, if that's what you're asking."

"Was she watching you while you worked?" Donegan said.

"Not that I noticed. I have a privacy shield on the laptop that blanks out the screen unless you're looking directly at it. Sitting beside me, she couldn't have seen anything, and the only time I was away from my laptop was when I went to the restroom a couple of times. I recall hearing the announcement that we were descending to land and all electronic equipment should be shut off. I was using my laptop, so I turned it off and put it into my computer bag."

"We walked off the plane together and through immigration and customs. I rechecked my baggage for my connecting flight to California. She didn't have any checked baggage, only a carry-on and her computer bag, which I thought was unusual for a woman."

Donegan groaned at his sexist comment, causing Palmer to chuckle to himself.

"Our flight from London arrived early. Alona told me how much she enjoyed meeting me and to my surprise, kissed me on the cheek. Then, she apologized for being forward and asked if I would like to get something to eat before we went our separate ways. We had three to four hours to kill before our connecting flights departed. Without hesitation, I said yes. She was insistent that we go into Philadelphia. She knew a fabulous restaurant. When I said I wasn't sure we had enough time, she said if we missed our flight, we could always catch one the next day. I'm sorry, but that seemed like an invitation to spend the night with her. No way was I going to pass that up."

Palmer nodded in affirmation.

"Men," Donegan muttered.

"We took a taxi to the restaurant, Buddakan, near the historic area of Philadelphia. We had a couple of drinks before dinner and a bottle of wine with the meal."

"Where were your computer bags while you ate?" Palmer asked.

"At the table with us. I rechecked my luggage after going through customs. Her carry-on was also at the table with us. By the time I paid the bill, we were cutting it close. We got to airport security about an hour before my scheduled departure, forty-five minutes before hers. This is the critical piece of the puzzle, so pay attention."

"We're all ears," Palmer said sarcastically.

With the jet lag, the drinks and wine, Fuller wasn't thinking clearly. They had their computer bags, and she had her carry-on. She was concerned she was going to miss her flight and asked if she could go through first. He recalled thinking it strange that she was now the one worried about missing the flight. As required, they took their laptops out of their bags and put them into separate trays. Green went through the scanner without a problem and was gathering up her things. When Fuller went through, the scanner alarm went off. The TSA agent asked him if he had any metal objects, like a cell phone or keys. He said no and stepped through again with the same result—the scanner alarmed. The agent took him aside for a pat down. Green was standing at the end of the belt, pointing to his computer bag. She made a motion, indicating she put his laptop in his bag and placed it in the same tray with his shoes and jacket. She smiled and blew him a kiss before she gathered her things and rushed away. The TSA agent wanded him and said his wallet seemed to be the problem. The only thing out of the ordinary in his wallet was Alona Green's card. When the TSA agent ran the wand across the card, the wand buzzed. The agent told him the card was metallic and that's what caused the problem.

"Do you still have it?" Palmer asked.

Fuller opened his desk drawer, found the card, and handed it to him.

Palmer examined it. "Alona G. Green, President and Chief Executive Officer, Green Consulting Group." Below that in smaller print were her address, phone numbers, and e-mail address, all of which he believed were fake. He held one end between his thumb and forefinger, careful not to touch it, and thumped it with the middle finger of his other hand.

"It's metallic all right. I'd like a photocopy of it."

"OK, but I want to keep it to show to the police."

"They may want it for fingerprints," Palmer said.

Fuller paused and looked away. "She had one of those cardholders in her purse. She held it out for me to take one at the restaurant. She didn't touch it."

"That's why the alarm didn't sound when she went through the scanner. The other cards were in her purse, not on her. She knew you would put it in your wallet or pocket and get stopped by the TSA when you went through the scanner."

"I was the last one to board the flight and slept almost all the way to the West Coast. After unpacking at the hotel, I was wide-awake. Around midnight I decided to check my e-mail, hoping Alona might have written after she arrived in Seattle. When I saw the log-on screen that came up wasn't LTG's, I panicked. I examined the laptop; and although it was the same make and model as mine, it didn't have an LTG security tag affixed to the bottom with a series of numbers and a bar code. I unzipped the compartment in my computer bag where I keep my pens, business cards, and other small items. They were all there. It was my bag. Then, I remembered that Green said she had a computer like mine. I was reaching for my cell phone to call her when it rang. It was Alona. She said she had gotten to her hotel in Seattle, took out her laptop to check e-mail, and discovered it wasn't hers. She knew she had picked mine up by mistake, blaming it on the drinks and wine and being in such a rush. She was very apologetic and asked if I had hers. She seemed genuinely relieved when I told her I did. She said she was flying to California on Saturday; we could exchange them then. I was scheduled to fly back that day but rescheduled my flight for Sunday. We arranged to meet at my hotel. I was excited about seeing her again, but when she didn't show, I was furious. I phoned the number she called me on, but no one answered."

"Why didn't you report it then?" asked Donegan.

"I felt like an idiot. I was embarrassed. Plus, because I didn't think she could get into the laptop without my ID and password, I didn't see the urgency to report it. When I got in from California Sunday night, I came straight here to check my e-mail and do some work. I tried to log on but was denied access. After three attempts, I was locked out. The next morning when I got in, someone from Security was waiting for me in my office and took me to see Wade Jansen. That's when he interrogated me."

"Why didn't you tell Wade all of this on Monday?" Donegan asked.

"It seemed easier and less complicated to say it was stolen. But after I got my badge reactivated and computer authorization reinstated, I thought more about it and decided to tell him the truth."

"But you didn't tell him everything you just told us, did you?"

Palmer said.

"I left out much of the detail. Whenever I started to ramble, he told me to cut to the chase."

Palmer looked at Donegan, then leaned forward and looked Fuller in the eyes. "You've been had."

"I know. I'm so stupid. I'm angry with her but more so with myself."

"What systems and data were accessed? Do we have a list of the dates and times?" Palmer asked.

Donegan pulled a spreadsheet from the folder she had brought with her and took a moment to scan through the information. "The first time Owen's e-mail account and the corporate intranet were accessed was Thursday for one minute, twenty seconds. Was that you?"

"No. I used the laptop on the flight from the U.K. with the wireless connection disabled. That access would have occurred after the laptops were switched."

"She was probably testing the ID and password," Palmer said. "If there had been a problem, she might have returned the laptop to you and said there had been a mistake."

"The next access was Friday morning," Donegan said. "She accessed some internal networks you were authorized to use. The first access to an account you were not authorized to use occurred that evening. Access continued through Sunday, even after Security blocked your ID and password. It stopped Monday afternoon."

"How would she have gotten my ID and password? Can a hacker get that from the laptop? How could she have done that?"

"You said you used your laptop several times during the seven-hour flight. Could she have watched you enter your password and ID?" Palmer asked.

"I suppose it's possible, but I don't see how."

"A final question: Where were you last night?"

"I worked until about eight and went home. With the project in the final critical stage, that's about the earliest I've left in a while. The field test is next week."

Donegan told Fuller he should call her immediately after Lieutenant Hawkins contacted him. She and someone from Legal needed to be present when he talked to Hawkins. Fuller's secretary made copies of Alona Green's business card for Palmer and Donegan.

After they left, Donegan asked Palmer, "Well, what do you think?"

"He couldn't have made up that story. Alona Green's a corporate spy and a damn good one at that."

20

WHEN PALMER AND Donegan returned to her office after meeting with Owen Fuller, Ed Taylor was behind her desk, leaning back in her chair with his eyes closed and mouth half-open.

"Ed!" Donegan said, startling Taylor awake.

Taylor opened his eyes and yawned, covering his mouth. "Sorry, I haven't slept all night. Your secretary said you and Palmer were meeting with Fuller. I sat down, thinking I would shut my eyes for a moment. I went out like a light. How'd it go?"

Donegan gave Taylor a topline summary of their meeting with Fuller.

"Sometimes I think the smarter people are, the less common sense they have—if you know what I mean," Taylor said. "Did you give him a heads-up about the cops wanting to talk to him today?"

"I told him to call me when they contacted him and to say nothing to the police without Legal and Human Resources being present," Donegan said.

"Any luck with the security video?" Palmer asked.

"The police wanted the disc last night. I convinced Lieutenant Hawkins to let me review it first. I could identify our employees and give them a list of their names along with the disc this morning. Since I saw you last night, I've only been home for a couple of hours to shower, change, and have an early breakfast. Alona Green is on camera signing in. Wade came down a few minutes later, and they walked toward the elevators."

"When did she leave?"

"She left alone at seven twenty-two, about an hour after she arrived. The guard wasn't at the desk."

"Was she carrying anything?"

"She had a computer bag with her both times."

"Did Wade escort her to the lobby?"

"He's not on the tape when she left. Because of the camera angle, we can't tell if he came to the reception area with her or not. It's possible he was on the elevator with her, said goodbye near the elevator doors, and watched her leave the building before he returned to his office."

"It's also possible she shot and killed Wade and then left alone," Palmer said.

"Of course. I also watched a couple of hours of the video on either side of the time she arrived."

"Did anyone sign in after her?"

"You were the first person to enter the building after she arrived. No one else entered until the ambulance arrived. Lieutenant Hawkins will be here in a couple of hours. He's already phoned this morning. They're putting out a 'Be On the Lookout' for Alona Green. He wants to issue the video to the local TV stations to help identify her. It's a little grainy, and she tended to look down, like she knew there were security cameras and didn't want to be identified. It's better than nothing, I suppose. The media is in a feeding frenzy. Hawkins is bringing a police sketch artist with him. The artist will work with Fuller and the guard to create a likeness of her face to issue to the press."

"Fuller will give them a detailed description all right. She's forever etched in his hormonal memory," Donegan said.

"Did anyone else leave after Green?" Palmer said.

"Twenty-six employees left after she arrived. We've identified all of them. Of those, only five, including our chief financial officer and our chief information officer, left after her."

"Was Owen Fuller one of them?" Palmer asked.

"Yeah. He left around eight o'clock."

"Last night, the guard told us that not all of the exits are monitored by cameras."

"A couple of exits aren't. Employees can leave through them, but they are farther away from the parking lot than the main entrance and seldom used."

"But if I was trying to leave or enter without being seen by the guard or security camera, I could use them. Right?"

"You could exit. To enter you would need a badge with authorization. Each door has a card reader mounted on the wall beside it. Or, you could wait outside until someone entered or left and grab the door before it closed. Because those exits are not used very often, you might have a long wait. After this, we are going to have cameras at all of the exits."

"If I left by one of those exits, would it be recorded?"

"No, only entries into the building are recorded by the card reader."

"There's a sign at the front entrance, stating that firearms are forbidden in the building. Do the turnstiles at the entrance have metal detectors that would detect a firearm being brought into the building?"

"If we did, the entrance would look like an airport security line in the mornings."

"I'd like to see those other entrances to the building."

Donegan took Palmer to the exits. The non-monitored doors had a push bar that released the lock, a Fire Department requirement. People had to be able to exit in case of an emergency. They stepped outside and let the door close behind them. Palmer tried to enter. The door was locked. On the wall beside the door was a small six-inch by six-inch card reader. Near the bottom was a small red light. Donegan held her ID badge against the reader. The box emitted a beep, and the red light changed to green. Palmer pulled on the door handle, and the door opened.

"Taylor said if someone enters, the information is captured."

"Date, time, and name of employee. However, since more than one person can enter once the door is open, that doesn't tell you everything. If you exit at one of those doors and someone is going to enter before the door closes, you're either supposed to ask them for their ID, if you don't recognize them, or shut the door and make them use their badge. Our employees don't always follow the procedure. They're too polite."

21

PALMER WAS IN the LTG break room having a coffee, wishing it were a gin and tonic, when Cora Donegan phoned him. Hawkins's meeting with Fuller was finished. He gulped down the rest of his coffee and was rushing to Donegan's office when his cell phone rang again. He didn't recognize the caller's number.

"Is this Jake Palmer?" the female voice asked before he could say anything.

"Who wants to know?"

She hesitated, and then said, "Alona Green."

Palmer came to a halt in the middle of the hallway. "A lot of people are looking for you, Ms. Green." He stepped into a vacant office and shut the door.

"I did *not* kill Wade Jansen. When I left his office last night, he was alive and well."

"The police just want to talk to you. You're not accused of anything."

"Do you really expect me to believe that?"

"How'd you get my number?"

"I told Jansen that two men were after me. He gave me your number and told me to call you if I needed help. He said he trusted you with his life. Was Owen Fuller's laptop in his office when they found him?"

"I was the one who found him," Palmer said. "There was a laptop in the center of his desk. The police took it."

"I was afraid of that. There's a lot I need to tell you. I don't want to do it on the phone, and I'm not turning myself in to the police. Can we meet?"

"Now?"

"This evening. Eight o'clock at One Fish-Two Fish restaurant near Lynnhaven Inlet. Come alone. If the police are there and I'm arrested, I'll lawyer up. It'll be months before you know what really happened."

"Fine. Eight o'clock at One Fish-Two Fish."

"How will I recognize you?" Green asked.

"I'll be at the bar. If there's not one, I'll be by the door. I'm wearing a white shirt, light-gray pants, and a blue sports coat. How will I recognize you?" There was no response.

"Alona? Are you there?" Palmer hit redial on the last received call—no answer. For what it was worth, he had descriptions of her from the guard and Fuller, and he could view the security camera footage of her arrival and departure. *She said someone was chasing her. Who? Why? Was it her laptop on Wade's desk? If so, where was Fuller's?*

^^^^

When Palmer arrived at Donegan's office, Hawkins was standing in the doorway, talking to her. They shook hands and went inside and shut the door.

"I was telling Lieutenant Hawkins what Fuller told us this morning. He said it was basically the same story Fuller told him," Donegan said. "Nothing new."

"What do you think, Lieutenant?" Palmer asked.

"Arrogance aside, I believe he's telling the truth. But I'm at a loss to see what motive Green would have to kill Jansen. I've viewed the relevant segments of the security video with Taylor. She had a computer bag with her when she arrived and when she left. There's no way of knowing what she had in it."

"Let's assume for a moment she brought Fuller's laptop with her to the meeting with Jansen, left it with him, and took her laptop," Palmer said. "Then who killed Jansen and why?"

"Your guys say the laptop on Jansen's desk is Green's. It has no LTG security tag on the bottom. I'll know more after our tech team has checked it. Green could have had a gun in the computer bag. When she reached in the bag to get the laptop, she took it out and shot Jansen before he could react. Green's my number one person of interest for the Jansen murder. The sketch artist is working with Fuller. We should have a good likeness of her soon, and I'll issue it to the press tomorrow morning."

"If the laptop on his desk is hers and she still has Fuller's, why would she kill him? That would mean she came to LTG with the sole intention of killing Wade. It doesn't make sense."

"How about Huntington?" Donegan asked.

"I met with Michael Sutton, your chief information officer this morning," Hawkins said. "The video shows him leaving around eight, long after Green left. He admitted to the affair with Huntington. He hasn't told his wife and doesn't intend to. According to Sutton, his torrid—his word—affair with Huntington began several months ago. During the course of things, he made a couple of calls at her request that resulted in her getting her dream job. After she joined the team, torrid became tepid. He knew he had been played. I asked if she threatened to tell his wife, and that's why he killed her. He said I had it all wrong. Huntington broke off the affair, not him. She had gotten what she needed out of the relationship. She had no reason to tell his wife. Besides, he said he didn't know what thallium was and didn't have access to it. Even if he did, he said he wouldn't know how to poison someone with it."

"Do you believe him?" Palmer asked. "He could have been furious that Huntington used him to get what she wanted and ended the affair. That's motive."

"As much as I would like him to be guilty, my gut says no. He could have had an attorney with him today, but he didn't. And their personal e-mail correspondence supports his story."

Donegan shook her head. "Of course, he didn't have anyone from Legal or HR there. He didn't want us to hear about the affair. After the sexual harassment seminar last year, he came up to me and said it was the third time he had attended the course. He joked that after the first two, he was no better at sexual harassment than he was before. The affair may not be pertinent to your case, but it is a serious matter. He's not heard the end of it. I'll see to that."

"Maybe Jansen became aware of the affair and threatened to report it. Sutton could be acting cooperative, believing it will throw us off," Palmer said.

"Possible, but not likely."

Palmer didn't tell Hawkins about the call from Green and their planned meeting that evening. If Hawkins knew, he would wire him, listen to their conversation, and take her in for questioning, regardless of what she said. Unlike Sutton, Green would invoke her right to an attorney. He couldn't risk it. Even if she didn't kill Jansen, she might hold the key to who did. Either way, he wanted to get to her first.

∧∧∧∧

"I need to see the video of Green coming and going," Palmer said as he stormed into Ed Taylor's office.

"What's the rush? The segments with Alona Green will be on the news tonight."

"I'm contracted to do this job. Show me the video. Now."

Without responding, Taylor went to the console on the table beside his desk and turned on the display. The relevant segments, which he had played earlier for Hawkins, were already queued up.

Palmer sat close to the screen, his hand on his chin, and watched the segments in silence, one taken when Green arrived, and the other, when she departed. The video was grainy. Just as Taylor said, Green kept her head down, not looking at the camera. He might not have an accurate description of her, but of one thing, he was certain: Alona Green's life depended on what she had to say tonight.

22

PALMER ARRIVED TWENTY minutes early for his meeting with Alona Green. The hostess who greeted him when he entered said there was a thirty-minute wait. He gave her his name and told her he would wait in the bar. They might not need a table; but if so, they were on the list.

One Fish-Two Fish was located at the end of a marina with an outdoor dining area that was part of a dock alongside the restaurant. Customers could eat indoors, at the outdoor dining area, or tie their boats up to the dock and have food served to them on their boats. It was a popular restaurant with the local, young professional crowd. Tonight, the outdoor tables on the water were in high demand; the sun was low in the sky and would be setting soon.

Palmer found an empty seat at the bar and ordered a double Glenmorangie. Ordering it reminded him of Fiona and made him smile. She had informed him that it was whisky, not Scotch, and then corrected his pronunciation when he ordered it at a pub. He took a sip of his drink and shifted in his seat, watching for Green and taking in the surroundings. The interior décor was contemporary, with blue pendulum lights over the bar and an open kitchen with a bar around it—the overflow space for those who didn't want to wait for a table.

Palmer nursed his drink, intent on maintaining a clear head. So far, no one who matched Green's description had arrived. He was getting impatient and beginning to wonder if she would show. He glanced at his watch: eight-fifteen. He drummed his fingers on the bar. *Where is she?*

An attractive woman with medium-length black hair, who had been with a man at a nearby table since his arrival, got up and walked toward the bar with her empty drink. He had noticed her and the man laughing and talking. He slid his chair over so she could get to the bar. As she brushed up against him, he caught the slightest whisper of her cologne. In his peripheral vision, he saw her set her empty glass on the bar and look at him.

"Jake Palmer?" she asked softly.

He turned to look at her. "Alona Green?" Palmer said with a note of surprise.

"Were you expecting someone else?"

"Where's the blond hair?"

"In my suitcase."

"How long have you been here?"

"Twenty minutes before you, long enough to make sure you were alone and not using a concealed mike. Funny thing about a wire—whenever someone's wearing one, they can't resist the urge to talk to whoever's on the other end."

Palmer was glad he had not told Hawkins about the meeting. "Who's the guy?" he asked, motioning with a nod of his head toward the man who was now talking to another woman.

"Just someone I allowed to enjoy my company while I watched you."

Dang, she's good.

Before he could say anything else to Green, the hostess who had taken his name when he arrived walked up and said, "Mr. Palmer, your table is ready when you are."

Palmer looked at Green. "Let's go. We'll have more privacy."

Green nodded her agreement, and they followed the woman to a table by the window. Both Palmer and Green moved to sit in the chair facing the restaurant entrance instead of the one facing the water. Palmer, rather than making an issue of it, pulled out the chair for her and sat beside her, where he had a view of the entrance and the door leading to the outdoor dining area. The hostess, looking a bit puzzled at their maneuvering for their seats, gave them a wine list and menus and told them their waiter would be right with them to take their drink orders.

"You're the prime suspect in the murder of a man who once saved my life."

"I prefer 'person of interest.' It's more provocative and open to interpretation."

"Don't be cute with me. If you don't have a good explanation, wire or no wire, I'm dragging you to the police," said Jake.

"When I got up this morning, I turned on the TV and watched the news. The lead story was about someone at Lynnhaven Technology Group being shot and killed last night. The reporter said the police were looking for a woman who met with the victim around the time of his death. I figured it had to be Jansen. I didn't know what to do. Then I remembered he gave me your number after I told him two men were chasing me to get the laptop, and I was afraid they would kill me. He suggested I call you."

Jansen would not suggest she go to the police. He was protecting LTG. He did not want the news media to get word of a stolen laptop. Even if the report was limited to the local media, over a hundred thousand members of the armed forces and military contractors lived and worked in the area. Naval Special Warfare Support Activity Two would hear about it soon enough.

"So, who *are* these two men?" Palmer asked, almost whimsically.

"I don't know. They looked like Arabs."

"Why should I believe you didn't kill Wade Jansen?"

"You have my word."

"Like Owen Fuller had your word?" Palmer leaned across the table and looked her in the eyes. "Why did you take his laptop? That was no innocent mix-up at airport security."

"I was hired to. Someone called and said he had a job for me, one where I could make a lot of money. It sounded simple enough—take Fuller's laptop and stick around while a couple of geeks trolled through his company's network."

"Why did they need his laptop to hack into the network?"

"LTG's systems are airtight. Only a handful of hackers are good enough to break through their firewall. But with a company-authorized computer, an ID, and password, you're in, and then the serious hacking begins. I'm guessing they wanted Fuller's because of the project he's leading at LTG."

He looked into her eyes. "Do you know Angela Huntington?"

Green looked puzzled by the question. "Never heard of her. Who is she?"

"What do you know about the LTG project that Fuller's leading?"

"Nothing really. He told me he was a project leader at LTG. I never asked why they wanted the laptop or what they intended to do with it. That was none of my concern. From what I could tell, it was—" Green stopped mid-sentence. "It's them."

"Who?"

"The two men. How did they find me? I found the tracking device on my car."

"In my experience, one tracker's good, two are better," Palmer said in a low voice.

"Crap! They've spotted me."

Palmer saw the genuine look of fear in her eyes. "Let's get out of here."

Green pushed her chair back from the table and started to leave. He grabbed her arm and looked around. One of the men pointed toward Green. The door to the outdoor dining area was near their table. Green was tugging to get out of Palmer's grip.

Palmer leaned close to her. "Stay calm. Go outside. Wait for me. I'll take care of this."

When Green got up from the table and hurried out the door, Palmer threw up his hands, pretending they had an argument. The men saw her leave and rushed toward the door. They moved quickly through the restaurant, snaking their way around the tables, and the waiters, and servers, paying no attention to Palmer.

He waited until they were two steps away from him. He spun in his seat and threw out his legs, tripping one man, who fell hard to the floor. The second stepped over him and took a swing at Palmer's head. Palmer moved to his left, grabbed the man, and then threw his elbow into the man's face. He went down. The other man had gotten off the floor and lunged for Palmer, who was ready and threw one punch that landed square on the man's nose. He went down like a rock. Palmer spotted a compact pistol in the man's belt when he hit the floor

Before either man recovered, Palmer was outside. Green had watched what had happened through a window. He shouted for her to follow him. He raced along the dock and jumped into a twenty-five-foot center console with twin outboard motors with the key in the ignition. Palmer started the engine as Green cast off the lines and leapt into the boat. Palmer pulled away from the dock before Green had a chance to sit. Ignoring the no wake zone, he pushed the throttles all the way forward. The outboards roared, the bow rose. Green stumbled backwards, grabbing on to the gunwale. Once she balanced herself, she walked the inclined deck to the console where Palmer was steering. Within a minute, he made the hard turn to starboard under an inlet bridge and into the strong current of the rising tide flowing in from the Chesapeake Bay.

∧∧∧∧

The two men, both blooded from their confrontation, watched in frustration as the boat sped off. Just then, a middle-aged man began maneuvering his boat into the open space vacated by the boat Palmer had hijacked. The two men motioned for him to throw them a line, indicating they would assist him in docking the boat. He did and as soon as they pulled the boat in close, the men jumped aboard. "What are you doing? Get the hell off my boat," the man yelled.

One of the Arabs punched the man in the stomach and then pointed a pistol. Within seconds, they pushed the man overboard and sped off after Palmer.

∧∧∧∧

After Palmer was away from the shoals and in deep water, he steered the boat westward under the bridge portion of the Chesapeake Bay Bridge-Tunnel, between the shoreline and the first island, where one of two tunnels descended into the bay. The sun had set, and it was getting dark.

Green shouted to be heard above the noise of the outboards. "Hey, tough guy, why did you run from them?"

"Ever hear the expression, 'Don't take a knife to a gun fight?' I'm no fool. I live to fight another day. And I will—on my terms."

The two outboards pushed the boat through the swells, the bow rising out of the water each time it cut through a peak, before slamming down into the trough. Green stood at the center console beside Palmer, who had one hand on the wheel and one on the throttles. He swung the boat in a wide arch toward the next inlet, staying clear of the shallow waters near the shore.

Palmer and Green spotted a bowrider also ignoring the no wake buoys as it sped through the inlet that was churned up with the incoming tide. They did not know who it was but assumed the two men had also hijacked a boat and were chasing them. Although they had a healthy lead, the distance between the two boats was closing.

"Where are we going? They're gaining on us."

"The next inlet," Palmer shouted.

When they were within a quarter mile of the entrance to the inlet, he heard gunshots from behind them. "Get down!"

Green dropped to the deck.

Palmer turned hard to port and into the marked channel that led to the inlet. Green grabbed the seat support post to keep from sliding on the deck as the boat banked.

Once in the inlet, instead of reducing his speed and taking the channel to the right, toward the marinas, Palmer steered the boat straight ahead at full throttle. He heard three more shots. One of the bullets struck the windshield of the boat, a foot from his head near where Green had been standing. Palmer looked over his shoulder. The pursuers were within fifty feet and closing in fast. He turned his head back to the front and saw another boat heading straight toward them with a blinking blue light. A warning horn sounded.

"Where are you staying?" Green shouted.

"What?"

"Your hotel—where are you staying?"

It was a strange question to be asked, considering the circumstances. Palmer backed off on the throttles. The engine slowed. "The Hilton."

Green pointed at the boat ahead of them and shook her head. "See ya." She ran to the stern, and without breaking stride, stepped on the gunwale and executed a perfect flat dive into the water. Palmer watched her slice through the relatively calm water of the inlet like a competitive swimmer. She was headed toward a row of townhouses on the right side of the inlet.

Palmer eased the Sea Hunt into neutral, a searchlight now pointed at him. Squinting, he put his hand up to block the bright light from his eyes. His smile burst into a laugh. He had entered the familiar waters of the U.S. Navy's Joint Expeditionary Base Little Creek, the world's largest naval amphibious assault base and the East Coast home of the U.S. Navy SEALs.

23

THE BOAT, WHICH was a type of Zodiac Hurricane used by the Navy to patrol harbors and ports, pulled alongside Palmer. The crewman who was steering was talking on the radio. The other asked, "Where are you headed, sir?"

"Into the base to seek shelter," Palmer said. "The men on the other boat were shooting at me." He pointed at the bullet hole in the windshield.

"Who were they?"

"Wish I knew."

"Permission to come aboard, sir?"

"Granted," Palmer responded.

Jumping aboard, the armed sailor said, "Steer in that direction." He pointed at the channel off the port bow. Neither spoke after that. The Navy boat followed close behind. Once the boats were tied to the dock, the sailor who had boarded escorted Palmer to a nearby building, while the other resumed his security patrol.

"I can explain," Palmer said.

^ ^ ^ ^

Palmer waited in a room while the sailor talked to a naval

officer. Like the two enlisted men, the officer wore Navy blue and gray camouflage fatigues. Jake noted he was a lieutenant junior grade. In a few minutes, he came into the room and shut the door.

"Jacob Palmer, U.S. Navy, petty officer first class, serial number—"

"Are you on active duty?"

"Not since 2002," Palmer said.

"Why did you pull into restricted waters, and who was shooting at you?"

Palmer proceeded to tell him what had happened, starting with meeting a woman at the bar at One Fish-Two Fish. He said he didn't remember her name.

"You don't know who the men were, and you can't remember the woman's name?"

"That's right. I just met her at the restaurant bar."

"Why did she jump off your boat and swim away?"

"I wish I knew. She was really coming on to me until those goons came into the restaurant."

The lieutenant folded his arms and leaned back in the chair. "Two boats were stolen from the dock at One Fish-Two Fish tonight. Both sped off, headed this way. That much we know from the police and marine scanners we monitor. We've notified the Virginia Beach Police Marine Patrol and Coast Guard. They're searching for the other boat and your jumper."

"Look, two Arab men came into the restaurant. One was carrying," said Palmer, referring to the pistol he saw in one of the men's belt. "I know cops. They weren't cops. It was either run or borrow a boat. I'm not as fast as I used to be, and I figured they had a car and could chase us, so I decided to borrow the boat. Next thing I knew they were behind us in another boat and closing fast. We took small arms fire. One of the rounds hit the windshield. The woman must have thought she had a better chance on her own. What else do you need to know?"

"You certain they were Arabs?"

"Yes, without a doubt."

An enlisted man entered and handed the lieutenant a note. He took a moment to read it.

"Your story agrees with witness accounts. And welcome

home, Palmer. I see you are a veteran and were with SEAL Team Two here at Little Creek."

"Affirmative and thank you."

"Wait here. The senior duty officer wants to talk to you."

The lieutenant left the room. Palmer glanced around. Framed photographs of various ships based at Little Creek were on the wall. He stood closer, looking at the photograph of a ship on which he had spent some time.

"Hello, Jake. Been a long time."

Palmer recognized that voice. "Twenty plus years by my count," he said before turning around.

Lieutenant Commander Lara Hamilton pushed his extended hand aside and put her arms around him. It was a quick, friendly hug, the kind relatives share, not one that expressed a great deal of emotion, just more personal than a handshake. "I didn't expect to see you tonight."

"That makes two of us." Palmer stepped back and took her in from head to toe. "You look great." Her Navy khaki uniform was fighting a losing battle to mask her femininity. She wore little or no makeup, and her hair was pulled back in a bun, the carefree style some female officers opted for rather than a drastically short haircut. From the size of the bun, he guessed her hair was only a little shorter than the shoulder-length style she wore when she was at the University of North Carolina. Lara Hamilton may have put on a few pounds, but she was still attractive, with the same smile, slightly upturned nose, and sparkle in her eyes.

"I'm sorry to hear about Wade Jansen. He was a good man."

"The best. I intend to find out who killed him."

"What have you gotten yourself into, Jake?"

"Nothing I can't handle."

"You stole a boat, two men were shooting at you, and some woman jumped from the boat when you entered restricted waters. Is that your definition of handling it?"

"Are you going to turn me over to the police?" Palmer asked.

"The police talked to the owner of the boat. As long as he gets it back, he's not pressing charges."

"I'll pay for the windshield and top up the gas tank. It's the least I can do."

"We found a pair of women's shoes on the boat. You told our

lieutenant you didn't know her name. Who was she, Jake? Who dove off the boat when base security approached you?"

"Alona Green, a suspect in Wade's murder. She called and asked to see me alone at a restaurant off Shore Drive. She said she was afraid for her life and couldn't go to the police. At the restaurant, she was about to tell me something when two men came in and rushed toward us. I delayed them long enough to borrow the boat."

"The police also wanted to know who she is. I bought you some time, but you have to tell them. I said you would be here for a while."

Palmer nodded his head, acknowledging he would contact the police.

"Wade called me a couple of days ago," Hamilton continued. "He asked if I would mind if he hired you to work Huntington's death. I told him I didn't have a problem with it.

"I had a feeling we would run into each other before my LTG contract was completed," Palmer said. "Just didn't think it would be this soon. What do you do for Naval Special Warfare? How did you manage to get assigned here?"

Hamilton told him that after graduation and commissioning at UNC, she reported to Naval Air Station Pensacola and went through Flight School and Electronic Warfare Operators School in Pensacola and was designated a Naval Flight Officer. She then went to Basic Airborne School and Military Free Fall School and became parachute-qualified, including doing a few HALO—High Altitude Low Opening—parachute jumps. Growing up in eastern North Carolina in a family of hunters, she knew how to handle guns. She had earned both the Navy pistol and rifle marksman ribbons. She wasn't a SEAL; there were no women SEALs, but she worked hard to earn their respect. She was the information operations officer for Naval Special Warfare Support Activity Two, integrating intelligence, surveillance, and reconnaissance with SEAL missions. Her primary role was matching the needs of SEAL teams with emerging technologies. In the past, they were given what the acquisition system and military-industrial complex thought they needed. Now, she worked with the teams to analyze tactical problems and identify solutions and then worked with defense contractors to refine and develop them.

Once a technology was ready, she deployed with the teams to test it.

"Sounds dangerous for a—" Palmer caught himself before he said it.

"Dangerous for what? A woman?" Hamilton laughed. "I'm used to hearing it. It makes my job all the more rewarding."

"I always knew you would excel at whatever you did. Since I'm here, I need to talk to you. Two LTG employees have been murdered. The only thing they have in common is some association with your project. Everyone I speak to at LTG says they can't tell me anything. Can you tell me what it is?"

"It's named Perseus. The project is one of the Navy's most important, possibly one of the military's more important, projects. Field tests begin soon. I'm leaving tomorrow for Afghanistan to manage it. After Wade told me you were going to work the Huntington case, I ordered a priority update of your security clearance. You have temporary limited authorization, enough for me to give you a high-level summary of the project."

"Good to know."

"The use of drones in Iraq and Afghanistan has been successful—more successful than anyone imagined. Building on that success, drones are now being deployed everywhere from battlefield to border patrol. The basic concept is simple: reduce risk while reducing costs."

"Motherhood and apple pie," Palmer said.

"That's right. In 2011, the Air Force trained more drone pilots than fighter and bomber pilots combined; and in two to three years, they will have more drone pilots than F-16 pilots." Hamilton explained that the most expensive way to deliver ordnance to a target is to have a fifty million dollar F/A-18 flown by a highly trained, highly paid pilot, take off and land from an aircraft carrier. Delivering that same ordnance by way of a drone from a carrier costs peanuts by comparison. And in the long-term, smaller carriers would be built to launch and retrieve them, saving even more money. The transition from a carrier-based strategy would take years; and even then, carrier-based fighter jets would continue to play a vital role."

"Where does the LTG project come into play?"

Hamilton told him that the Navy's interest was the

N-UCAS—Navy Unmanned Combat Air System—drone that would be capable of taking off and landing on aircraft carriers. The public had been told that production and deployment of the first N-UCAS drone would be in 2018. Working with defense contractors, including LTG, the research and development of the drone had been accelerated. Perseus, the prototype, could fly at over four hundred knots for fifteen to twenty hours without refueling, and was capable of in-flight refueling from both Navy and Air Force tankers. She asked him to imagine a strike group of drones with the capability of seeking out targets identified by the smallest of electronic signals or by the physical characteristics of the target.

A few months earlier, Hamilton accompanied a SEAL team to a forward Marine operating base in Afghanistan. They placed the tracking dots on munitions that they allowed to fall into the hands of Taliban fighters. Two days later, a land-based Reaper drone, retrofitted with LTG's targeting system, locked onto multiple signals. A SEAL team had tracked the main group from the base and confirmed the target before the order to fire the missile was given. It flew low and undetected, and destroyed the target.

"Was LTG involved in the test?" Palmer asked.

"Not directly. They were involved with the modifications to the Reaper and provided the dots but were not aware of when and where the test would be conducted. The upcoming field tests will be the first live-fire use of a new stealth drone launched from a carrier and using DoSTA and physical recognition targeting technologies with missiles more advanced and powerful than the Hellfires. To top it off, the team will be controlling the drone from the ground. I can't begin to explain the leap in technology and firepower this represents," Hamilton said. "It's bigger than Doolittle's B-25s taking off from the carrier *Hornet* to bomb Japan in World War II."

"Can you delay the test, at least until we figure out what is going on? I'm convinced the deaths of Wade Jansen and Angela Huntington are related. There's also a recent issue regarding LTG's network security."

"We know about the security breach, although LTG doesn't know we do. We believe another company is attempting to steal their drone navigation and target acquisition/tracking technology. Not everyone's a fan of the cost-effective use of drones. Companies vested in fighter jet development and manufacturing stand to lose billions, if not trillions, when drones replace them on carriers. Drone technology is evolving faster than flat-screen televisions. Companies spy on each other to stay ahead of the curve. Governments spy on companies and other governments for the same purpose."

"Fuller's laptop was used to breach LTG's secure networks," Palmer said. "Whatever was gleaned from that breach might be used to sabotage the test."

"The tests are too controlled for that to happen," Hamilton responded with assurance. "Only a small select group of LTG engineers, along with engineers from the aerospace company that is manufacturing Perseus, will be involved in the field test. Besides, no company would endanger their defense contracts by sabotaging a test that is crucial to the country's future. If they were caught, the company execs would be wearing orange jumpsuits. We believe a company is attempting to steal LTG's technology to leapfrog them in development of the next generation drone navigation and targeting systems. First to market isn't always a good thing. Sometimes, it's faster and cheaper to be second on the market, especially if you can steal the technology instead of spending millions to develop it through your own research and development. We don't know which company is responsible, but we're working on it."

"That's a lot to absorb. Where does Huntington's death fit?"

"Our theories range from unrelated to her being the mole, the corporate double agent."

24

THE PRIVATE MARINA near the naval base was filled almost entirely with sailboats. On the rear of one of them Green saw a stack of towels. The boat appeared to be empty. She reached over the railing and grabbed one. After drying off, she shook her head and ran her fingers through her hair. She reached into her trousers pocket for her cell phone. The screen was dark. After unsuccessfully trying to switch it on, she threw it into the water. She'd buy another one. She put her hand into her other pocket to confirm car keys and cash were still there. She tossed the wet towel onto the boat and walked to the marina office.

A girl, who looked to be about eighteen, was behind the desk, reading a glamour magazine.

"Mind if I use the phone? I'm so stupid. I slipped and fell in the water and lost my keys. I need to call a taxi."

The girl looked up from the magazine only long enough to respond, "Sure."

"Do you have the number for a taxi?"

The girl, who looked annoyed by yet another interruption, pointed to a couple of cards for taxi companies stuck on a corkboard beside her.

Green dialed the number for one of them. She gave the dispatcher the name and address of the marina she got from the stack of business cards beside the cash register. She thanked the girl, who without looking up said, "No problem."

Her clothes were almost dry when the taxi arrived about thirty minutes later. She told the driver to take her to One Fish-Two Fish. Within twenty minutes, they were within sight of the restaurant. Ahead of them was another restaurant.

"Stop here."

The driver responded in an Eastern European accent, "One Fish-Two Fish there." He pointed to the restaurant ahead of them.

"Stop. Let me out here. I changed my mind."

Green paid him, stepped out of the taxi, and sat in one of the chairs by the restaurant door, watching her car and looking for anything suspicious in the parking lot. She was confident the police would be unable to trace the car to her, so she was not concerned about them. If the men who had chased Palmer and her were lying in wait, she needed to spot them before they saw her. Her eyes darted to each car parked in the lot.

She waited thirty minutes before she walked nonchalantly to her car, listening for any movement. Once there, she worked fast. She walked around the car, checking all the wheel wells. The tracking device she found the day before had been in the front driver's side wheel well. She found another one in the second wheel well she checked. Palmer was right. One's good; two's better. She checked the other wheel wells, just to be sure. Then, she got on her knees and looked under the car, half-expecting to see a bomb.

Green slipped into her car and inspected the tracking device. It was a different shape and size than the other one. That gave her pause. If someone were clever enough to plant two devices on her car, the devices would be twinned, sending out the same signal to a single receiver. If one malfunctioned or was found, the other would keep transmitting the same signal to the receiver. *Why plant two devices?* There could be only one explanation. Different people had attached the devices to her car. Shaun and Graham had planted the first one, which she found and crushed under her shoe on the floor of the parking deck. The Arab men, who killed Shaun and Graham, had planted this one. That's how they followed her to Virginia Beach and found her at the restaurant.

Green turned the ignition key, holding her breath even though she hadn't seen anything unusual under the car. The car started, and she exhaled a sigh of relief. A black Ford King Ranch pick-up truck was parked nearby with a vacant space beside it. She pulled out of the space she was in and parked next to the truck, checking to make sure no one was watching. It only took a moment for her to place the device in the wheel well of the truck and drive away. *Follow that, assholes.* She smiled to herself.

25

"A VIRGINIA BEACH Police Marine Patrol Unit boat found a Chaparral bowrider aground on a shoal off Chick's Beach less than a mile from the inlet," Hamilton told Palmer. "They dusted for fingerprints, but the boat had been wiped clean."

"They broke off the chase when the patrol boat came toward me with its blue lights flashing," Palmer said. "Once they were back in the bay, they couldn't risk being caught by the Coast Guard, police, or a flotilla of vigilante pleasure boaters from One Fish-Two Fish, all full of wine and catch-of-the-day.

"I need to talk to Hawkins anyway," he continued. "I'll call him in the morning."

"The lieutenant agreed to cover the remainder of my watch," Hamilton said. "I assume you need a lift somewhere."

"I can take the boat back to the restaurant."

"Not a good idea."

Hamilton offered Palmer a ride back to the restaurant, giving him even more details on her upcoming trip to test the drone. The pair was comfortable together, straddling a line between flirting and business.

If all went well in Afghanistan, Hamilton would be back soon after the test. If it didn't, she would be away for a couple of months. She would be with the SEAL team at a remote base near the Afghanistan-Pakistan border.

"Don't go. Send someone else," Palmer said.

"How would that play out? *Admiral, may I be excused from the field test? A man I used to date, and whom I haven't seen or heard from in twenty years, is worried something is going to happen to me.*"

"Then I'm going with you."

"You're what?"

"You're not doing anything on the mission I haven't done a hundred times before. If I can't go as a member of your team, I'll go as a member of the LTG team."

"You're not going."

"I'm worried about you."

They were at the exit to the building. Hamilton stopped, folded her arms in front of her, and shook her head. "Why, after all this time, do you give a crap, Jake?"

"I just do."

"That was ages ago. I'm not one to dredge up the past, but you're the one that broke things off, not me. A week before you graduated, you told me you were joining the Navy as an enlisted man. I was a junior, a Navy ROTC midshipman, only a year away from graduation and my commission. You said it was going to be complicated."

She was right. He had made choices; she had made choices. Those choices, like the branches of a tree, had taken them in different directions. "I enlisted with the goal of becoming a SEAL. Even if you weren't going to be an officer, I wouldn't have wanted to put you through the anxiety of wondering whether I was dead or alive for weeks at a time when I was on a mission. And I wouldn't have wanted you in my head when I was."

Hamilton laughed.

"You know what I mean," Palmer said, curious at her reaction. "You work with those guys, and you know the pressure they're under each time they go out. It's just as hard, if not harder, on their wives. When you're on a mission, you're in reactive mode. If I had a wife and family to consider, I might have hesitated for a fraction of a second. That hesitation might have gotten me or one of my teammates killed."

"You really believe that rationalization bullshit, don't you?"

"What do you mean?" Palmer said.

"You really don't know, do you? No wonder you're still single. You can't commit to a relationship. That happened to us, and I bet it has happened to your other relationships. From your perspective, there's always a reason, like you're worried about putting a wife through too much stress."

"You don't know what you're talking about."

"After we broke up, I thought a lot about why it had happened. I questioned what I had done to lose you, all the while assuming it was my fault. Then it hit me. You had never gotten over your parents' divorce. You didn't want the same thing to happen to you, and one way to be absolutely certain it doesn't is never to fully commit to a relationship, to find an excuse why it won't work."

Is Lara right? Palmer thought about his failed relationships. He had strong feelings for Fiona, maybe even loved her. But since his last trip to London, he kept telling himself that long distance relationships do not work, and his relationship with Fiona was taking too much time away from his cases. *Is it all a self-fulfilling prophecy?* He looked at Hamilton's hand. Jansen had told him she wasn't married.

Hamilton saw him check out her ring finger. "I've had my share of serious relationships. I was engaged once."

"Didn't work out?" Palmer smirked.

Hamilton took a deep breath and exhaled. "He was killed by an IED in Iraq—five years ago."

"Damn. I'm sorry, Lara."

She paused for a moment before continuing. "I kept up with you, at least while you were in the Navy. You made quite a name for yourself. People here still remember you. Some of them even remembered hearing you talk about me."

"Your name might have come up on occasion, after a drink or two."

"You remember Mac McKiernan?"

Palmer laughed. "Mac? Of course I do." He and Jansen had reminisced about the "third musketeer" the day before Jansen was murdered. The three of them had spent many nights in bars, drinking until last call.

"Mac is a member of the SEAL team I'll be with. Do you remember Smitty?"

"Is that old fart still around?"

"He's on my team. He'll be on the carrier. The *George H.W. Bush*, with the Perseus drone aboard, left a couple of weeks ago. Smitty, along with the key members of the project team, will be flown onto the carrier for the field test. Smitty and Mac would both love to see you. Mac has a full schedule right up to our departure at sixteen hundred. Smitty's tied up in the afternoon but has some free time in the morning. Why don't you stop by? He can give you a demo of the Perseus navigation and targeting systems. Ten o'clock OK?"

"Works for me. Can't wait to see him."

"I'll brief him on what he can tell you. He can go into a little more detail about the technology."

Palmer was eager to see the Perseus system. He believed understanding it might provide a clue as to how the project might be linked to the two deaths. *Was Huntington somehow involved in industrial espionage, maneuvering her way onto the Navy's top-secret project at LTG? Had Huntington and Alona Green been working together?*

26

HASSAN ASWAD AND his nineteen men left the tribal village north of Peshawar. Crammed into several old cars and trucks, they would drive until the road narrowed into a wide path. To avoid discovery, the final leg of the journey to the abandoned Marine forward operating base Hammerbeck in Afghanistan's Kunar Province would take a day by foot. At last, the mission was underway. The enemy's capabilities exceeded theirs in almost every way. Aswad's primary advantage was surprise. They must gain the upper hand quickly, because it would last for only a brief time, after which the advantage would be lost, and the Americans might overwhelm them.

The men left the vehicles and began walking two at a time, as planned. Aswad and Abdul-Wajid Shadid, his next in command, were the last to leave. Aswad wanted to be certain the men left in the proper order and with the right amount of time spaced between them. If unexpected trouble arose, the men ahead of him would encounter it, not him. Aswad and Shadid waited until nightfall, drove two of the smaller trucks farther down the path, and hid them near the base under an anchored down, camouflage tarp. If something went wrong, they would use the trucks to escape with as many of the men as possible.

After the trucks were hidden from view, Shadid said, "When

will you tell the men the purpose of our mission?"

"An hour before we begin, when we are together."

Aswad restrained his excitement. He was close to achieving his sole personal ambition: to become to the Taliban what bin Laden was to al-Qaeda. The success of the mission was critically important to him in achieving that goal. He had put in his time, serving the jihad for many years. His reputation as a strategic tactician and superior field commander was well recognized. He had been on the U.S. terrorist watch list, until the news broke that he was killed in the drone strike. The only thing missing from his resume was a high profile, newsworthy mission to cement his name into history and make him the most visible, most feared terrorist leader since bin Laden. Soon, he would have his victory, and his place in history would forever be secure.

27

"I WISH YOU weren't going," Palmer said, standing by the driver's side door of Lara Hamilton's car in the parking lot of One Fish-Two Fish.

"Wish all you like. I'm going. I'll see you when I get back. In the meantime, stay out of trouble."

"That sounds more like a direct order than a request."

Hamilton winked and saluted him from her open car window.

Palmer watched her drive away before he got into his car. By the time he got to the Hilton, it was almost midnight—two late nights in a row. He needed some sleep. He threw his car keys, wallet, and watch on the table and was starting to undress when the bedside phone rang. He picked up the receiver, expecting it to be Hamilton.

"About time. I was beginning to think you were in the brig," said a cheery female voice. It was Alona Green.

"And I was wondering if you were fish food. Where the hell are you?"

"In the lobby on the house phone. I saw you go by. I waited to see if you were being followed before I called."

"Are you sure you weren't?"

"Of course. When I got back to my car, I found the other tracking device. No one followed me here."

Palmer gave her his room number. A few minutes later, there was a soft knock on the door. He looked through the peephole. Green was there, arms crossed, head cocked to the side. He unlatched the door and let her in.

"I need a shower. You mind?"

"Make yourself right at home. There's a bathrobe on the back of the door."

While she showered, Palmer poured a Scotch and sat in one of the two chairs in the room. He had spent less than an hour with her, most of which was on a boat eluding two Arab men, who were trying to kill them. *If she murdered Jansen, why would she want to meet with me earlier and come here now? She admitted she switched laptops with Owen Fuller, and his laptop was used by someone to access LTG's secure networks. What happened? Did the plan go sour? Who were those Arab men? Maybe a Middle Eastern government ran the operation, not another company. Was it the plan all along to keep her around until they got all they could from LTG's networks and then kill her?* His gut told him she did not kill Jansen, but he still would not allow himself to trust her. Sun Tzu, the Chinese military philosopher and author of the *Art of War,* is often credited with saying one should keep his friends close but his enemies closer. Whichever she was, he would not let her out of his sight.

In about fifteen minutes, she came out wearing the hotel bathrobe. She sat on the bed, drying her black hair with a towel.

"Thanks. Ever since I got out of the water, I've been itching like crazy."

"Crabs."

"Beg your pardon."

"They're baby crabs—megalops."

"Whatever. I feel much better. So, what happened after I left?"

"Abandoned ship is more like it. The Navy grilled me and let me go. They found the other boat run aground near the Little Creek amphibious base inlet. No sign of your friends."

"Really? They weren't with the boat, arms raised, waiting to be arrested."

"Smartass."

Palmer looked at her. She sat on the edge of the bed with wet hair and the terry cloth robe opened, exposing much of her thigh. She needed no makeup to cover her flaws; she had none to conceal. By anyone's standard, Alona Green was a beautiful woman.

"Thanks for getting me out of that restaurant and away from those men."

"If I had thought you murdered Wade, the only reason I would have rescued you was so I could kill you myself."

"So you believe me?"

"It's more that I don't *not* believe you. If you had killed him, you wouldn't have contacted me before and again now. You have a story to tell, and you want me to hear it."

"How long have you got?"

"You're in my room. I'm not going anywhere."

28

GREEN TOLD PALMER that her job was to steal Fuller's laptop, get his ID and password, and do it without him suspecting it had been stolen. Stealing it was easy; getting his ID and password and stringing him along for a few days to keep him from reporting it stolen distinguished her from the pack. Airlines, like defense contractors, have extremely tight computer system security, but very few corporations book their own travel; they outsource it to a travel group that sends itineraries to the company by e-mail. She hacked into the travel agency systems and reviewed Fuller's travel history for the past year. When she saw the itinerary for his London trip, she knew it was a perfect opportunity. Fuller's layover was long enough to lure him away for dinner and give him a metallic business card.

"You had those cards made with the sole purpose of giving him one, didn't you?"

A sly grin came across her face. "I switched laptops while he was being frisked and wanded by the TSA agent. I didn't have any checked baggage, so after I switched the laptops in security and confirmed the password and ID I gleaned from him on the flight worked, I left the airport. My contact had given me an address and told me two men would be waiting for me. I was to give them the laptop and stay until they finished their work.

Once the job was complete, I would receive the other half of my fee."

"How much?"

"Fifty thousand, half up front, plus expenses, and the other half when they finished. After I gave them the laptop, the two geeks—Graham and Shaun—went to work. I stayed in the house with them. They printed reams of documents, which they never let out of their sight. On the few occasions when they both left the room, they secured the computers and took the printed material with them."

"You had plenty of time to observe them. What were they up to?"

"Some type of corporate espionage. As long as I was getting paid, I didn't care."

"Why did they wait to pay you the second half of your fee?"

"I've thought a lot about that. I guess they wanted to make sure I was doing all I could to string Fuller along for the longest possible time before he reported his laptop stolen or before LTG discovered what they were doing and shut off access."

Palmer took a drink of Scotch and leaned back in the chair. "What happened the day you left?"

"They went to another room and shut the door. They were arguing. Their voices were muffled. I couldn't tell what they were saying. Then I heard something. It sounded like the front door shutting. I was in the back of the house, so I peeked down the hall toward the door. I saw the two men, the same two who were at the restaurant. One of them had a gun. They moved slowly toward the room Shaun and Graham were in. I had to get out of there. I grabbed the laptop and was crawling out the window when I heard gunshots. I ran around the house to my car and was pulling out of the driveway when they came out the front door. I was able to get away before they could stop me."

"If Shaun and Graham were killed, the police will have a report on the murders. I'll look into that. Why didn't you leave the laptop at the house or destroy it?"

Green said that although she was not certain that was what the men were after, she was not going to leave it behind. When she called LTG's main number and asked for the head of corporate security, she was transferred to Jansen, and he agreed to meet with her. She figured if she returned Fuller's laptop, he would help her, but he told her LTG wasn't in the protection business and suggested she contact Palmer.

"Why didn't you call Fuller?"

"I didn't think he would be very understanding of the situation."

"Fair point."

"Neither was Jansen for that matter, until I talked to him."

"So, where's Fuller's laptop?"

"I gave it to Jansen. He set it on the desk on top of mine."

"Did he return yours?"

"I told him he could keep it. I was pretty sure LTG installed some tracking software. The computer was clean except for the pre-installed software. I bought it solely for the purpose of switching it with Fuller's. I ran the set-up program, created an ID and password, and wiped it clean before putting it into my computer bag. I picked it up with my scarf when I put it in the tray on the security belt and when I took it from the tray and slid it into Fuller's computer bag."

"When you left Wade's office, were both laptops on his desk?"

"Yes."

"When you left LTG, did you leave alone?"

"Jansen rode on the elevator with me to the ground floor and told me to sign out. He was in a hurry to get back to his office and make a couple of calls. The guard wasn't there, so I just left."

Her story matched the security camera video of her leaving the building alone. Palmer thought about the note he found on the floor beside the desk. Green said Jansen was in a hurry to return to his office to make a couple of calls, one of which may have been to him. Jansen was murdered before he had a chance to call. Palmer was not going to be her bodyguard, but he was going to use her as bait. The two men would try to find her—and when they did, Palmer would be waiting.

"Where did you stay last night?"

"A hotel in Norfolk, nowhere near as nice as this one. I've been there two nights. I checked out this morning after I heard about Jansen."

"Stay here tonight," Palmer said.

"A little forward, aren't you?"

"Don't flatter yourself. I'll book a room for you under my name."

"Are you throwing me out?"

"Against my better judgment, yes. The police want to see me tomorrow morning about the incident at the restaurant. I also need to stop by LTG and go to the Navy amphibious base to see a friend. I should be back by one or two o'clock. Wait for me. Call room service for breakfast and lunch and watch TV. Do not leave the room. Do you understand?"

"No, could you repeat it?" Green said, rolling her eyes.

"Listen, dammit. My friend has been murdered. This isn't a game. You have my cell phone number. Call me if anything happens."

"I will. Don't get your boxers all in a twist."

Palmer phoned the front desk. While he was talking, he watched Green open the sliding glass door and step out onto the balcony. She opened the front of her robe and rested her hands on the rail, allowing the ocean breeze to blow her robe back and caress her naked body as she gazed at the moon's reflection glimmering on the water. When he got off the phone, he poured both of them some Scotch and joined her. He cleared his throat when he stepped out. Green closed her robe, tying the terry cloth belt in front.

Palmer handed her a glass. She smelled it and took a drink. "I'm not a Scotch drinker, but tonight I'll make an exception."

He stood close to her, looking at her and then at the moon. "The adjoining room is vacant. The bellman's bringing up the keys."

"It is beautiful here, so peaceful."

29

THE NEXT MORNING, Palmer saw Lieutenant Hawkins walking toward the Virginia Beach Municipal Center. He hurried, catching up with him just before he entered the building.

Hawkins glared at Palmer. "Seeing you just made my bad mood worse. This is the second night in a row you've cost me a good night's sleep. What the hell were you thinking?"

"This woman—"

Hawkins interrupted. "I'm willing to bet most of your stories start out with those two words. They teach you anything about obstruction of justice at law school?"

"She said if she saw any sign of the police, she'd disappear. One of the men was armed, so we borrowed the boat and got out of there before he started shooting in a crowded restaurant."

"You're stretching the definition of borrow, counselor."

"All right, commandeered a boat."

They were still standing outside the entrance to the building when the roar of jet engines drowned their voices out. Palmer looked up to see two Navy F/A-18 Super Hornet fighter jets flying low overhead, making their landing approach at Oceana Naval Air Station, the Navy's East Coast master jet base. As the second circled around to land behind the first, the noise began to subside.

"Let's go inside where we can hear each other," Hawkins said. On the way to his office, Hawkins told him that one of his officers talked to the girl who was on duty at the marina at Little Creek Inlet. She remembered a woman, who was soaking wet, telling her she had fallen overboard and lost her keys. She said the woman called a taxi and waited for it outside the marina office. The officer located the taxi driver, who told him the woman asked him to take her to One Fish-Two Fish, but changed her mind and had him drop her off at another restaurant near One Fish-Two Fish.

"Green probably wanted to make sure the men weren't waiting for her."

"What did she have to say?"

"She said Wade escorted her downstairs, but didn't get off the elevator. The guard was away when she went by the desk, so she left without signing out."

"And you believe her?"

"If I didn't, she'd be dead. She gave Fuller's laptop to Wade. He tried to return hers, but she told him to keep it. She suspected LTG installed some tracking or monitoring software on it. She said Jansen set it on top of hers on his desk. Have you examined it?"

"We have. Other than the standard pre-installed programs and some tracking software, the laptop was empty, just as it comes off the shelf. We found Jansen's fingerprints and some others we're still trying to identify. They may belong to the LTG employees who checked it out. Since we don't have Green's fingerprints, we've nothing to compare them with."

"She said she wiped her laptop down before making the switch at the airport."

"That figures."

"But I brought you a present." Palmer handed Hawkins a brown paper bag he had been carrying.

Hawkins took the bag and started to reach inside.

"Don't touch it," Palmer said.

"What is it?"

"A glass with Alona Green's fingerprints and DNA." The glass was the one she had drunk Scotch from in Palmer's room at the Hilton. He let Hawkins assume it was from One Fish-Two

Fish. "Can you run it?"

Hawkins looked inside the bag. "Sure. It may take a few days."

"Let me know what you find."

"Maybe she took Fuller's laptop after she shot Jansen. Did she tell you what she was doing with it?"

"She was hired to get Fuller's laptop and deliver it to two men, Shaun and Graham—she didn't know their last names—at a house in Conshohocken, near Philadelphia. The men used the laptop to access LTG networks. A couple of days ago, they got into an argument and went into another room to talk. While they were in the room, two Middle Eastern men entered the house. One of them had a gun. She grabbed the laptop and was jumping out a window when she heard gunshots."

"The same two men who were at the restaurant?"

"Right. Can you contact the local police and confirm her story about the two men in Conshohocken being shot?"

"Give me a minute," Hawkins said.

They had been standing outside Hawkins's office. He went inside and shut the door. Palmer waited nearby in a vacant cubicle. Fifteen minutes later, Hawkins motioned for him to come in.

"What did you find out?"

"Two men were killed in a house in Conshohocken a couple of days ago. The crime scene investigators found some drug paraphernalia and traces of crack cocaine."

"Any computers?"

"Nothing. Only a few pieces of furniture and some beer in the fridge. The victims were identified as Graham Willett and Shaun Tuttle, two self-employed information technology consultants. They paid cash in advance for a three-month lease on the house. Forensics found their prints in the house, as well as some others they couldn't identify. It boils down to this: Do I believe her story? Or, do I believe she got the money for the laptop theft from someone else, went to score some drugs, and killed Willett and Tuttle."

"She killed two drug dealers and takes Owen Fuller's laptop to LTG, where she killed Wade. That's ridiculous. They were either IT consultants or drug dealers. They weren't both."

"It's just a theory. I didn't say it was a good one."

Palmer thought about what Hawkins had said. Assuming Green was telling the truth, the two Middle Eastern men shot Shaun and Graham, cleared out the computers, and staged the scene to make the murders look like a drug deal gone bad. Maybe that's why they failed to chase her when she drove away from the house. They were in a hurry to stage the crime scene in case someone had heard the gunshots and called the police. Regardless, the police now wanted Green in connection with three murders.

"Why did she contact Jansen?" Hawkins asked.

"She knew she was in over her head and thought LTG might protect her."

"And you believe that?"

"Actually, I do. Can you match the bullets that killed Willett and Tuttle with those that killed Jansen."

"The investigating officer in Conshohocken will fax me the ballistics report. They're running a trace on the weapon to see who owns it. It's probably unregistered."

"Anything new on the Huntington death?" Palmer asked.

"Michael Sutton, LTG's chief information officer, stopped by. He brought printouts of all the e-mail correspondence he had with Huntington on his personal computer. I've compared it with the e-mails from her personal computer. They match up. The past few indicate there was trouble in paradise. Just like he told me when I interviewed him at LTG, Huntington wanted out. He accused her of using him to get on the Perseus project team."

"So his wife doesn't know about the affair?"

"No, and I see no reason to destroy his marriage without more evidence. He gave us permission to run a check of his office e-mails and cell phone calls."

"How about his personal computers and phones?"

"With his permission, we're searching the records for his home and cell phones. For now, I'm holding off issuing a warrant and confiscating his computers. Look, Palmer, we've had four murders, if you count the two in Philly. Ms. Green is a person of interest in three of them. If the ballistics report from Jansen's death and the Pennsylvania deaths show the same gun was used, she's on the hook for those."

"I'll admit she's probably guilty of a lot of things, but not murder. Even if she shot Jansen and the two men in Pennsylvania, which I don't believe she did, it would be a huge stretch to think she also poisoned Huntington."

"Why are you defending her?"

Palmer stood and walked to the window. His mind raced with questions and doubts. *Why am I defending her? If Green murdered the men in Pennsylvania, why contact Wade? Why return the laptop? Why not leave it in the house or throw it in the Schuylkill River? Was it because of the murders in Pennsylvania? If so, why murder Jansen? She had the opportunity, but what could have been the motive?*

"You've fallen under her spell, just like Fuller, haven't you?"

"Hell no!" Palmer responded emphatically, turning around to face Hawkins.

Hawkins rose from his seat and walked over to Palmer. "Personally, I don't care if you have fallen for her. But if you know where she's hiding, you'd better tell me, or you'll find yourself in jail facing some very serious charges."

30

WHEN PALMER ARRIVED at the Navy amphibious base, he was directed to an area adjacent to the gate to have his car inspected. While one guard checked his ID and confirmed his name was on the list of visitors, another searched his trunk and then used a mirror on a pole to check under his car. When they finished, one of the guards waved him through. Chief Petty Officer Howard E. Schmidt was waiting for Palmer at Naval Special Warfare Support Activity Two and was at his car door before he could get out. They shook hands and hugged, clinging together a little longer than usual before vigorously thumping each other on the back with the other hand. They spoke briefly about Jansen's death, recalling the days when the three of them served together on the team.

"It's been too long, Smitty. How's it going?"

"Business is good. There's no legal limit on the number of terrorists you bag these days."

"As long as you read them their rights first."

Palmer followed Schmidt through the building to a room with a secure entry panel beside the door. Schmidt bent down slightly so that his eyes were even with a scanner on the panel. An electronic female voice stated, "Cleared for entry." The room resembled a small theatre with rows of seats, enough for between twenty and thirty people, elevated behind a very contemporary mock-up of a cockpit. The cockpit had two seats with multiple electronic panels in front of each, and over them were several large flat-screen monitors.

"You're looking at something very few people have seen, my friend: the future. This is a test and training facility. For now, most of the observers are Navy and civilian bigwigs. They watch the large screens overhead, while a narrator explains what they're seeing. The cockpit is a prototype of the Navy drone pilot's cockpit. The pilot sits on the left, just as he would in an airplane. The person responsible for day and night sensors and target tracking sits on the right. The Air Force pilots live and work in Nevada, far removed from the battlefield. That causes all sorts of problems, both ethical and personal. The plan is for Navy drone pilots, for the most part, to be based on the carriers with the drones. The number of the drone cockpits on a carrier will be based on the maximum number of drones the carrier may have in the air at one time."

Palmer had used flight simulators in the past. This one was nothing like any he'd ever seen. They sat in the two cockpit seats, Schmidt on the left. Palmer shifted in his seat and watched Smitty go through the start-up process. The screens on the consoles in front of them sprung to life. On the center screen were video images that to Palmer looked like Iraq or Afghanistan.

"The videos are from previous drone flyovers in Afghanistan. This area," Smitty said, pointing to the monitor, "is near where the ground portion of the field test will be run." Schmidt picked up an electronic tablet about twice the size of an Apple iPad. He flipped through the images on the display, swiping his finger across the screen. He explained that a Navy pilot trained by the drone manufacturer would fly the drone until Hamilton acquired control at the op site. Project team members from the manufacturer and LTG would be on the carrier to ensure everything went smoothly and to resolve problems, if any occurred. Once Hamilton took over, she would direct the drone from a remote unit like the simulation tablet.

Palmer watched Schmidt go through a series of steps to get the demo loaded. The process took about ten minutes. On the screen, a convoy of military vehicles came into view. Schmidt picked up the electronic tablet and activated the targeting module. He maneuvered the crosshairs over the lead vehicle, locked it onto the position, and sat back in his chair. The crosshairs stayed on top of the vehicle. He followed it for a while before tapping the screen to enter some commands. When he tapped the final time, the vehicle exploded.

Other than the use of the electronic tablet to pilot the drone, Palmer didn't see anything he had not seen on countless news reports in the past five years.

"That was simple old-school technology—nothing too exciting. Now watch this." Another video appeared—a road in the desert. Schmidt touched an icon on the screen labeled "Targeting Mode" and touched an icon labeled "DoSTA." A keyboard appeared on the screen. He typed in a series of numbers and letters. The image changed as the drone altered its course. In a minute or two, an armored vehicle appeared at the bottom of the screen with the crosshairs locked onto it. A message popped up on the screen: "DoSTA Signal Acquired." Two icons were within the pop-up window. One was "Fire," and the other was "Continue to Track." Schmidt touched the "Fire" icon and another window popped up, asking to confirm the Fire command. He tapped the "Fire" icon once again, and the armored vehicle exploded.

"Son of a bitch," Palmer exclaimed. "Are you kidding me?"

"You haven't seen anything yet. This is my favorite."

Schmidt brought up another video, this one of a town with several buildings, similar in size and shape. "This is a purpose-built town in Nevada that we used for testing." He touched TARGETING MODE on the screen, tapped PHYSICAL CHARACTERISTICS RECOGNITION TARGETING and then, from a menu of options, pulled up a photograph of one of the buildings in the town. He tapped the photograph and hit AUTO FIND AND FIRE. Then he sat back. The crosshairs on the screen moved from building to building and flashed before settling on one of the buildings that appeared slightly larger than the others. The photographic image merged over the video image, the screen flashed green, and a missile fired, destroying the building.

"What the hell was that?" Palmer asked.

"You're aware of facial recognition software, right?"

"Of course."

"This is physical characteristic recognition. For example, a SEAL team can snap a photograph of a building or any physical object and upload it to the drone. The drone locates and confirms the likeness at 99.9% accuracy. Perseus can either be set to either FIND AND CONFIRM, which requires human confirmation and firing of the missile, or AUTO FIND AND FIRE, meaning the drone finds and fires automatically without operator confirmation. If the likeness is less than ninety-five percent, it will not fire without human intervention."

"How does it work?"

"It's a combination of GPS and electro-optical/infrared technology, along with passive millimeter wave imaging, a military application of the technology used to scan passengers at airports that can penetrate fog, dust, smoke, light rain, and some physical objects. Don't ask me to explain how it all works. I just know it does."

"That's amazing."

"Once Perseus is in production, there will be a confirmation protocol requiring authorization before weapons are fired or set to auto fire."

"So if you can run the operation from the carrier, why put the SEAL team in harm's way?" Palmer asked.

"We're testing the ability of a SEAL team in the field to take control of a Perseus drone launched from a carrier and to upload images of targets they locate while in the field. On this mission, they will first launch missiles at real targets marked with tracking dots fired from what, for all practical purposes, is a very expensive, high-powered air gun, as well as some non-essential, unoccupied buildings. The plan is to use a former Marine forward operating base as the op site. Other SEAL team members, working in pairs, will mark and monitor the targets for twenty-four hours leading up to the test. After that portion of the test is complete, the team will use the base itself as a target to test the physical characteristic recognition technology. Our intel is that insurgents are using the base as a stopover when going to and from Pakistan. After this mission, it will be a pile of rubble."

"What's your role?"

"Perseus was loaded by crane onto the USS *George H.W. Bush* at Norfolk Naval Base last month, the day before the *Bush* deployed to the Persian Gulf. I'll be flown onto the carrier prior to the test. Most of the civilian project personnel are already on board. Once the field test commences, I'll be in the combat direction center, where I'll be the primary liaison between the LTG team, the SEAL team on the ground, and the Navy personnel on the ship. My job is to keep everyone advised of everything that happens up to and including the point at which control of the bird passes to the field team."

"I want to be with you during the test."

"Sorry. Only a handpicked contingent of civilian project team members and Navy personnel will be in the control room."

"When do things start happening?"

"As early as next week, if the team's in place, the bird's ready to fly, and the weather cooperates."

"I have a bad feeling about this mission, Smitty—like a symptom you can't describe to your doctor, but it's there all the same. With Angela Huntington and Wade being killed within days of each other, I need more time to investigate the connection to this project. I'm worried about Lara and the team. You know what I mean."

"You've been away from the action too long. Don't worry. Everything is under control."

"Is there any way I can contact you or you can contact me?"

"Satellite phone is the only way. Hamilton told me the mother hen was worried about her chicks. I have one for you." Schmidt extracted a black satellite phone from a small satchel from under the table and handed it to him. Palmer held it in his hand and examined it.

"Sweet."

"Don't call me for the weather report. And don't run up the Navy's phone bill calling your friends all over the world. Only use it for a dire emergency."

31

PALMER TOUCHED HIS new LTG ID badge to the sensor on the turnstile, waited for the green light, and walked through to the elevators. Ed Taylor's secretary told him that he was meeting with someone and asked him to wait in the vacant office next door. From there, Palmer could hear the conversation in Taylor's office, not well enough to understand what was being said, but well enough to know it was heated and animated. In a few minutes, the conversation ended. He heard the door open and someone leave. Taylor's secretary motioned to him that Taylor was free to see him. Palmer closed the door behind him after he entered and sat in the chair in front of Taylor's desk.

"What was that all about?" he asked.

"You," Taylor said. "That was our senior vice president of Legal, chewing my butt out. To say he wasn't pleased by your antics yesterday would be a huge understatement. Did you really steal a boat and get arrested by the Navy?"

"I commandeered that boat, and the Navy doesn't actually arrest you."

"Don't be flippant with me. LTG doesn't need that kind of publicity. We've had two murders in a short period of time, and now one of our independent contractors steals a boat and charges into the Navy amphib base. Are you crazy?"

"I assume that's a rhetorical question. Are you interested in hearing my side of the story?"

While Palmer told Taylor what had transpired the previous day, Taylor sat back in his chair with his arms folded across his chest. He listened in silence, occasionally shaking his head. By the time he finished, Taylor had begun to relax somewhat, although he was, by no means, calm.

Taylor stood, placed his hands on his desk, and leaned toward Palmer. "I should terminate your contract and send you packing."

Palmer stood and faced him. "You can terminate my contract if you like. That's your choice. But I'll continue to search for Wade's killer until I find him."

"Or her."

"She didn't kill him."

"How can you be certain?"

"I just am."

Taylor turned away from Palmer, pacing the length of the room as he continued. "The only thing saving your ass is the call I received from Hawkins about an hour ago. He called you unconventional, in a good way, saying you might be an asset to his investigation."

"I knew we hit it off," Palmer said.

"Though he warned me that if you are hiding Alona Green, he would arrest you. Where is she?"

"She's not the kind of person who stays in one place for very long."

Taylor stopped pacing and stood facing the window, his back to Palmer. "When you find her, and I know you will, turn her in."

"Alona Green is the least of your problems. Something's going on with the Perseus project. I tried to convince Hamilton to postpone the field test."

Taylor whipped his body around, glared at him, and shouted, "You what?"

"I told her to postpone it, at least for a few days, to give us more time to investigate Wade's death."

"Who the hell gives you the authority to ask the Navy to postpone the Perseus field test?"

"She said the same thing—well, not in those exact words."

"What could possibly happen?"

"Huntington was working on the project. Fuller is the Perseus project leader, and his laptop was stolen and used to access LTG secure networks. After Green gave Wade the laptop, he was murdered. No matter which way I turn, I run into the Perseus project."

Taylor faced Palmer. "You'll need more than paranoid speculation to delay the field test. When you have something specific and some evidence to support your wild-ass theory, let me know. Until then, I don't want you to so much as fart without my approval. Now, get the hell out of here."

32

PALMER STOPPED BY Cora Donegan's office at LTG. The Human Resources director was on her way to lunch and invited him to join her. It was her only free time for the rest of the day. After going through the cafeteria line, they sat at a table in the far corner to lessen the likelihood of someone joining them or stopping by to ask her a question.

"I heard you had an exciting day yesterday," Donegan said.

"Word spreads fast. Taylor's not too happy with me."

"Neither is Legal. Did you expect them to be?"

"I'm not being paid to make everyone happy. If Alona Green's telling the truth, and I believe she is, the Perseus project is the common denominator in the two murders at LTG. When the guard and I found Wade's body, there was only one laptop on his desk. It was Green's, not Fuller's. Green said when she gave Fuller's laptop to Wade, he set it on top of hers in the middle of his desk. Both laptops were there when she left. Therefore, if you believe her, whoever killed Wade took Owen Fuller's laptop. Fuller is the project leader for Perseus, and Huntington worked on the project."

"All based on your assumption that Alona Green's telling the truth, someone we know to be a thief, con artist, corporate spy, and God knows what else."

"Do you run security checks on your employees?"

"Before we extend a job offer, we check references and request security clearance, if required. References are a formality. Because the applicant provides us with the names, we assume they will give a positive recommendation to hire. It's still worth doing. On occasion, a reference will surprise us. Depending on the applicant's role and responsibility, we also request a security clearance. The Defense Industrial Security Office conducts those. The applicant is told at the time that the offer is contingent on the outcome of the reference check and security clearance. Because the security clearance process takes so long, we normally obtain an interim clearance first in order to proceed with the hiring process. Why do you ask?"

"Did you review the security checks for the Perseus project team members to see if anything unusual came up?"

Before answering, Donegan took a forkful of salad and chewed like it was a piece of cheap steak. "Such as?"

"You'll know it when you see it. We're missing something."

"If there's anything unusual, we would have followed though to resolve it, or we wouldn't have hired them."

"Check anyway."

"I don't have time for this."

"It's important, or I wouldn't be asking. I have a hunch and want to follow it through."

"The results are in each member's personnel file. I'll have my secretary pull the files, but I'll have to review each of them. It will take a couple of days."

"The Naval Special Warfare team flies out today and will be in Afghanistan and on the carrier with the LTG team a few days from now to conduct the field test. If my hunch is correct and something happens to the team—something that could have been prevented if you had reviewed the files—would you want that on your conscience?"

Donegan set down her fork and leaned back in her chair. "I'll call you if I see anything out of the ordinary."

^^^^

On his way to the Hilton, Palmer stopped at Jansen's home. The children had arrived and a neighbor, who had dropped off some food, was just leaving. He talked to Carol in general terms about the police investigation. She put on a brave face, but he could see she was distraught.

Palmer stayed longer than he intended. Before he left, Carol spoke more about Wade Jansen's memorial service at their church in Virginia Beach and asked him to give the eulogy. Jansen would be buried later at Arlington National Cemetery. Palmer accepted but immediately began to dread the thought of trying to hold himself together while speaking of his friend in front of what would likely be a large Navy and civilian crowd, paying their last respects.

33

GREEN WAS BORED silly staring at the four walls of the hotel room. The view of the beach from her balcony only worsened the sense of confinement. She needed a new phone and knew she could find one in the stores near the hotel. She pulled her hair back and left, stopping at a shop across the street that sold beach towels, boogie boards, and other items tourists needed for their beach vacations. She paid cash for a pair of large sunglasses and a floppy hat, donned them, and walked until she found a shop that sold prepaid phones.

Green liked her unconventional life. Hers was as unpredictable as it was exciting—one that did not conform to what most people might expect from a bright, attractive woman. It had not begun that way. At MIT she spent more time working in the library and computer lab than enjoying the Cambridge and Boston nightlife. She dated no one for more than a few months. Whenever she saw that certain look in a man's eyes or whenever his talk turned to settling down or moving in together, she broke off the relationship. Serious relationships took time and energy. Falling in love was a major distraction. Someday, she would be ready for that, just not now. Her dream had been to accomplish things no one had ever done—discover the unknown, explore the uncharted, invent the unimaginable, and travel to exotic places.

She had spent very little time with Palmer, yet was drawn to him—perhaps, because he seemed to be the male version of her. That could spell trouble in the long run, but she knew her time with Palmer was limited. There was no future. She planned to enjoy the next few days and not think about what she might have to do beyond that. For someone who always worked alone, having him close felt good. She knew he did not trust her and had no idea who she really was. Yet, for whatever reason, he seemed convinced she did not kill Wade Jansen

^^^^

Palmer opened the door to his room at the Hilton and saw an envelope on the floor. He picked it up and read it. "Completely stir crazy. Gone for a walk on the boardwalk. Back soon. A.G."

The door to the adjoining room was locked. He knocked. She didn't respond. He called her room from the phone by the bed. No answer. He stepped onto the balcony. The boardwalk was jammed with people taking advantage of the warm, sunny day—walking, biking, and skating. In the distance, he thought he saw her. The woman was wearing a large hat, so he could not see her face; and although he was not a hundred percent certain, he recognized her walk. He looked carefully at the people around her. Behind her, farther down the boardwalk, two Virginia Beach bicycle policemen were headed in her direction.

Palmer rushed out the door and took the elevator to the ground floor. He stepped quickly through the restaurant and out the door leading to the beach. Running would catch the policemen's attention. He walked fast until he met the woman on the boardwalk. It was Green.

"Are you crazy?" he said.

"I couldn't stay in that room another minute. Besides, I needed to buy a new phone. Don't worry—I bought a prepaid phone and paid cash."

"If the Arabs don't find you, the police will." Palmer motioned in the direction of the policemen with his head.

Green looked over her shoulder and saw them. They had stopped to help a skateboarder who had wiped out on the concrete boardwalk.

Palmer and Green walked straight ahead, not looking back.

"What did you do today?"

"Got my ass chewed out by Wade's replacement at LTG."

In a few minutes, the policemen rode by on their bikes without noticing them.

"I'm waiting for someone to get back to me. In the meantime, there's not much I can do here over the weekend. If I'm going to keep you out of sight, we need to get away from Virginia Beach."

"Where are you taking me?"

"The North Carolina Outer Banks—an hour or so away. It's quieter there, and we'll be safer."

34

HASSAN ASWAD STOOD alone, his arms crossed over his chest, in the middle of the abandoned compound, situated on a narrow corridor through which travelers passed between Pakistan and Afghanistan. He remembered the day last December when, after months of fighting, they had taken control of the U.S. Marine forward operating base. Their celebration was short-lived. The Americans had tricked them. He believed the ammunition they left behind had been used to provide the drones with targeting information that resulted in the death of many of his men. Their lives were a small price to pay for the ultimate revenge and victory that would soon be his. Still, Aswad was angry with himself for not following his gut instinct. He should not have taken the munitions the Marines left behind. His information source had known of a planned test but did not know where or when the test was to be conducted and knew nothing of the details. Aswad was an unwilling accomplice in an American plan and only through Allah's grace had he been spared.

Aswad and his men had entered the compound one or two at a time over the course of a day to prevent drawing the attention of the American drones. If drones were monitoring the base in advance of the operation, this level of activity would not seem unusual. Had twenty armed men entered at the same time, it would have. The challenge now was to keep them out of sight for the next seventy-two hours. Since the base was abandoned several months ago, travelers—mostly insurgents who came upon it in their travels—went through every building in search of something of value. Some used it as an overnight stop. It had been picked clean.

Aswad walked in a tight circle, observing all and seeing nothing, although all nineteen of his men were within five hundred yards. As instructed, they went inside the buildings and remained hidden after they arrived. He was pleased. Aswad had detailed information about the Navy's plan to test the new drone and its navigation and targeting system.

Abdul-Wajid Shadid approached Aswad. "The men are getting restless, a combination of nerves and boredom."

"Tell them I will kill anyone who steps outside."

35

PALMER WAS READING the Sunday paper while he drank his morning coffee on the back balcony of the appropriately named Tranquil House Inn in Manteo, North Carolina, on Roanoke Island.

He felt the warmth of the early morning sun and watched the sea birds flying over the water. He looked to the marina below and across Scarboro Creek, an offshoot of Shallowbag Bay, to the replica of the *Elizabeth II*, one of seven ships on which English settlers sailed the Atlantic to reach the new world in 1585. They had come in to establish a permanent and profitable colony in a land of hope and opportunity. So much had changed in four-hundred-plus years, not all of it for the better.

Alona Green was still in her room. She was a late sleeper, like many people without a regular job. Palmer was an early riser, always had been. He enjoyed the morning, the time of the day before most people in the sleepy resort town were moving around. Palmer set the newspaper on his lap, took a sip of coffee, and thought about the weekend.

Manteo had turned out to be a perfect choice for keeping Green out of sight of the police and the two men who were after her. They meandered about the restaurants, pubs, and shops. On Saturday morning, they purchased swimsuits and beach towels.

She modeled several one-piece swimsuits for him in the store, asking his opinion about each. He was surprised at her lack of visible tattoos, although he considered the possibility that the one-piece suit hid a tramp stamp on her lower back. That was a mystery that would remain unsolved, or so he thought.

They had driven south on Highway 12 and found an undeveloped, almost deserted beach on the barrier island. After they spread out their beach towels, he watched her step out of the shorts and T-shirt she was wearing over her black swimsuit. It was cut low, exposing enough of her breasts for him to be unable to resist imagining what the rest looked like.

Lying on their towels, Palmer flipped through a magazine while Green read a novel. No one was in sight, and the only sounds were the waves and sea birds. Without a word, Green stood and walked toward the water, as she had done a couple of times before, jumping into the refreshing Atlantic to cool off. He looked up from his magazine and sat up, peering over his sunglasses to watch her. She walked the runway walk of a model, her arms swinging loosely by her sides, as she placed one foot directly in front of the other, causing her butt to twist invitingly with each step. At the water's edge, where the waves were lapping on the shore, she stopped, slipped off her swimsuit, and tossed it on the dry sand behind her. She walked into the ocean as calmly as if she had stepped out of a pair of flip-flops. There was no tramp stamp in the small of her back.

He watched her swim for a few minutes, fighting the urge to join her. She slipped out of the water and ran her fingers through her hair, pulling it behind her neck. Her figure was flawless, and her pubic area cleanly shaven. She turned her back to him and, keeping her legs straight and slightly apart, picked up her swimsuit and shook off the sand before returning to the water's edge to put it on. When she came out and walked toward him, he turned on his side, cocked his head, and watched her saunter back. Standing beside him, she wrung the water out of her hair before patting her face dry with a towel.

The ring of Palmer's phone jarred him from his daydream about the weekend with Alona. Annoyed by the interruption, he glanced at his phone. It was Cora Donegan from LTG.

"What have you got?" he snapped.

"What's with the attitude? I spent all day and night yesterday going over the files for the Perseus project team members for you."

"Sorry, Cora. I have a lot on my mind."

"I didn't see anything unusual until I got to Angela Huntington's file."

Donegan had found a sealed manila envelope stamped "Personal and Confidential." Inside was a report entitled, *Risk Analysis of the Use of Multiple Controllers in the Navigation and Target Acquisition/Tracking Systems for the Perseus Drone.* Huntington authored the report and sent it to Perseus Project Team Leader Owen Fuller. Huntington concluded that the use of multiple controllers resulted in unacceptable risks, including the issuing of conflicting commands. The biggest concern, however, was the risk of the drone controller falling into the wrong hands.

"Now we're getting somewhere. E-mail me the report as a PDF."

"I can't e-mail a confidential document to a non-secure number," Donegan said. "You can read it in my presence tomorrow."

"What did Fuller do with the report?"

"I called Owen last night. He wasn't happy. He said Huntington threw the report on his desk and demanded he do something. Fuller read it, found that Huntington made some valid points, and then he presented it to the LTG committee that oversees our projects. Fuller told them that changes at this stage would delay the project timeline and result in cost overruns. Instead, he recommended that Huntington's concerns be addressed after the field testing. The committee supported his recommendation and thanked him for bringing it to their attention."

"Why was the report in her personnel file?"

"Not sure. Huntington asked that the report be placed in her personnel file. Maybe she felt it was an achievement that needed to be recognized at her annual review."

"Or maybe it was the only place she felt the report would be safe," Palmer said. "At least Fuller didn't just round file it. At least he presented her concerns to the committee."

"Anything else? Palmer asked. "How about Owen Fuller?"

"His file looks fine," Donegan said. " He was born in England. Moved to the U.S. to attend MIT."

"If he is not a U.S. citizen, how did he get security clearance?"

"The Defense Industrial Security Office contracted out his security check, as they seem to do with most of them these days. According to the official report, he's a naturalized U.S. citizen. His security clearance is limited to LTG defense projects."

"There has to be something about him we don't know. Request an update of the clearance."

"That would require high-level authorization, and I don't have sufficient justification to request it," Donegan said. "Owen is an employee, and he's leading the Perseus project. And if I had authorization, it would take several days to get company approval. Even then, the government might not reopen the case."

"Maybe I can help. What are his parents' names? Are they still in the U.K.?"

"Fuller was born to an unwed mother. He listed his father as unknown. His mother is Deborah Elizabeth Fuller. The only address I have is Beckenham, Kent. I have her telephone number, the one he gave us when he joined the company. It might have changed. She might also have moved."

"Give me the number you have," Palmer insisted.

"What are you going to do with it?" Donegan fired back.

"I know someone in London who can make you tell things you didn't know you knew."

"Not another of your ex-Navy friends, is it? We can't go around interrogating people, frightening them half to death."

"No. She's a corporate auditor and a very pleasant person."

36

PALMER LOOKED AT his watch. London was five hours ahead of Eastern Daylight Time. His girlfriend, Fiona, might be out on a summer Sunday afternoon; or knowing her, she might be working at home. He had not spoken to her in the past two to three weeks. Out of sight, out of mind. He thought about what Lara Hamilton had said about his avoidance of commitment. *Is she right? Am I making excuses for not calling?* He scrolled through the address book on his cell phone and found her number, including the international dialing digits. He tapped the screen on his phone, initiating the call.

"Jake," she exclaimed. "Where are you? Are you here?" Fiona seemed excited to hear from him and not bothered that he interrupted whatever she was doing.

"I wish I were. I miss seeing you. I'm in the States."

"I miss you too," she said with an air of disappointment.

"Fiona, I need your help."

She hesitated before responding. "Oh." Her single word transmitted her disappointment across the Atlantic as clearly as if she were sitting beside him, looking into his eyes. "What do you need?"

"I'm working a case at Lynnhaven Technology Group in Virginia. An old friend of mine was murdered."

"Murdered?! How awful. I'm sorry to hear that." Fiona's tone changed. She was interested and empathetic.

"One of the company employees may have been involved in his death. He was born to an unwed mother in the U.K. His mother still lives there. Her name is Deborah Elizabeth Fuller. I would like for you to contact her. Her son, Owen Fuller, is a project leader for a classified Navy project. Fuller was in the U.K. a couple of weeks ago. Tell her LTG is following up on his security clearance, and it's very important. Mothers are always happy to talk about their sons. Just start her talking and see what she says. You auditors are good at that."

"You auditors?"

"OK, you're good at it. According to the company's personnel records, Owen Fuller was born in London on June 26, 1973."

"Do you have his father's name?"

"He listed it as unknown on the job application. That would be a good starting point. Tell her LTG needs his father's name on file."

"Maybe she doesn't know who his father is. It happens. A woman has multiple partners and falls pregnant, not knowing who is the father."

"That's something you can confirm with his mother."

"Where does Deborah Fuller live?"

"All I have is Beckenham, Kent, and a telephone number. How far is that from your home?"

"Beckenham is only twenty miles or so from Sevenoaks Weald. What does his father's name have to do with the murder of your friend?"

"I don't know. Maybe nothing. It's one of the leads I'm working on. I really appreciate this."

"When are you coming to the U.K., Jake?"

"I want to see you. I just can't get away. Can you come to the States?"

Palmer listened, awaiting her response.

"I haven't had any time off in months. I need a break. Let me check my schedule and see what I can do. When I call you about Fuller's mother, I'll let you know."

"There's another reason to check your schedule. Can you come to New York at Christmas for a few days? My father is getting married. I'd like you to be with me."

"I'd love to," Fiona responded enthusiastically.

"I don't know the exact date. When I find out, I'll call or drop you an e-mail. I can't tell you how much I appreciate this, Fiona."

"I love you, Jake Palmer."

They said goodbye and hung up. Palmer smiled at the prospect of her visit. He had asked her to come to New York to attend his father's wedding and meet his family. *I hope she didn't read anything into that.*

37

PALMER AND GREEN checked out of the Tranquil House Inn and had lunch before leaving Manteo to drive to Virginia Beach. "This was the most pleasant weekend I've had in a long time. What a beautiful part of the country," Green said.

"Glad you enjoyed it."

Palmer had enjoyed it too. Alona Green was intelligent and had a good, albeit sarcastic, sense of humor. The fact she was a little like Fiona had not escaped him. Both used their intelligence and good looks to achieve their goals. Fiona, a regulatory and compliance auditor for Blackwell & Anderson Pharmaceuticals, used hers in a legal, ethical, and socially acceptable way. Green, on the other hand, seemed to have taken an almost opposite path. Although he found her attractive—what heterosexual male wouldn't—he kept his feelings to himself.

"There's just one thing niggling at me," she said.

"Oh. What's that?"

"You didn't hit on me. If you had, I might have been receptive."

"Don't you have a boyfriend, someone you care about?" Palmer asked, not taking his eyes off the road.

"I haven't had a steady boyfriend since high school. When I need companionship, I have no difficulty finding an attractive man—no strings attached."

"To be blunt, Alona, you're not my type."

Palmer lied. He was attracted to Green in a big way, but he was not going to get involved with her, not for one night, not for a weekend, and definitely not for a long-term relationship. If there were those you play with and those you stay with, she was neither. She was one you ran like hell from. Like a powerfully addictive drug, one taste and you were hooked. And if he later discovered she murdered Wade Jansen or played a role in his murder, he would never forgive himself for having made love to her.

Green squinted her eyes and cocked her head. "Really?"

"Really."

"Oh," she responded, dragging out the word.

"What do you mean by that?"

"I just assumed you were straight."

"So if a man's not attracted to you, he's gay?"

"I've never been wrong before. And you didn't react at all when I came out of the water naked yesterday."

Palmer shook his head. "There's a first time for everything. I'm straight. You're just not my type. And to set the record straight, I did react. You just didn't see it."

"What's your type then?"

"The motherly, nurturing, stay-at-home-on-a-Saturday-night-and-watch-a-movie-curled-up-on-the-couch kind of woman."

She twisted around in the seat, facing him. "Who says I'm not that type?"

"That doesn't even warrant an answer."

"Seriously, what type do you think I am?" Green asked.

"You're the kind of woman a man first dreams about, then is later haunted by in his nightmares.

Green paused, cocked her head toward him, and squinted. "You're full of crap, Jake Palmer. Admit it. I am your type."

"That, Alona, is something you'll never know."

"We'll see about that. What are we going to do when we get back?"

"I booked rooms at the Hilton."

"Not where are we going to stay. What are we going to do?"

"*We*," Palmer emphasized, "are not doing anything. I'm finding Wade's killer. You are going to stay in your room and try to keep from being arrested."

"Who do you think did it?"

"I have two or three people on my list. You're one of them."

"You're kidding. What motive would I have?"

"And there's Shaun and Graham in Conshohocken. Who's to say you didn't kill them too?"

"If I had killed any or all of them—and I didn't—I would've disappeared. I certainly wouldn't have called and arranged to meet Jansen and then you."

"Yeah, I haven't worked that out yet. Maybe that's what you want me to think. You're good at manipulating people. Did you ever hear Shaun or Graham mention Angela Huntington?"

"No. You asked me about her at the restaurant. Who is she?"

"Another LTG employee who was murdered before you turned up."

"What?"

"Someone working on Fuller's project team. She was poisoned."

^^^^

Miles of the rural countryside passed by without a word being spoken. Then Green said, "Owen seemed to be an okay guy. He was attracted to me. I actually felt bad about what I did."

"You have a conscience?"

"I know, right? It surprised even me."

"I feel a *but* coming."

"But something's not right. I got a bad vibe from him."

"What do you mean?" Palmer asked.

"It's a feeling, nothing more. On the surface, Fuller's a nice enough guy, quiet and intellectual. Under the surface, I sensed something else, like a tightly controlled, raging fire."

"If there's a raging fire, I didn't see it," Palmer said. "He has no arrest record or history of violence—not even a speeding ticket. He's in a high-paying corporate job and heading up one of LTG's most important projects. Why would he do anything to screw that up?"

Green shrugged. "Any suspects on Huntington's poisoning?"

"She was having an affair with one of the execs."

"Aha."

"That's what the police suspected too. The exec may, in fact, have had a motive to off his mistress, but not Wade and certainly not your two friends in Conshohocken."

"They weren't my friends. Do you think her death is connected to Jansen's?"

Palmer's cell phone rang, interrupting their conversation.

"Palmer, it's Hawkins. I have the ballistics report from Pennsylvania."

38

LARA HAMILTON HATED flying in CH-47 Chinook helicopters. She was never totally at ease on the missions with the SEALs, but she felt especially vulnerable and exposed in these loud, lumbering, low-flying choppers.

On the long journey to Afghanistan, Hamilton had plenty of time to think about Jake Palmer. How strange that he had reappeared in her life. After their college breakup, she fought the urge to contact him. Although she would have liked to see or talk to him, she was not going to make the first move. She was stubborn that way. She realized now that it was not just his commitment phobia—he also had a history of walking away from the past and never looking back. He had done it to his family, to his Navy teammates, and to the women in his life, including her. Perhaps it was a defense mechanism developed as a child after his mother ran off with their pastor. She recalled that he had perceived that as a betrayal by his mother and by the church.

After she learned Palmer left the Navy, she applied for a position with Naval Special Warfare at Little Creek, an assignment she had wanted for years but was not going to pursue as long as he was stationed there. Her initial request for transfer was declined. Between then and the next time she applied, she got herself into shape. She might not have to go through basic underwater demolition/SEAL training, but she needed to be able to hold her own and gain the respect of these extraordinary men. After two more rejections, she convinced Naval Special Warfare Support Activity Two that there was a need for someone with her background and experience in information technology, and her application was accepted.

The night Palmer was taken into custody at Little Creek, she took a few deep breaths and calmed herself before entering the room where he was being held. She entered, feeling each distinct heartbeat in her chest. On the exterior, she maintained her professional demeanor. A naval officer knows how to control emotions, remaining objective and keeping feelings in check. On the inside, she was a ship aground on an uncharted reef.

Hamilton looked forward to returning home and seeing him. Although she was no longer in love with him, he would always have a place in her heart. And she would always wonder what might have been. Maybe they could go out when he was in town working with LTG. She would like that. They had much to talk about.

^^^^

Lieutenant John "Gator" Nelson, the officer-in-charge of SEAL Team Two's Squadron Firestorm, gave the order to get ready to disembark. To lessen the time the helicopter would be stationary and an easy target for any Taliban fighter, the pilot would hover about fifty feet over the landing zone. Everyone got his gear together and moved to the door. The six-member SEAL team was a polished, well-rehearsed unit that moved fast, gracefully, and with little talk. Seated to Hamilton's left was Petty Officer First Class Tom "Mac" McKiernan, the team sniper.

Everyone had a call sign or nickname. Hamilton's was "AJ," given to her soon after joining Navy Special Warfare, which stood for Angelina Jolie, who played a pistol-totting protagonist in the movie *Tomb Raider*. The team crowded near the open helicopter door. Team leader Nelson held up one finger and shouted, "One minute." His words were drowned out by the incredible noise of the twin rotors. The Chinook dropped fast above a flat and open area a few hundred yards across. The team fast-roped to the ground in a predetermined order. Hamilton was the third one out. As soon as the last man's boots hit the ground, the pilot revved the engine, and the helicopter was gone. The dust storm created by the downdraft of the helicopter's rotors provided momentary cover for them to move away from the exposed landing site.

The distance to the abandoned forward operating base Hammerbeck, where the test would be run, was relatively short; but the hike through rugged, mountainous Kunar Province would take six hours. They had been to the base several months earlier after Hamilton had learned of the plan to close the outpost and put forward a plan to use the opportunity to plant the tracking dots on the ammunition and leave it behind for the Taliban. Like ants taking ant poison back to their interconnected nest, she knew if the Taliban took the bait, the ammunition would be distributed to a network of insurgent cells within a few days and become a target for the new drone target acquisition and firing system.

A few hundred yards from the base's outer perimeter, the team took up positions. The base seemed lifeless and bleak. What the villagers had not stripped away, the windblown sand had begun to bury. In another year, the last remnants of the base would be gone. Lieutenant Nelson watched the site, looking for signs of movement. After a couple of hours, he motioned for two of his men to move out. Their approach did not draw any fire. Nelson had not expected it would. For the past seventy-two hours, drone aerial surveillance had been in place. Nothing unusual had been observed. At the entrance to the base, the two men surveyed the situation and signaled for the team to join them. Hamilton walked behind Nelson and in front of the other men.

McKiernan stayed behind in a position where he could watch the team's rear flank while they conducted the test. He was armed with a Navy MK11 Sniper Weapon System, a 7.62mm round sniper rifle accurate to fifteen hundred yards and equipped with a detachable sound suppressor that muffled the noise and muzzle flash. In this supporting lookout role, a spotter was unnecessary.

"AJ, wait here while we clear the buildings," Nelson said. "Notify the flattop we're on site."

Although Hamilton's rank was a grade above the team leader's, the lieutenant was in command. She was a member of his team on this mission, and she followed his orders.

"Calling the carrier now," Hamilton said. "Runway, this is AJ. All boots are on the ground and in position. Launch the bird."

"Roger, AJ. This is Runway. Launching the bird—T minus one."

39

"WHAT DOES THE ballistics report show?" Palmer asked Virginia Beach Police Lieutenant Hawkins.

"Perfect match with the 9mm gun used to kill Jansen. Alona Green is my suspect for the three murders. I need to talk to her. Where are you?"

Palmer held his finger to his lips, indicating for Green to keep quiet. "On the way back from the Outer Banks."

"Find Green and bring her in."

"I'm confused. Isn't that your job?"

"You know where she is; I don't. I've issued an all-points bulletin for her arrest. If you're hiding her, I'm going to hang you by your balls."

"I get the point."

"Don't forget it."

"I'll be in Virginia Beach in about an hour. If I run into her, you'll be the first one I call."

"Don't screw with me, Palmer."

"Wouldn't think of it."

"One more thing. We ran Green's prints from the glass you gave me. They matched prints at the house in Pennsylvania, the ones we couldn't identify."

"Anything on the official record."

"Nothing in IAFIS," he said, referring to the national Integrated Automated Fingerprint Identification System. "The DNA results from the glass aren't back. Since we struck out matching her fingerprints, I seriously doubt we'll find a DNA match. Without either of those, we have little hope of identifying who she really is."

∧ ∧ ∧ ∧

"Who was that? You were talking about me, weren't you?" Green said after Palmer finished the call.

"Lieutenant Hawkins, Virginia Beach Police. The gun used to kill Jansen was the same as the 9mm handgun used to kill Shaun and Graham."

"How can that be?"

"You tell me."

"OK, Sherlock. How about the two men who killed Shaun and Graham and chased us out of the restaurant also killed Jansen."

"Why?"

"To get the laptop."

"Am I to believe they simply strolled into LTG, killed Wade, took the laptop, and are now looking for you?"

"Makes sense to me," Green quipped.

"How did they know he had the laptop?"

"They were following me. Remember? I'd located and destroyed one tracking device on my car, but it wasn't until you suggested there might be another that I found a second one. They were still tracking me the night Jansen was killed."

"You might have led them to LTG. How would they have known you were there to see Wade? How would they have known he had the laptop?"

"Good point," Green said. "They could have looked on the visitor's log and seen I was there to see him."

"The security video shows no one entered LTG after you until the EMTs arrived." Palmer thought for a moment. "How about this? You were part of a corporate espionage scheme. Your job was to get the laptop, along with Fuller's ID and password. Once they had everything they needed, the three of you became liabilities. They needed to get rid of you."

"Actually, that's a pretty good theory," Green said, looking impressed.

"I can see why they would want to kill you. Some people might be cheering them on."

"Not funny, Palmer."

"But why would they kill Wade?" Palmer asked.

"To get the laptop?"

"Why would they need it? It's only use would be to link to LTG's systems, and they wouldn't have the current ID and password."

"On that last day, Shaun and Graham saw something on the laptop that disturbed them. They went into the other room to make a call. That's when they were killed."

"Do you have any idea what they saw?" Palmer asked.

"No. One of them, I think it was Graham, was more disturbed by it than the other one was. Maybe it was something on the laptop, something the two Arab men wanted."

That's it, Palmer thought. *Something they wanted was on the laptop. That's why they killed Shaun and Graham and why they tracked Green and the laptop to LTG, killed Wade, and took the laptop. It's all tied to the Perseus project. And maybe, just maybe it's not about industrial espionage. Maybe Huntington's death has nothing to do with the other three.* Palmer needed to see the report in her personnel file. He also wanted to hear what Fiona learned from Fuller's mother. *Maybe one or both will provide the key to this complex puzzle.* He hated waiting; he was not a patient man. Lara and the team should be in place. Time was running out.

40

THE USS *GEORGE H.W. Bush* (CVN-77), a Nimitz-class nuclear-powered carrier and home to six thousand Navy men and women, cut through four-foot seas in the Persian Gulf like they were ripples on a farm pond. Captain Lawrence Quateraro stood on the ship's bridge, looking out at the other ships that comprised the strike group. Weather would not be a factor in today's schedule. The sky was clear, and winds were light over the region.

The plan was simple. This would be the first real fire test of the jet-powered stealth drone launched from a carrier. Now that the SEAL team was in place and ready, the countdown had commenced. About fifty technical representatives from the drone's manufacturer and from Lynnhaven Technology Group that had developed and manufactured the navigation and targeting systems were on board. The steam catapults used to launch the F/A-18s would be adjusted to compensate for the slightly lighter weight of the drone. On future *Gerald R. Ford*-class aircraft carriers, an electromagnetic aircraft launch system built to launch manned and unmanned aircraft of all sizes and weights, would be used.

A container about half the size of a railroad car was tied down on the flight deck near the ship's island, the superstructure where the bridge and flight deck operations were located. Stored inside was a large variety of technical equipment and replacement parts for the drone, as well as communication equipment and high-definition cameras. The container had been brought up from the hangar deck and would be moved back after the drone returned to the carrier. This reduced the risk of parts and equipment being left on the deck by one of the civilians on board who was unaccustomed to carrier flight operations and the requirement to keep the flight deck free of debris. A fighter jet would sustain tremendous damage if even a small bolt left on deck were sucked into the engine intake.

Lynnhaven Technology Group engineers and Navy personnel would control the drone from the carrier's combat direction center, or CDC. When the drone was in place over the test area in Afghanistan, Lieutenant Commander Lara Hamilton would assume control, maneuvering the drone to an area where microdot targets had been placed. Once the drone acquired the signals, Hamilton would fire the missiles at the targets.

"Smitty, are we ready to launch?" Captain Quateraro asked, calling down from the bridge to the CDC.

"Yes, sir. Firestorm is in position, and communications are confirmed. The test safety officer has given us a go. Perseus is in position for launch. Countdown underway. Ready to launch in five, sir," Schmidt said.

"Let's do this. I've got flight ops to run," Quateraro commanded, looking down on an almost empty flight deck. Flight operations had been halted and the flight deck cleared of most of the eighty combat aircraft on board the carrier. The aircraft had been moved to the hangar deck until the Perseus field test was competed. For the carrier, the test was a small, almost insignificant task on an otherwise packed schedule. The carrier's planes provided air support and reconnaissance for military operations in the Gulf. The flight deck, normally a cramped and dangerous place full of electromagnetic energy for air traffic control that could conflict with the signals used to operate the Perseus drone, was quiet and would remain so until the drone returned to the ship.

Quateraro looked down from the bridge at the drone. The triangular-shaped, futuristic drone bore little resemblance to the loud and powerful F/A-18s. It was shorter in length but its wingspan was wider. At about forty thousand pounds, it was not much lighter than the fighter jet. The drone had no tail, and the shape of the trailing edge of the wings made it resemble the bat plane.

When the countdown reached zero, Quateraro and the senior members of the Perseus project team watched from the bridge as the catapult launched the drone down the runway to the end of the flight deck. The drone dipped ever so slightly toward the water before it rose and began its gradual upward trajectory. Watching from the bridge, the ship's captain shook his head, knowing he had just witnessed the unmanned future of naval aviation and the beginning of the end of the Navy fighter pilot.

41

THE SEAL TEAM moved toward the buildings, their weapons raised and ready. Their task was to clear the buildings before "AJ" Hamilton set up the equipment for the test. The current intelligence reports stated that the base was used as an overnight rest stop by small groups of travelers. Although the report did not say the travelers were armed, in Kunar Province, you assumed everyone had a weapon and the basic skills to use it.

The team was moving toward the first building when gunfire erupted. One SEAL was hit, then another. Team leader Nelson radioed his marksman. "Taking fire from multiple locations. Two men down."

"Roger. I have a visual on you. Shots coming from every building," McKiernan radioed back.

A man shooting from a doorway of the building fell backwards. McKiernan scanned the compound for another target. None were in the open; there were no easy targets. Seeing muzzle flashes at the door of another building, he focused in on that location and waited. When the shooter inched out to fire, McKiernan picked him off, a direct hit to the head. McKiernan waited patiently until he pinpointed the location of other shooters, killing or wounding three more. With the sound suppressor in place, they would assume his teammates had shot them or perhaps even their own men in the wild firing. The firefight stopped. He ceased firing and watched though his binoculars.

∧∧∧∧

Hamilton had just set her pack on the ground when she heard the first shot. Her immediate thought was that one of the SEALs had encountered a couple of insurgents. But when the gunfire persisted and the SEALs began returning fire, she knew it was more than an isolated encounter. The gunfire seemed to be all around her. She looked to the team. They were returning fire in deliberate, short bursts and backing toward a wall of sandbags ten yards behind her. She brought up her M4A1 long barrel rifle, fired five shots in rapid succession at a door where she saw muzzle flashes, and joined the team behind the wall. She dropped to the ground with her back against the sandbags. The sound was deafening, and she was unable to concentrate. Only Lieutenant Nelson and three others were behind the wall with her. That meant two of the SEALs were still out there.

Hamilton had been on several non-combat missions with the team and knew the rules. When she was out with the team, she was one of them. She carried an M4 rifle and a Sig Sauer P228 9mm pistol, a smaller version of the 9mm carried by the SEALs. Although she was an excellent marksman and had spent far more than the required hours on the firing range, this was her first firefight; and as she had been told numerous times, nothing prepares you for that. Stationary targets on a range do not return fire. You do not hear bullets sail by your head. You do not see your teammate ripped apart by a bullet. She looked at Nelson, her eyes communicating her silent plea for his guidance.

"How soon can you take control of Perseus?" Nelson asked.

"About two hours. The Perseus controller, antenna, and satellite phone are in my pack, out there." She pointed to the open area on the other side of the wall, halfway between them and one of the buildings.

"Stay behind the wall," he said. "Let us take care of this."

"Like hell," she replied. Hamilton took a deep breath, exhaled, and stood. She saw a rifle jutting from one of the windows on the building to her right. She pressed her rifle into her shoulder and fired four quick rounds. The insurgent's weapon fell onto the ground outside the building. Several bullets thudded into the sandbags close to her. As she dropped back behind the sandbag wall, she saw the two men motionless and exposed on the ground between the buildings and the wall.

Hamilton was aware the situation was dire. She didn't have to ask Nelson, nor would she ask him. Even if the two men were alive, they would either bleed to death or be killed where they were by the insurgents. She also knew the unwritten code: No SEAL has ever been captured. A SEAL fights to his death. If they continued to fight, that would be the outcome. She believed they had little chance of surviving. In advance of the Perseus test, the drones that monitored the area had been pulled back. No one was watching.

42

"LET'S SEE IT," Palmer said, walking into Cora Donegan's office, a large cup of Wawa convenience store coffee in his hands.

Donegan was seated at the small table in front of her desk, a stack of files in front of her. "No pleasantries? Right down to business?"

"Don't want to run up my consultant fee with idle chitchat."

"I'm pleased you're so mindful of the company's money," she said with a smirk.

Palmer sat beside her.

"These are the personnel files for the core project team members. Because I had a limited amount of time, I reviewed them first. If needed, I can also review the files for the peripheral members." Donegan took two file folders off the top of the stack and set them in front of her. "This is Fuller's file." She opened it and flipped to his employment application. She pointed to the next of kin and emergency contact lines. On both was the name of his mother, Deborah Elizabeth Fuller, with the residence listed as Beckenham, Kent, England. "Here's his security clearance report." She handed him the file to read.

Palmer scanned through the documents. Fuller had moved from the U.K. to the U.S. to attend MIT, graduating near the top of his class and staying on to obtain his master's degree. He then worked at a couple of other technology companies before applying for the LTG position. Several years ago, he applied for and received American citizenship. The only issue of note was that his father's name and address were unknown. "Fuller" was listed as his mother's maiden name.

"I've asked my friend in London to contact her," Palmer said. "She'll be polite and discreet."

"She'd better be. I can only imagine the shitstorm if Legal finds out we have an unauthorized person conducting a security check on an employee without his knowledge or permission. My job is on the line."

Donegan closed the Fuller file and opened the next file, sliding it in front of Palmer. The file was tabbed "Huntington, Angela." The first item in the file was the Huntington envelope Donegan had told him about on the phone. He opened it and extracted the report. The report was entitled *Risk Analysis of the Use of Multiple Controllers in the Navigation and Target Acquisition/Tracking Systems for the Perseus Drone.* Palmer flipped through the ten or so pages of the report and returned to the first page, the executive summary. LTG had designed and developed navigation and target acquisition/tracking systems to allow operation by remote controllers, those apart from the primary controller. The system allowed active and passive handoff. For example, the primary controller could be on the carrier or as far away as a base in the U.S. The field team could request control of the navigation or targeting system, or they could assume control without requesting it. This allowed precise targeting of the missile by the team on the ground that might have the target within sight. Huntington stated in her summary that although this functionality had the potential to reduce collateral damage and civilian deaths, it came with great risk because the field team's controller could fall into enemy hands. Huntington recommended the field team controller be designed to prevent it from taking unilateral control of the navigation or targeting system. She also criticized the omission of a self-destruct mechanism to destroy the drone in flight should the need arise.

"She's right, you know. Multiple controllers present a significant risk," Palmer said without looking up from the report.

He continued to read.

To support her case, Huntington described two incidents involving security issues with drones. The first incident occurred in December 2009. Iraqi militants used off-the-shelf software to intercept live video feeds from U.S. Predator drones. Videos of the feeds were found on a Shiite militant's laptop. Militants used the information to evade the U.S. military.

The other occurred in August 2010. The Navy lost control of a MQ-8B Fire Scout unmanned helicopter. According to official reports, the Fire Scout flew twenty-three miles, entering the National Capital Region restricted airspace, part of the Air Defense Identification Zone around Washington. Control of the helicopter was restored when the Navy shifted to another ground control zone. The Navy's investigation concluded the incident was caused by a "software anomaly that allowed the aircraft not to follow its pre-programmed flight procedures," even though the UAV had over a thousand flight hours prior to the incident.

The military dismissed both as isolated incidents and assured the public that the technological issues that caused them had been resolved. Huntington speculated both incidents were part of a more widespread problem related to control and use of unmanned aerial vehicles. She surmised that the defense contractors and military were not being completely open with regard to the magnitude or extent of the risk associated with the use of drones.

"To Fuller's credit, instead of dismissing her report as flawed and inaccurate, he presented it to the LTG project committee. After I spoke with him yesterday, he e-mailed me a copy of the committee minutes for that meeting." Donegan slipped a copy of the minutes in front of Palmer. "The committee agreed the current design and security protocol carried some risks, but they decided to proceed with the project as planned. They also agreed that the recommendations should be addressed after the field test, along with any additional concerns that might be identified during the test. As for the self-destruct mechanism, they agreed with the project leader, concluding it would add too much weight and bulk to the aircraft to be considered even at a later date."

"Can you check Fuller's bank accounts for any unusual transactions?"

Donegan cocked her head and squinted, looking at Palmer as if he had lost his mind. "Sometimes I don't know if you're serious or not."

"I'm serious."

"Then the answer is absolutely not."

Palmer glanced at his watch. "I need to see Ed Taylor. I haven't talked to him in a couple of days. He's going to be on my ass."

"He's under a lot of pressure," Donegan warned. "Be careful. It won't take much to set him off."

^^^^

When Palmer arrived, Ed Taylor was pacing the length of his office. Palmer leaned against the doorjamb and told Taylor about Huntington's risk evaluation report and the ballistics report from Pennsylvania. When he finished, Taylor shook his head.

"Check with me before you do things, not after you've done them," Taylor snapped.

"I'm an ask-for-forgiveness, not ask-for-permission, kind of guy."

"Well, I'm not."

"Man, you need to chill a little. No harm, no foul."

"I'm catching hell from all directions: the CEO, Legal, the cops, and the press. Even the wife's on my case. She says I'm spending too much time at work. Can you believe that?"

"What doesn't kill you makes you stronger. Hang in there."

"Spare me your witticisms, Palmer."

"Just trying to help."

"Screw you. I don't need your help."

"Have you heard from the LTG team on the carrier?"

Taylor sat down at his desk and looked down, rubbing his temples. "At the management meeting this morning, the boss said everything was ready. Our team is on the carrier. We're getting periodic updates from them. No one at this facility is directly involved."

"Where's Fuller?"

"He was on the roster for the carrier team. At the last minute, he backed out and sent a replacement engineer. He said he wasn't a good sailor and preferred his project engineers run the show and get some of the limelight."

Palmer finally walked into the office and sat in one of the chairs in front of Taylor's desk. "That's odd. How about the SEAL team? Everything okay with them?"

"They were dropped off on schedule. That's all we know. We're not privy to the details of their location, mission, or test target. It doesn't matter. Our systems get the bird in place, lock onto the target once identified, and fire the missiles. They could be blowing up a pile of camel shit for all we care. What's up with Alona Green? Do the police have any leads on her?"

"None so far. She didn't murder Wade, though."

"How can you be sure?"

"I just am. I need to see Fuller. Where is he?"

"How the hell should I know?"

43

THE FIREFIGHT WAS in its second hour. SEAL team leader Nelson told the men to check their ammunition. Hamilton ejected the magazine on her M4 and checked it, four rounds remaining. They were all running low.

"You're outnumbered, surrounded," an amplified voice said in English. "You have no chance. Drop your weapons. You can attend to your wounded."

Nelson was puzzled and angry. How the hell did this happen? The insurgents were waiting for them. They knew the mission was today. That was impossible. They had not simply stumbled upon a Taliban encampment. No, the insurgents were well-hidden, waiting to engage them. He knew he and the team had only a few options: fight to the death, surrender, and then concentrate on escaping, or continue the fight and hope that Perseus would arrive overhead, and the team on the *Bush* could see what was happening.

Nelson moved beside Hamilton. "Where's Perseus?"

She glanced at her watch and shook her head. "About an hour out. If I don't assume control, Smitty will attempt to contact us. When he can't reach us, he'll use Perseus to investigate."

"We don't have an hour," Nelson said.

"Let me make this easier for you," the amplified voice said.

"If you do not surrender in five minutes, we will kill one of your wounded men. Five minutes after that, if you do not surrender, we will kill the other."

Nelson used a small mirror on a rod to look above the sandbags to confirm what he had suspected. One of his men was motionless on the ground, and a second, who appeared wounded, was crawling toward him.

"You have five minutes."

Nelson considered their options once again. It was time to make a decision. McKiernan was the wild card. If they surrendered, McKiernan could pick off a few of the insurgents, possibly the leader; but they, too, would be killed. Or he might wait and attempt to rescue them, if they were still alive. Navy SEALs would be a prize catch for the Taliban. He envisioned a video of their execution being broadcast on the Internet. As grim a thought as that was, being held captive for even a few hours would allow more time for a rescue. He called McKiernan on the team radio.

"Mac, we're going to surrender. Hold your fire, observe, and act based on what you see unfold."

McKiernan's reply was immediate. "God be with you."

The men and Hamilton were watching Nelson, who, with his eyes straight ahead, set his weapons on the ground in front of him and stood with his fingers interlocked behind his head, fully expecting to be shot. If he were, then they would know the only option was to fight to the death. No one fired.

^ ^ ^ ^

Hamilton's heart was pounding in her chest. Nelson and the others were standing near her. Nelson looked at her, motioning with his head for her to stand.

The controller was in her backpack between the wall and the dead and wounded SEALs. Even if she couldn't get to it, she could not allow it to fall into their hands. A grenade would destroy the pack; however, it would also kill the other SEAL. She took her Sig Sauer P228 9mm from her holster, switched off the safety, and chambered a round. She took aim at the backpack, and took a final look at Nelson. He shook his head and mouthed, "No."

She realized he knew if she fired a shot, they would be killed where they stood. She could use her team communicator and tell McKiernan to shoot it, giving away his position and going against Nelson's orders. She cursed herself for not taking care of this earlier, during the firefight. With Nelson watching her out of the corner of his eye, she shoved the pistol into her belt and joined them with her hands behind her head.

"Come out from behind the wall."

The five of them moved outside the wall and stood close to her pack, waiting for what seemed like an eternity before the insurgents stepped a few at a time from the buildings and began to circle them. This was her last chance. She knew where in the pack the controller was located. One shot was all she needed. She lowered her right arm and reached behind her.

"If you want to live, put your hand back behind your head," said the man whose amplified voice they had heard. She was about to reply when something struck her helmet.

44

FIONA COLLINS PARKED in front of Deborah Elizabeth Fuller's house, near the New Beckenham railway station. After talking to Palmer, Collins had confirmed Fuller lived at 66 Park Road in Beckenham, which was south of London and in the general direction she took on her way home to Sevenoaks Weald. She stepped close to the door and listened. The television was on, so she knocked and waited.

Even though Collins had obtained Deborah Fuller's telephone number, she had not phoned ahead because she did not believe Fuller would agree to meet with her for a chat about her son and his father, and Collins wasn't going to lie about why she needed the information. It would be more difficult for her to say no to a kind-looking, non-threatening woman standing on her doorstep than to a faceless voice on the phone. She had, however, a more important reason for not calling. If she had phoned Fuller that afternoon, whether she agreed to meet with her or not, she would have called her son, inquiring as to why someone was asking questions about him.

Collins heard footsteps. The door opened. Deborah Fuller was in her mid-fifties, wearing a long black skirt and white blouse, as though she had just gotten home from work and had not yet changed into more casual clothes.

"May I help you?"

"Are you Deborah Elizabeth Fuller?"

"Yes. What do you want?"

"I'm Fiona Collins. I work with B&A Pharmaceuticals in London."

"You lot aren't selling door-to-door now, are you?"

Collins held back a snicker. "No. I'm a director of clinical research auditing at B&A." She handed her a business card.

Fuller took the card, briefly glanced at it, and looked at Collins with a puzzled expression on her face.

"I apologize for stopping by unannounced. Please, let me explain. A friend of mine called today. He's working with Lynnhaven Technology Group in the States."

"That's where my son works."

"That's right—Owen Fuller."

"Is he all right?" Fuller said with an intake of breath, placing her hand on her chest.

"He's fine."

"Thank God. What is it then?"

"LTG is conducting routine follow-up security checks on their top level staff, only the ones who are most valuable to the company." Collins played to the mother's pride. "Instead of turning it over to one of those impersonal government agencies, my friend asked if I would stop by and speak with you."

Fuller looked at her again, taking in everything she had said. "I'm sorry. I commute by train to and from my job in London. I got home just a half-hour ago. Won't you come in?"

"Thank you. I'd love to. The traffic was horrible."

They went into the living room. Fuller picked up the remote from the table and turned off the television.

"Please have a seat. Cup of tea?"

"No, thank you. A bit late for me."

"Ms. Fuller—"

"Please call me Debbie."

"Debbie, I understand Owen was in the U.K. recently. Did he have a chance to visit you?"

"Oh, yes. He was working in London. We met one evening for dinner. He seemed to be under such stress. It's that project he's working on. I'm worried sick about him."

"How long was he in London?"

"I'm not sure. I didn't know he was coming. He called my mobile phone one afternoon and surprised me."

"You must have been over the moon to see him."

"I was indeed."

"Debbie, I won't take much of your time. I'm going to ask a couple of questions regarding some gaps in his security clearance. Your son is a critically important employee at LTG. From what I've been told, he's leading one of their most important projects with the U.S. government."

Fiona was as good as any at putting people at ease and reading them. She watched auditees and assessed their reaction to her statements and questions. Some of her co-workers were trained in NLP, neuro-linguistic programming, a skill believed to assist in the interpretation of an individual's body language and speech. Fiona preferred to trust her own observational skills. Debbie Fuller beamed with pride when talking about her son coming to see her; however, at the mention of the U.S. government project, she sat back in the chair and crossed her legs, arms folded over her chest.

"Perhaps I should talk to him before I speak with you. Do you mind?" Fuller asked.

"That's what I would expect a mother to say. It might influence your answers and, as a result, the validity of the security check. That might have a negative impact on his career at LTG."

"Well, I guess it's OK."

"When Owen was hired at LTG, a routine security check was done. There were a couple of gaps. According to the information I was provided, you were a single mum, raising Owen on your own."

"There weren't many professional jobs for women then. I did what I could to make ends meet. He was a good boy."

Collins leaned toward her and said softly, "I know it must have been difficult. Did his father help out at all?"

"He provided some financial support at first." Fuller hesitated.

Collins had asked the not so innocent question in an empathetic tone, precipitating Debbie Fuller to answer in an unguarded moment. She could not retract the words. She knew who his father was.

"He stopped after the first couple of years. Over time, however, he asked to spend more and more time with Owen."

"I'm going to read the questions I've been given to ask you. There's only a couple. What is Owen's father's name?"

Fuller looked at Collins without responding.

"Debbie?" Collins said, prompting Fuller to say something.

"Is that really necessary? It's personal."

"I'm only asking the questions I've been given. You don't have to answer any of them. Shall I indicate you preferred not to answer?"

"What effect will it have on Owen if I don't?"

"I don't know. It could impact on his responsibilities at LTG, or they might contact the government agency that conducts these security checks to investigate further. I think they're trying to save some time and money by asking me to do it."

Deborah Fuller nibbled at the fingernail of her index finger. Collins leaned back in her seat and waited patiently. She had learned long ago not to yield to temptation to fill the void when someone was considering a response to a question. Doing so provided them more time to think of an answer. Waiting out the silence put subtle pressure on the person to say something.

"Is it really necessary?" Fuller repeated.

"LTG needs the information. If you are unwilling to provide it, they will simply find it through other means, such as medical records or certificates of birth."

Collins used another auditor trick. If Fuller believed she would eventually find out about his father and there were other means to validate the information, she would be more likely to tell her the truth now.

"I was contacted in reference to his security clearance after Owen applied for the job at LTG. I said I didn't know his father's name. Owen warned me in advance and said it could cost him his job."

"I understand, but he's proven himself now. He's a valued and trusted employee."

"I suppose it's less important to keep it secret now anyway."

"Why's that?"

"His father passed away recently."

"I'm so sorry."

"Owen's father was Hassan Abdul-Bari Aswad."

Collins did not react to her answer. That alone, especially in greater London, was not unusual. London was full of Arabs. More revealing was that Owen Fuller had not wanted his mother to provide his father's name when the initial security check was conducted, though Collins understood why someone applying for security clearance in the U.S. would want to keep secret the fact his father was an Arab.

"Did Mr. Aswad reside in the U.K.?" It was a matter-of-fact follow-up question.

Fuller did not respond right away. She looked down when she answered. "No, he was killed in an American drone attack in Afghanistan."

"When?"

"Several months ago. Hassan and I hadn't seen or talked to each other in many years. The last time I saw him was just before he left the U.K. in 2003."

"When your son was here, did he talk to you about his father's death?"

"He mentioned it, but we didn't dwell on it. After he was grown, I never talked to him about his father or about what they did when they were together. Owen met a friend of his father's for dinner. He said they talked about it."

"Why did Mr. Aswad leave the U.K.?"

"At the time, he said Allah was calling him to return to his homeland, Afghanistan." Fuller said she met Aswad at Oxford. Soon after graduation, she became pregnant. They got jobs in London and moved in together. The fairytale was short-lived; she was not the subservient woman he expected or wanted, and he was not the loving, attentive man she had fallen in love with. Owen was just a toddler when they separated. As he got older, his father spent more and more time with him, making her fear that he would steal her son away to some Middle Eastern country, and she would never see him again.

Collins had the information Palmer needed but stayed a bit longer to chat before leaving. She enjoyed talking to Debbie Fuller and hoped for her sake her son was not a murderer. Just because Hassan Aswad was his father did not mean his son was a Muslim extremist.

Collins had no doubt that Debbie would phone her son and tell him about her visit. She called Jake on her hands-free mobile phone in the car. After several rings, it went into voicemail.

"Jake, it's Fiona. I talked to Debbie Fuller. Call me immediately."

45

OWEN FULLER'S OFFICE door was closed and the lights were off. Palmer saw Fuller's secretary returning to her desk with a cup of coffee and a Danish.

"Where's Owen?" Palmer asked.

"He called and said he wasn't feeling well. He's working from home today. He's going to teleconference into the morning management meeting to present the Perseus status update."

Palmer stared at her in disbelief. If he were in Fuller's shoes, he would not, under any circumstances, call in sick while the field test was underway. He would drag his butt into the office even if he were puking up his guts.

"Do you have his home number? I need to talk to him. It's urgent." He held up his contractor ID badge so she could see it.

Answering while she looked at his badge, she said, "I can't give you his number. I'll ask him to call you when he checks in."

Palmer gave her one of his business cards and circled his cell phone number. "I understand. This is a big week for him. I'm sure he would rather be here. Can he monitor the progress of the Perseus field test from home?"

She took a bite of her Danish and a sip of coffee before answering.

"Oh, yeah," she said with her mouth still half-full. "With the computer and the other techno gadgets he has at home, he can monitor just about everything here."

"Technology, eh? I can't keep up with it. I don't even know how to use half the functions on my cell phone."

"I know, right? He even has one of those control units at home to monitor the actual Perseus systems. Imagine that—thousands of miles away and you see and control everything."

"On second thought, don't bother him. I'll talk to him later in the week."

Palmer left and marched straight to Ed Taylor office.

^ ^ ^ ^

In the hallway, Palmer ran into Taylor, whose mood had not improved.

"What is it now, Palmer?"

"Fuller's working at home. He doesn't feel well."

"I'll send him a get well card."

"Doesn't it strike you as strange that he's not here on one of the most important days for the Perseus project?"

"Welcome to the electronic age. People aren't tied to an office. They can work from anywhere in the world, even access e-mail and the Internet from thirty-five thousand feet on a plane."

"This is not right," Palmer said, his jaw clenched as he pounded his fist into his hand.

"Fuller can do almost anything from home that he could do here. He has a Perseus control unit with him."

"How many Perseus control units are there?"

"Three. Lieutenant Commander Hamilton has one with the SEAL team. There's one with the team on the carrier, and Fuller has one. They are under tight inventory control and electronically tracked. You'd think they were blocks of gold."

"Who tracks them?" Palmer, his eyes on the floor, paced back in forth in front of Taylor.

"Information Technology Risk Management. They report to me. You're letting your imagination run away with you. I can tell you have a problem with Owen. What's he done to piss you off?"

Taylor had a point. He could not name a single thing, and he had no evidence to support his accusations. Everything was circumstantial.

"Where are the controllers at this moment?" Palmer asked.

"Do I have to repeat myself? One's with the SEAL team, one's with the carrier team, and Fuller has one at home."

"Are you sure?"

"Positive."

Palmer stormed out of Taylor's office. Worry gnawed at his gut. He felt helpless and hated the feeling. He racked his brain, trying to sort through the ominous thoughts he was having. What could he do? He had not checked in with Green since he left the hotel. He reached in his pocket for his cell phone to call her. It wasn't there. Then he remembered. He left it in the car.

46

OWEN FULLER SAT in the upstairs study of his house near the waterfront south of the town of Cape Charles on the southern end of the Delmarva Peninsula. With fewer than one thousand full-time residents and surrounded by water and farms, Cape Charles felt like a remote island. Yet it was only about a half-hour's drive on the Chesapeake Bay Bridge-Tunnel to metropolitan Hampton Roads and the one and a half-million residents of its cities, including Virginia Beach, Norfolk, Portsmouth, and Newport News. The relative isolation of the house was ideal for Fuller.

He navigated through his laptop's security levels to get to his personal partition. Everything appeared as it had before Alona Green took it. How could he have been so stupid? Too much was at stake. Green had no idea what she had done or who she was screwing with. She would pay for it with her life as Jansen had done.

Fuller recalled the wide-eyed look of shock on Wade Jansen's face when Ragheb Ata' Allah Nazari entered his office with a gun. Nazari shot Jansen before he could react. Fuller watched the light in his eyes dim, his face relax, and then nothing except the empty, open-eyed look of death.

Someone tapped lightly on the doorjamb.

"Sir, everyone is here. We're ready to begin," said Nazari.

"This is a glorious day, Ragheb."

"I've lived for this all my life."

"Prepare the men. I'll be down soon."

Like Nazari, Fuller had lived all his life for this day. He thought about his boyhood in London. His father and mother had never married and separated not long after his birth. Although his father lived and worked in London, he never saw him. As Owen grew older, his mother allowed him to spend time with his father. At first, the visits were only for a few hours each week, but over time, they became longer and more frequent. Soon, he was spending weekends with him or even weeks at a time during school breaks. His mother was a Christian, but not a religious person, so his father's talking to him about Islam and the Koran filled a void. His father convinced Fuller that Muslims had been persecuted by Christians for centuries and read to him about the atrocities committed by Christians against Muslims during the Crusades. His father warned him that his mother would be upset if she knew he was studying Islam and very angry if she knew he had become a Muslim. She might insist he stop seeing his father. So, Fuller prayed in private when he was at home and kept his prayer rug and copy of the Koran hidden from her.

When he was with his father, they attended the *Masjid ibn Taymeeyah* or Brixton Mosque and Islamic Cultural Centre in south London, where extremists recruiting for the jihad had befriended his father years earlier, saying they needed someone of his intelligence and charisma. By the time the Americans attacked Afghanistan in 2001, he and his father had become obsessed with the jihad. His father told him Islam's "Battle of Britain" would be won without a shot being fired. The Muslim population in the U.K. was growing much faster than the rest of British society, the result of a liberal immigration policy and an apathetic, dwindling Christian population. In 2003, his father, believing he could put his talents to better use in the fight to rid his homeland of the Americans and reclaim it for the Taliban, said goodbye to his son and flew to Pakistan for indoctrination and training, never to return.

Fuller had wanted to join his father, but his father would not allow it. He stressed the importance of an American education and pushed him toward the defense industry after he graduated. His father did not want him to become a soldier. Instead, he suggested he work his way up within the defense industry and become a corporate spy for the jihad, advising the jihadists of the technologies the West was developing to use against them. When it was time to go to college, Fuller persuaded his mother to allow him to attend MIT in the U.S.

The years of preparation and planning had come to fruition. It was time for a historic strike against the Americans. Like December 7 and September 11, today's date would soon be stamped into the hearts and minds of Americans.

47

LARA HAMILTON'S VISION was blurred, like looking through a glass smeared with ointment. She rubbed her eyes and saw men collecting the weapons and gear from the SEAL team. As her vision cleared, she saw a man holding a pistol standing over her. "Get up," he shouted, kicking her in the side. She pushed herself off the ground. He was barking orders in Arabic to some other men. She had some basic knowledge of the language but only caught a word or two. One of the men, whom the others called Shadid, stripped off her flak jacket and helmet and threw them on the ground. Hamilton stared straight ahead and stood motionless while he patted her down, putting his rough hands under her bra and down her pants. His hand grasped her crotch. She winced and closed her eyes when he forced his dry, rough finger into her vagina and let it linger there. She remained expressionless, never blinking, when he removed his hand and wiped his finger slowly across her face, then slapped her. He moved close, whispering in her ear, "I'll see you later, whore." After Shadid was finished, he gathered up her things, including the backpack, and escorted her into a makeshift building, where he shoved her onto the floor.

Shadid handed Hamilton's backpack to the man with the pistol, who set it on the table and opened it. He shuffled though the contents until he extracted the Perseus control unit, including the satellite antenna and other peripherals. Others brought the squad's weapons and gear into the room, dropped them on the floor beside a table, and left.

Hamilton's mind was filled with a thousand thoughts, few of them good. The temperature inside the building was easily over one hundred degrees, and the air was as still as death, even though the windows were open. Sweat poured from her body. How did they know about the mission? How did they know about Perseus? She watched the apparent leader examine the control unit. It was useless without her assistance; and although they would do whatever was necessary to make her cooperate, she would not help him. Hamilton had read field reports of the sexual torture by these extremists and prepared herself for the worst.

He handed the satellite antenna components to Shadid and said something in Arabic. Shadid took the equipment outside.

The man stood over her and said, "I am Hassan Abdul-Bari Aswad. I'm America's worst nightmare."

Hamilton recognized the name. Aswad was supposed to have been killed in the drone attacks following their mission to apply the tracking dots to the Marines' ammunition at this very outpost. She had seen the intelligence and news reports. "You're supposed to be dead."

"You believed the missile that killed my men also killed me, didn't you? That was a couple of days after you put tracking devices on the ammunition in the munitions bunker. I saw you with the others that day, wearing the same type of helmets and body armor you are wearing today. I thought at the time how strange it was for a woman to be here."

"What do you want?"

"Nothing," Aswad said, holding the control unit in front of her.

Hamilton didn't respond.

"This is the greatest gift I've ever received. How kind of you to bring it to me, my own control unit for the Perseus drone."

"The what?"

"Don't be coy. You were going to have a little fun with this, weren't you?"

Hamilton saw the subdued rage in his eyes and remained silent.

"I don't harm women. Perhaps I spent too much time in the West. I lost my taste for it. On the other hand, Shadid rather enjoys it."

"Death comes to us all. We're prepared for it."

"I'm sure you are. But you are not prepared for what precedes it."

Shadid entered the door of the building and said something to Aswad in Arabic.

"The antenna and communications are operational," Aswad said to Hamilton. "Now, let's turn on this device."

Hamilton watched in silence and waited. He could activate the unit, but without her ID and password and assistance, he would not be able to pilot the drone and launch the missiles. The window of opportunity was narrow. If she did not communicate with Smitty and request control of Perseus within a reasonable time after Perseus entered the test zone airspace over the base, the test safety officer and captain of the *Bush* would abort the mission and return the drone to the ship.

Aswad pushed the power button and looked into her eyes. What he did next shocked her and made her realize there was nothing she could do to stop him. He entered her ID and password and activated the controller.

48

NAVY CHIEF SCHMIDT had been on numerous missions. Seldom did one go without a hitch. No matter how much one plans and trains, the unexpected always occurs. Most have a hiccup or two that are easily overcome. Every once in a while, however, things go completely pear-shaped. Was this one of them?

The Perseus drone had entered the designated airspace, thirty thousand feet above western Afghanistan, close enough for the team to take control. The time to pass over to the field team had come and gone and still no word from them. In thirty minutes, he would have a visual over the former forward operating base and could see what, if anything, was happening.

Captain Quateraro approached him. "Smitty, where the hell is the team?" Quateraro asked, keeping his voice down but pronouncing each word with such quiet force that it had the same effect as shouting.

"Calling them now, sir."

The protocol was for Hamilton to contact Schmidt on the satellite phone two hours after launch from the carrier. She was to use the code phrase: "Firestorm ready to fly the kite." Schmidt would respond: "Roger, Firestorm. Cutting the string." He called Hamilton on the satellite phone, which was linked to an external antenna on the ship, allowing it to send and receive calls within the ship.

The ship's captain and members of the drone team stood anxiously.

"No answer, sir," Schmidt reported to the captain.

"What do you mean *no answer*?" the captain barked.

"They're not answering their sat phone."

"I get that. Where's the drone?" Quateraro tugged on his ear.

"Perseus is within the test zone, sir."

"You've got ten minutes until the test safety officer stops the test and I give the order to return the drone to the ship."

Schmidt told the LTG team to put the drone in a holding pattern.

Instead of continuing to fly past the site, the drone would be placed in a circular pattern over the SEAL team location. He tried Hamilton again—still no answer. It was five minutes until the captain might give the order to abort the test. The captain had command of everything related to the ship, including the field test. It was his order to give; and if he gave it, they would return the drone to the carrier.

A test safety officer stood beside Schmidt, ready to give his approval to proceed or to stop the test and return Perseus to the carrier. He glanced at his watch. "Time's up, Smitty."

"Firestorm ready to fly the kite." Hamilton's voice crackled over the satellite phone speaker.

"Thank God," Schmidt shouted. He looked to the test safety officer, who nodded his approval to proceed. "Roger, Firestorm. Cutting the string."

"They have it," said one of the Perseus team members. "They've taken control."

Schmidt saw the message on the screen: "Control acquired by remote unit."

"Now we wait," Schmidt said to the team.

49

PALMER SPRINTED FROM the LTG building to the parking lot. He hit the remote and unlocked the doors on the run. The phone was on the console, where he had left it. He had four missed calls, one from Alona Green and three from "Unknown Number." Since international calls showed no caller identification on the telephone, he assumed—he hoped—it was Fiona. He pressed Fiona's speed dial number and waited for the international call to go through.

"Hello, this is Fiona—"

"Fiona!"

"... please leave your message at the tone. Beep."

He disconnected without leaving a message. "Damn, damn, damn." Palmer pounded his fists on the steering wheel.

His phone rang.

"Fiona!" Palmer said, without looking at the screen.

"No, it's Alona. Where are you?

"I'm at LTG. What's up? Make it quick. I'm waiting for another call."

"Yeah, like I know. Fiona. What's she got that I haven't?"

"What do you want?"

"I'm going out for a while. I have some things to do."

Palmer was not in the mood to argue with her about staying

in her room.

"Stay close to the hotel. And be careful."

"I will, daddy," she replied in a little girl voice.

"Take your phone with you."

"Look who's talking."

^^^^

As soon as Palmer disconnected, his phone rang again.

"What is it now, Alona?"

"Alona? Is she someone I should be concerned about?" Fiona said.

"Fiona, I'm sorry. I left my phone in the car this morning. I just saw you had called."

"First things first. Who's Alona?"

"A woman I'm working with on this case."

"Is that supposed to make me feel better? Kind of like you worked with me on a case."

"No, I mean, yes. You know what I mean."

Fiona laughed. "I'm not the jealous type, Jake. Did you listen to my voicemail?"

"Who under the age of fifty uses voicemail?"

"You mean Americans under fifty, don't you?" Fiona said, placing a bitter emphasis on "Americans."

If there was one thing that annoyed Palmer about Fiona it was that she often went out of her way to correct his American English or to say something sarcastic about Americans. He usually played along, but right now, he had no time for playful banter.

"Did you talk to Deborah Fuller?"

"I met with her."

"What did you find out?"

"She's really nice."

"I don't care if she's the reincarnated Mother Teresa. What did she tell you about Fuller's father?"

Fiona said nothing for a moment.

"Fiona, I'm sorry. This is urgent and extremely important. I don't intend to sound dramatic, but lives are at stake—a lot of lives."

"Do you want the long or short version?"

"Short, please."

"Fuller's father is Hassan Abdul-Bari Aswad. She said he was killed in an American drone attack."

Palmer had not known what to expect, but that was not it. He got out of his car and walked fast toward the building. He had to let Smitty know, but first he needed to tell LTG security chief Taylor. This would convince him they had a serious problem.

"Are you sure?"

"That's what she said. Do you know who he was?"

"Not right off hand. I'll check with my Navy contacts. If Aswad was killed in a drone attack and it was on the news, he had to have been a high-value target."

"He was. While I was waiting for you to call back, I did some research on the Internet. He attended Oxford and was working in London until around 2003 when he left for Pakistan to train with the Taliban and al-Qaeda, about the same time those responsible for the July 7, 2005, suicide bombings in London were there to train. They immediately recognized his potential value. He rose rapidly through the ranks and was a Taliban commander at the time of his death." Fiona continued, telling Palmer what she had learned from Owen Fuller's mother. She told him when Owen applied for the job at LTG, he had warned his mother a security clearance investigation would be conducted, and that if it were known his father was an Arab, it would jeopardize his job.

"Anything else?"

"She had dinner with her son when he was in London recently. She said he looked stressed."

"Did they talk about his father's death?"

"Yes, but they didn't dwell on it. She said her son gave her an envelope at dinner and told her not to worry, said he'd done some estate planning. She opened the envelope on the train to Beckenham. It was a will and a list of his assets."

This was still circumstantial, but withholding the fact that your father is an Arab on an application with a firm that does military contracting is *not* a simple administrative oversight. Having an Arab father might not be a deal breaker for security clearance, but having a father who was an Arab extremist would be. Fuller's interest in getting his affairs in order was also a red flag.

"Do you think he's your murderer?" Fiona said.

"It's possible." As an afterthought, he asked. "Are you going to be able to come to the States at Christmas?"

"I'm working on the dates. I'll let you know. I may be able to visit next month as well."

"That's great. Can't wait to see you," Palmer said, rushing through the words. He needed to let Smitty know about Aswad. "I have to go."

50

"I'M A LITTLE busy here, Jake. What's up?" Schmidt said into the satellite phone.

"Ever heard of Hassan Abdul-Bari Aswad?"

"You bet I have. Aswad was near the top of the terrorist list. We set up the drone attack that killed him several months ago. Why do you want to know?"

"Hassan Aswad was Owen Fuller's father."

"Oh, shit!"

"My sentiments, exactly."

"What's your source?"

"On LTG's employment records, Fuller's father is listed as unknown. On a hunch, I asked a friend of mine in London to contact his mother. She met with her a few hours ago. Fuller's mother told her his father was Hassan Aswad, and he was killed in a drone attack. Fuller kept his father's identity secret. When the initial security clearance investigation was conducted, he warned his mother in advance that she would be contacted and told her to say she didn't know who his father was. Now, believing Aswad was dead, she opened up."

"The test is underway. We launched the bird, and Firestorm has control."

"Stop the test, Smitty. Fuller has a controller. He's not at work today. I think he's going to use Perseus to avenge the death of his father."

"I'll notify the captain and advise the team. Hold on."

Palmer could hear voices in the background. He waited. One minute, two minutes, five minutes. What was going on?

"Smitty!"

Another five minutes went by. He could still hear voices.

"We can't reach the team on the sat phone," Schmidt said.

"Was that the plan, for them to go dark?"

"No, but we had some difficulty with it earlier. The LTG engineers called Fuller on the satellite phone. He didn't answer."

"Abort the test."

"We can't. We tried to reacquire control of Perseus. We can't get it back. The tracking function is also malfunctioning."

"I have to go. I'll keep the phone with me."

Palmer sprinted back to the LTG administration building and punched the elevator button before looking at the floor numbers displayed overhead. Both were going up. He took the stairs, taking two steps at a time and rushed down the hallway to Ed Taylor's office. It was empty. His secretary was at her desk.

"Where's Ed?"

"Management meeting."

"Where?"

"Executive conference room, top floor."

Palmer pivoted and hustled back to the stairwell. When he got to the top floor, he burst into the room. Taylor was seated at the head of the table, briefing his management team. Every head jerked toward him.

"Owen Fuller's father was Hassan Abdul-Bari Aswad, a Taliban commander. He omitted it from his employment application. Aswad was killed in a U.S. drone attack. Stop the field test," Palmer demanded. "Fuller's going to sabotage it to avenge his father's death."

Taylor stood. "How do you know who his father was or is?"

"A friend of mine in London talked to his mother."

"What?" Taylor's face and ears turned red. "That's it," he shouted. "I've had enough. You have no right to contact an employee's family. You're fired. Your contract is terminated."

"I don't give a shit about the contract. Can't you see what's happening?"

"Give me your badge." Taylor extended his hand toward Palmer.

Palmer took off the badge and threw it at him. It hit Taylor's chest and fell to the floor.

"Now, get the hell out of here. You have ten minutes to get off the site. If you're not, I'll call the police."

^^^^

"You can't go in there," Cora Donegan's secretary said as Palmer stormed by her and reached for the closed office door. "She's meeting with someone."

Palmer opened the door and walked into Donegan's office. She was the only person at LTG whom he felt he could trust and who could help him.

Donegan stopped mid-sentence. The woman she was speaking to turned around and looked at him.

"I need your help," he said to Donegan.

"Can it wait? I'll be through in a few minutes."

"No."

Donegan apologized to the woman in her office and asked if she minded stepping out for a moment. She left and closed the door.

"What's going on?"

"I need Fuller's address."

"I—" Donegan began.

"Fuller's father was Hassan Abdul-Bari Aswad, a high-ranking Taliban militant who was killed several months ago in a drone attack. He's supposed to be working at home. Can you believe that? Working at home on one of the most important days for the Perseus project."

"Have you told Ed Taylor?"

"Yes."

"What did he say?"

"He terminated my contract." Palmer looked at his watch. "I've five minutes to leave the site, or he's calling the police."

Donegan reached into her desk drawer and pulled Fuller's file.

"Let me try his home number." Donegan called him on her

desk phone. She bit her lip while she waited for Fuller to answer. She shook her head. "No answer."

He opened his eyes wide, extended his arms out to the side with his palms up, and shrugged in an "I told you so" gesture.

"I shouldn't do this. I'll probably end up getting fired too." Donegan wrote Fuller's home phone number and address on a notepad, tore off the page, and handed it to Jake.

"I'll print the directions."

"I have a GPS. I'll find it. No, print it anyway, just in case."

He paced while Donegan printed a map with directions to Fuller's home near Cape Charles. While it was printing, she said, "Don't do anything stupid." She jerked the page from the printer and handed it to him. "And when you do, be careful."

51

"WHAT'S THE SOURCE of the information?" Captain Quateraro asked Schmidt.

"Jake Palmer, former SEAL. He's doing some contract work for LTG. A friend of his talked to Fuller's mother a few hours ago."

"That's it? That's all you have? You expect me to ignore our intelligence data and believe some civilian's theory based on something Fuller's mother told a friend of his? Do you have any credible information that Fuller is plotting to avenge his father's death or that there's a threat to U.S. or foreign assets?"

"No, sir. But Palmer's not just any ex-SEAL, sir. I'd trust him with my life."

"Give me the upside and downside of the situation," Quateraro said to the team members in the combat direction center.

Smitty responded, "Best case is that the team is fine and have control of the drone, and they and Fuller are out of contact with us for whatever reason. We had trouble with communicating with the team earlier."

"Worst case scenario?"

"Worst case—the SEAL team's been eliminated, the Taliban have control of the drone, and Fuller's somehow involved."

"A satellite communication problem would explain your inability to contact the SEAL team and Fuller. Is that correct?"

Quateraro asked.

"Yes, sir."

"As a precaution, let's recall the drone and sort this mess out later."

"We tried. We can't reacquire control, and the tracking mechanism is malfunctioning."

Schmidt felt like Quateraro's eyes were burning a hole in him. He had a stern, determined look on his face, and his hands were on his hips. Quateraro was one of only ten men who commanded a nuclear-powered aircraft carrier, and Schmidt was confident he would make the right decision. The annals of naval history, however, were full of senior officers who had plummeted from grace after inattention, poor management, or a solitary lapse in judgment resulted in disaster.

Quateraro looked at the test safety officer. "Do we have the ability to order it to self-destruct?"

"No, sir," said the test safety officer. "That mechanism is too heavy and bulky for the drone."

Quateraro then turned to Schmidt. "How easy would it be for the Taliban to take control of the drone?"

"If, and it's a big if, the Taliban have the unit, they would have to enter Lieutenant Commander Hamilton's ID and password and have some knowledge of how to use it in order to control the drone. They have a variety of unpleasant means to get her to talk. If she's tortured or otherwise coerced, she might cooperate. Also, if Fuller's behind this, he may have communicated Hamilton's ID and password to the Taliban. The thing is we heard Hamilton on the phone say they were ready to assume control. The message on the screen confirmed control had been acquired by the remote unit."

"She may have been forced to say that." Quateraro rubbed his forehead. "I must assume there is at least a chance that the Taliban have control of the drone. I'll confer with Admiral Edwards, commander of the carrier strike group."

"Before you do, remember Perseus uses a new stealth technology, one more advanced than that used by the future F-35 fighter and, in theory, a step ahead of what our radar systems can reliably detect. We've not tested the ability of a ship's Aegis combat radar system to detect and track Perseus."

"What?" Quateraro's head moved forward as his eyes narrowed.

"The location we have is based on calculations using the drone's last known speed, heading, and altitude. If someone has redirected it, all bets are off."

Quateraro did not respond. Instead, he looked past Schmidt, again pulling on his earlobe. Schmidt knew what was going through his head. Stealth aircraft technology and the ability to detect it were an arms race unto itself. The gap was narrowing between the development of new stealth aircraft technology and the development of new radar technology, including combinations of existing radar systems that could detect them. Perseus was the U.S. military's next step in the technology race, and it was a step ahead of existing radar systems' capability to detect it.

"Give me a max speed and range plot for Perseus for the next twelve hours based on its last confirmed location," Quateraro snapped.

"That's thousands of square miles, sir," Schmidt said.

"Better get started then."

Quateraro left the combat direction center. While he was gone, the Perseus team continued to attempt to retake control of the drone and contact the SEAL team. Several minutes later, Quateraro returned.

"Before I talked to Admiral Edwards, I contacted the commanding officer of Naval Special Warfare Group Two. He put me on hold while he contacted LTG. Apparently, they think Palmer's lost it and gone rogue. They fired him."

"With all due respect, Palmer's no nutjob," Schmidt said.

"I gave Admiral Edwards all the information we have, and he escalated it up the chain of command. He does not believe a credible terrorist threat exists at this time. However, as a precaution, he's alerted all ships in the strike group. We'll have a couple of the Hornets do a low pass of the SEAL team's location and see what's there. On the way, if they get a visual on the drone, they'll let us know and one will follow it. We're also sending another special ops team to their location. Admiral Edwards advised the Air Force and CIA of the situation. They are returning all drones within the maximum range of the Perseus for the next twelve hours. Let's pray to God we're right."

52

OWEN FULLER WAITED for the electronic notification that Hamilton's Perseus controller was switched on and that Hamilton's ID and password, which he had passed on to his father through a third party, had been entered and accepted. Once he saw that, he relayed the message to Schmidt's satellite phone—"Firestorm ready to fly the kite"—using a recording of Hamilton's voice giving the notification during a dry run in the Perseus simulator at Little Creek. Once Fuller confirmed the team on the *Bush* had relinquished control of the drone to Hamilton, he disabled the carrier team's controller. Until they tried to use it again, they would believe they could resume overall command control of the drone at any time. He had also disabled their ability to track Perseus.

The phone rang in Owen Fuller's home. He turned his head away from the computer screen and glanced at the caller ID. It was Ed Taylor. He had let previous calls roll into his voicemail. Answering any call was a calculated risk. He pressed the talk button.

"Calling to see why I'm not at work?" Fuller faked a laugh. "I have a terrible head cold. I'm monitoring the field test from home."

"It's not that. I thought you should know that Jake Palmer's gone off the deep end."

"What's he done?"

"He claims your father was an Arab, Hassan Aswad."

Fuller needed only a couple of hours at the most. Taylor didn't have enough time to follow up on Palmer's accusation. "That's absurd."

"He claims he got the information from your mother."

"My mother raised me. She never told me who my biological father was."

"He wants us to postpone the Perseus field test."

"You're not going to, are you?"

"Of course not."

"Jansen's death hit him hard," said Fuller. "He's lost touch with reality. You have to stop him."

"I have. I terminated his contract. He knows you're working at home and may come there."

"Did you tell him where I live?"

"No, but Palmer has a lot of contacts. He'll find you."

"I really don't have time for this, Ed. The test is underway, and some issues need to be resolved."

Palmer had to be stopped. Fuller hesitated, carefully weighing his response to Taylor.

"I'm worried, Ed. Can you report this to the Cape Charles Police? Tell them he's upset, and you're concerned he may physically assault me. Tell them he may have a gun."

"Consider it done. Call me if you hear from him."

After Taylor hung up, Fuller struck the table with his clenched fist. Why had his mother revealed his father's name? He had told her never to tell anyone. She believed his father was dead. Even when he learned that his father had survived the drone attack, he didn't tell her. Maybe, believing his father was dead, she thought his identity was no longer an issue.

Fuller turned his attention back to his laptop and refocused on the task at hand. The screen was divided into four sections. On the top were replicas of the three control unit screens, including the one on the table beside him. He looked at the fourth section, the live video feed and display showing the current speed, direction, and altitude of the drone, as well as the status of the drone's ordnance.

The laptop was vital to the success of the plan, so he had panicked after Green switched hers with his. His father's terrorist plot seemed doomed before it had even begun. He had convinced LTG to allow him to use his laptop for business and personal use, even though it was against company policy, saying that he traveled extensively and was not going to carry another laptop for personal reasons. The head of research and development approved a policy exemption because Fuller was the Perseus project leader. Fuller partitioned off a section of the LTG laptop's hard drive for his personal use. His personal partition was password protected and contained programs related to his true mission and purpose, which was to give his father command and control of one of the military's most lethal weapons of war, a Perseus drone. Using the laptop, he could link LTG's own systems to the programs he had created. The result was total control of the Perseus command, navigation, and targeting systems. Communication with his father had been painstakingly orchestrated, taking place face-to-face with a third party when he traveled to Europe.

If all had gone well at the former Marine forward operating base, his father was now piloting the Perseus drone and nothing could stop him from carrying out the mission. Fuller would have confirmation once he saw the course change. Meanwhile, he had to go downstairs and warn his men, who were members of a terrorist cell that had been operating in the area for years and with which Fuller had secret ties. If the police didn't stop Palmer, these men would. His most militant two were of Arab descent and shared a common hatred for the establishment, which they believed had disowned them. They, like others who feel lost and abandoned by society, longed to be part of something meaningful.

Fuller heard a beep that signaled the Perseus drone had made a significant course change. Fuller studied the new course and smiled. His father was piloting the Perseus drone. No one could stop him now.

53

A POLICE CHIEF and four officers provided law enforcement services for the thousand or so residents of Cape Charles. When the call came in from Lynnhaven Technology Group that a man, Jake Palmer, was on his way to Owen Fuller's house, patrolmen Billy Turner and Sam Giddens were winding down the day in the police station lounge.

The dispatcher shouted from the other room, "The caller's worried about Mr. Owen Fuller's safety."

Turner looked at the wall clock and then at Giddens.

"He said this fella Palmer might be armed," the dispatcher said.

Turner gulped down the rest of his coffee, sat up straight in his seat, and looked at Giddens. "Armed and dangerous. Let's roll."

"Probably has a slingshot or air rifle," Giddens said, with a disbelieving grin.

In the year since they were hired to replace a couple of retirees, they had responded to lots of emergency calls. Other than a few automobile accidents with serious injuries, none were worthy of mention. This one felt different; it could be the one where they made a name for themselves.

"I'm right behind you," Giddens said, stretching out his arms and yawning.

Turner jerked the piece of paper with the address of Fuller's house from the dispatcher's hand and rushed out of the station. He was in the driver's seat, drumming his fingers on the steering wheel, by the time Giddens strolled out the door.

Turner rolled down the window and shouted, "Hurry up, dammit."

Before Giddens could buckle up, Turner hit the emergency lights and siren and sped off.

^^^^

When Fuller heard the siren, he went downstairs and ordered his men to keep away from the doors and windows and remain quiet. He waited in the front room until he heard knocking on the door. He unlocked the door and stepped outside.

Two young men wearing Cape Charles Police uniforms introduced themselves.

Patrolman Turner asked, "Are you Owen Fuller?"

"I am."

"We've been advised that a Mr. Jake Palmer is on his way here," said one of the patrolmen. "Do you know him?"

"Thank God, you're here. My company's head of security called and told me he might be coming. He was concerned for my safety and said he was going to call the police. I'm frightened."

"You should be. Palmer's armed and dangerous," Turner said.

Fuller held back a smile. Turner appeared to enjoy saying the words.

"You could be in danger, sir." Turner leaned his head to the right and left as he talked, looking past Fuller into the house.

"Whose are those?" Patrolman Giddens asked, pointing at the cars parked in front of the house."

"My colleagues.

"May we come in?"

"I'd rather you didn't. I can't give you the details, but as you know from speaking with Mr. Taylor, I work with LTG, a defense contractor. We're working on an extremely important Defense Department test and can't be interrupted. It's related to our national security." Fuller knew his rights. Without a search warrant, they could not enter his house without his permission.

"Mind if we have a look around the property?"

"Of course not. Could you stop Palmer before he gets here? He'll be coming from Virginia Beach. You know the make and model of the car he's driving, right?"

The policemen looked at each other with blank faces. "The caller didn't say," Giddens said.

Fuller had seen Palmer drive away from LTG. "It's a silver Toyota Camry. I'm pretty sure it's a rental car. Maybe you could set up a roadblock at the turnoff from the highway."

"There's not much we can do since he hasn't actually committed a crime," Giddens said.

"We can stop him and ask to search the car for a weapon," Turner said to Giddens.

"I would appreciate anything you can do," Fuller said. He closed the door, locked the deadbolt, and watched them through the windows. They were talking to each other as they began walking around the house. In a few minutes, they returned to their patrol car and drove off.

Fuller walked into the room where his men had gathered out of sight of the front door.

He looked at one of the men, Ahmed Akbari.

"It's time, Ahmed," Fuller said.

The Arab dutifully nodded and walked to a car parked in Fuller's driveway.

54

PALMER'S EYES DARTED between the rearview mirror and side mirrors. He was speeding and weaving in and out of traffic. A driver blew the horn. *Screw you*, Palmer thought. He was more worried about the police pulling him over. Although convinced a terrorist plot was underway, he hoped this was all for naught, that he would find Fuller at home, working on his computer and monitoring the field test. Maybe Taylor was right. Was he so attuned to the doomsday scenario that he was smashing pieces of this insane puzzle together to create what he believed the end result would be?

He exited Shore Drive onto the entrance ramp to the Chesapeake Bay Bridge-Tunnel. He stopped, paid the toll, and sped off on the twenty-three mile journey across the Chesapeake Bay. Palmer entered the first of two tunnels, the one that ran beneath the fifty-foot deep Thimble Shoals Channel. A mile later, he was back on the surface and the bridge again, heading north. He phoned Fuller. The call went into his voicemail. He disconnected and set the phone on the console. It rang.

"Where are you?" Cora Donegan asked.

"The Chesapeake Bay Bridge-Tunnel, on the way to Cape Charles. Why?"

"Taylor stormed into my office and told me he fired you. He

warned Fuller that you might be coming and phoned the police."

"What?"

"He phoned the Cape Charles Police. They're sending a car to Fuller's house. Be careful, Jake."

"They're walking into a shitstorm."

Palmer was not concerned about the local police stopping him. He was worried that they might be walking into a deadly situation without warning. Why did Fuller answer Taylor's call? He had not answered *his* calls. Was Taylor working with Fuller? He picked up the satellite phone from the passenger seat and called Schmidt.

"Smitty, talk to me."

"It's FUBAR, Jake. The strike group commander isn't convinced there's a credible threat or that the SEAL team's in trouble. He's taking some initial actions as a precaution. The carrier strike group is on alert. We've lost control of the drone. Perseus is stealth, so we can't track it by radar. The tracking function has malfunctioned, or someone's tampered with the tracking signal or our ability to receive it, so we can't track it on our controllers either. The captain's scrambled a couple of F/A-18s to the team's location. If they see the drone on the way, they'll advise us. The possibility of getting a visual of an object the size of a car in the airspace Perseus can cover is about as likely as a blind man catching a fly ball in Fenway Park. I just heard that the State Department has notified countries where important political and military targets exist. Perseus covers a lot of ground."

"Fuller is at his home in Cape Charles. He's not answering my calls but has talked to Ed Taylor, the LTG interim head of security. I'm headed there now. ETA thirty minutes."

"I'll tell the captain. Keep me informed."

55

LARA HAMILTON SAT on the dirty wooden floor with her forehead resting on her knees and her eyes half-closed. Her arms and legs were bound. Palmer's intuition had been right. Something bad happened, just as he feared, but Hamilton was almost certain she would not survive to hear him say, "I told you so." What had gone wrong? How could they have known when they were coming? How had Hassan Aswad known her ID and password? She watched him enter them and take control of Perseus. She heard her recorded voice give the notification to the team on the *Bush*. Only one thing explained it all: There was a spy in their midst.

Hassan Aswad dragged a chair across the floor and sat down a few feet in front of her. She raised her head enough to see what he was doing. He held the Perseus controller in front of him, turning it around in his hands. He tapped on the screen. His taps were deliberate, not random.

Aswad looked up from the screen. "Impressive device."

"What the hell are you doing?" Hamilton said.

"Watch your mouth."

"How did you know we were coming? How did you know my ID and password?"

"My son told me. Maybe you know him—Owen Fuller."

"Lying asshole."

"I told you to watch your mouth. Next time, I'll have Shadid cut out your tongue and shove it down your throat. Owen resembles his mother more than me. She's English.

"They're tracking the drone. They'll abort the mission and crash Perseus into the sea."

"The tracking mechanism on the carrier's controller has been disabled, and there's no self-destruct mechanism. According to the time and distance calculator, my first target will be destroyed in less than an hour and soon after that, the USS *George H.W. Bush.* Since I won't be able to see their faces when they die, I want to watch yours, a single American face, contorted in grief over the deaths of six thousand men and women aboard the carrier. But first, just in case the attack on the *Bush* fails, I have another more convenient, less protected target in mind."

Hamilton sat motionless and speechless. If what Aswad said was true and the tracking function had been disabled, Perseus had almost no radar signature to follow. The team on the aircraft carrier would have lost the signal and could not monitor the drone's flight path. Owen Fuller had the only other operational controller, and he was working with his father. Given the range and firepower of Perseus and the target rich environment of the Middle East, she could only imagine the devastation that was in store—Israel, the Green Zone in Iraq, the presidential palace in Afghanistan, to name a few. Hundreds of strategically important targets were all in play. Would the carrier task group even consider the *Bush* a target? If the *Bush* had no advance warning, it had little chance of stopping the attack. She thought through what the LTG team would do once the signal was lost and they could not raise the SEAL team on the satellite phone.

Protocols had been in place for notification of the President, U.S. military, and Middle East leaders since the days of Saddam Hussein and his Scud missiles. Over the years, the protocol had been refined; it was now faster and more efficient. With Perseus's speed, firepower, and stealth radar signature, however, there was little anyone could do. Its missiles would strike without warning.

"Did your son teach you how to use the controller?" Hamilton spoke more calmly now.

"He met with my colleague in London and taught him. Because the controllers are tracked and monitored, my son couldn't take his controller to London. Instead, he delivered a copy of the user manual to my colleague on a jump drive and demonstrated a simulation of the controller that was installed on his laptop. That's when he passed along your ID and password. You did not have the ability to change them because in the test mode, he controlled ID and password changes."

Hamilton was struggling to hold back her anger and her fear. How could Fuller do this? He was a successful man, one who had reaped the benefits of living in America with its freedom and opportunities.

56

AHMED AKBARI DROVE the old Buick south on Route 13 toward the Chesapeake Bay Bridge-Tunnel. The drive took fifteen minutes. He had passed the policemen who had stopped by Fuller's house. They were parked in their Cape Charles Police car at the intersection of the highway and the road to Fuller's house. If everything went as he planned, their wait would be in vain. He paid the toll and continued on the southern approach toward Virginia Beach.

The second span of the CBBT was built in the 1990s, providing separate and parallel bridges across the Chesapeake Bay: one for two lanes of northbound traffic and one for two lanes of southbound traffic. However, because funding was not sufficient to build additional tunnels, the parallel bridges funneled into single, dual-lane tunnels at two points, running under the deep-water shipping channels.

Akbari descended into the Chesapeake Channel tunnel, the northernmost tunnel and the first of the two encountered when driving south from the Eastern Shore to Virginia Beach. Traffic was light and Akbari drove well below the speed limit, waiting for the right opportunity. About halfway through the one-mile tunnel, he saw what he was looking for. A tractor-trailer truck barreled toward him in the opposite lane, the top of the truck inches from the top of the tunnel. Akbari pushed the accelerator pedal to the floor, roaring from fifty to seventy-five miles per hour. He would soon be in paradise, a martyr for the cause. What a glorious death. Fifty yards from the truck, he veered into the opposite lane.

"*Allahu Akbar,*" Akbari shouted the instant before the truck slammed head-on into his car.

∧∧∧∧

Palmer was two miles from the second tunnel when he saw brake lights ahead. The cars in front of him were not budging. He heard a siren. Had the authorities closed the Bay Bridge-Tunnel in order to apprehend him? That was illogical; they would wait for him at the tollbooths, not close the Bay Bridge-Tunnel. He looked into his rearview mirror. An emergency vehicle was coming from behind him.

Palmer called Schmidt.

"Smitty, I'm stuck in traffic on the Bay Bridge-Tunnel. I think there's been an accident in the tunnel.

"We're screwed," Schmidt said.

57

ALONA GREEN WAS on Shore Drive, driving toward the Bay Bridge-Tunnel less than a mile from the entrance ramp, when her phone rang again. Her contact told her of the accident and the closing. His final words were "Get Palmer." She did a U-turn across the grassy median and sped toward North Great Neck Road.

In less than five minutes, Green was at a busy marina on Long Creek, a deepwater creek that fed into the Chesapeake Bay. Green parked in a space close to the dock shop. A sign "Boats for Rent" was on the side of the shop, a long list of available boats posted below it. The paperwork process for renting a boat would take too long. She kept walking and stood over the slips where several boats were docked and where, on a busy summer day, boat owners, guests, mechanics, and employees came and went without notice. She glanced at the boats in the slips. A center console, about thirty-feet long with twin two-fifties, was in the slip closest to the dock shop. She glanced inside and saw the keys. She was familiar with the workings of a dry storage facility. There was no formal check-in process when returning a boat. The staff moved the boat to its designated space within the boatel when they got around to it, anywhere from ten minutes to an hour. Most of the summer workers were high school or college kids. They would never question someone who looked like they belonged.

If Palmer can do it, I can. Green pushed one of the carts leaning against the dock shop to her car. She looked around before opening the trunk. No one was watching. Within a few seconds, she put her Smith & Wesson 9mm pistol, an assault rifle, ammunition, and some other equipment into the cart and covered them with a couple of beach towels.

She pushed the cart down the ramp to the floating dock, again looking around to see if anyone was watching. She quickly unloaded the cart and started the twin four-cycle outboards. The gas gauge needle indicated the tank was full. She cast off the lines, engaged the outboards, and steered the boat out of the slip and into Long Creek, passing One Fish-Two Fish, where she had first met Jake Palmer. She kept her speed down in the no wake zone. A Virginia Beach Police boat going in the opposite direction approached. She smiled and waved. Once past the other seafood restaurants on the right side of the channel, she passed through Lynnhaven Inlet, under Lesner Bridge, and into the Chesapeake Bay, just as she had with Palmer during their escape from the two men who had been pursuing her.

Nearing the end of the inlet's no wake zone, Green jammed the throttles all the way forward. Once past the last channel marker, she reached for the pistol and ejected the magazine, confirming it was full. She pushed the magazine back into the pistol and chambered a round.

58

PALMER SAT IN his car drumming his fingers on the steering wheel. After a few minutes he got out, just as other drivers were beginning to do. He paced, hands on his hips, in no mood to speak to anyone. Any other time, it would have been a beautiful place to be stranded in traffic. Not today. Not now.

"Dammit!"

A uniformed Chesapeake Bay Bridge-Tunnel policeman walked down the line of traffic with a bullhorn, announcing a crash in the tunnel. He said it would take hours to clear the wreckage and reopen it to traffic. He instructed the drivers to turn their vehicles around and drive back to Virginia Beach, assuring everyone that all traffic coming onto the CCBT had been stopped and they were free to drive in what would normally be the wrong way.

Palmer stormed up to the policeman. He composed himself before he spoke. Being demanding or angry to a law enforcement officer who was in an emergency situation served no purpose and would make matters worse.

"I have an emergency situation," he said calmly. "I have to get across. I'll walk through the tunnel if necessary. Have the police meet me on the other side. I need to get to Cape Charles."

The policeman lowered the bullhorn by his side. "You're not

allowed in the tunnel, and the police do not provide a chauffeur service. You can go back to the restaurant at the first island and wait, or you can get off the bridge—your call."

A voice crackled on the policeman's VHF radio.

"Looks like vehicular suicide. Witnesses say a car jerked in front of an eighteen-wheeler. The truck overturned. Two other cars piled onto the crash. This is going to take some time to clear."

"Roger that."

"Crap!" Palmer exclaimed, overhearing the conversation.

"You heard him, mister. There's a fatality. We had a similar accident several months ago. Took about three hours before everything was cleared and the tunnel was reopened. We can't begin the recovery operation until everyone is off the bridge. So either go to the restaurant at the first island or leave the bridge."

Was this really an accident, or was it the intentional act of someone who wanted to block traffic from Virginia Beach and Norfolk? Palmer glared at the policeman before walking to the edge of the bridge. He leaned against the rail and looked down at the water. He estimated the bridge was about thirty to forty feet above the water. If he jumped in, he could swim ashore, but then what? It was miles to the other side. When Palmer turned around, the policeman was standing behind him.

"You don't understand," Palmer shouted, holding out his arms.

Before he could say anything more, the policeman got within inches of Palmer's face and pointed to a parking area on the island near the entrance to the tunnel. "Sir, for the last time, either drive your car back to Virginia Beach, park it off the roadway at the restaurant, or get yourself arrested."

Palmer said nothing. Dejected and frustrated, he walked slowly back to his car. As he reached for the car door, his cell phone rang. *Please be Smitty with news that the SEAL team is safe and the drone mission was aborted.* He glanced at the screen before answering. It was Alona Green.

"What do you want?" Palmer snapped.

"And a nice freakin' day to you too. Where the hell are you?"

Palmer was taken aback. This was not the silky sweet voice he was accustomed to hearing.

"I'm stuck on the Chesapeake Bay Bridge-Tunnel. That's where the hell I am. There's been an accident."

"I know. I see the cars driving south on the northbound bridge. I'm in a boat coming up on the west side of the third island, where the tunnel descends under the Chesapeake Channel."

With the phone still at his ear, Palmer went to the west side of the bridge. In the distance, he saw a large center console boat, bow up and running fast. He heard the boat's horn and squinted to see who was driving it. The woman at the wheel waved frantically.

Palmer waved back. "Is that you?"

"It's not the Coast Guard."

"What are you doing?"

"I'm coming after you. Get ready to jump."

"I'll wait until you're here."

He had no idea of what she was doing in a boat coming to rescue him, but he did not care. As far as he was concerned, Alona Green was his guardian angel. He looked down to the water again, by his estimate about eighty feet to the surface. Water depth was another issue.

Palmer watched Green slow the boat as it neared his location then stop and back away from the bridge, far enough to clear the space immediately below him. He looked over the edge of the bridge. The wind was blowing from the west at about ten to fifteen knots. He would have to allow for that.

"What's the depth?" He saw Green look at the gauges.

"Over thirty feet. Jump!"

"Just a moment."

Palmer ran to his car. He got the map with the directions to Fuller's house. He opened his padded pistol case, put the map, his phone, and satellite phone inside, and closed it. He ran back to the side of the bridge.

"Sir, return to your car and exit the bridge," shouted the Bay-Bridge policemen, walking toward him. The policeman was talking into his radio.

Palmer looked down at Green, who was motioning for him to jump.

"The keys are in the car," Palmer shouted. He stepped onto

the wall that ran along the side of the bridge and clutched the case to his chest.

The policeman shouted, "Stop!"

59

HASSAN ASWAD TAPPED the controller screen with his finger, bringing up the targeting screen. He pulled up a photograph of the first target with associated latitude/longitude navigation coordinates that Owen had previously set. For the second target, he tapped the button designated to return the drone to the location from which it had been launched. The USS *George H.W. Bush* was moving. He returned to the home screen and tapped the "camera monitor" button. The controller screen flashed on and off until a live black-and-white feed from the Perseus camera appeared. At the bottom of the screen were the zoom-in and zoom-out buttons and the time and distance to the two destinations.

Without looking away from the screen, he said to Lara Hamilton, "This technology is incredible—so simple to use yet so technically complex and deadly."

This was his day, and he was enjoying it immensely. The prospects for the future were daunting. How could the jihadists compete against such weapons? Perhaps they had brought this upon themselves.

After the World Trade Center buildings were destroyed, no self-respecting, patriotic congressman dared question the multibillion dollar defense budget, at least not one who wanted to be reelected. As a result, the development and use of drones accelerated exponentially. The destruction of the *Bush* would likely bring a similar response from the U.S., along with a reversal of planned defense budget reductions. On the other hand, the attack would create a huge boost in recruitment for the Taliban, al-Qaeda, and other jihadist groups.

"Do you know what you're doing?" Lara Hamilton asked.

"Like our heroes of 9/11, I may not know how to take off and land this aircraft, but I know enough to use your airborne drone to destroy whatever I wish."

"You'll never get away with this."

Aswad cocked his head and looked at her. Deep furrows developed in his brow.

"Of course, I will. But if I don't, I've fulfilled my life's work. My only regret is that there are not enough missiles to destroy everything and everyone I would like to see vanquished from existence."

^^^^

Hamilton prayed the captain and crew of the *Bush* were aware of the threat and had gone to general quarters. The LTG team on the carrier should have recognized they had a problem and notified the ship's captain, who would have launched the jet fighters. Locating the stealth drone would be next to impossible. The crew would be on full alert, ready to engage all of the ship's missile defense systems, including electronic countermeasures, and Vulcan Phalanx. However, if a DoSTA tracking device had been planted somewhere on the exterior of the ship, the missile might seek the lowest level approach and remain hidden from the *Bush's* defenses. Even if Perseus were detected, there would be only seconds to respond and take out the missile.

She also wondered if the Navy had launched a rescue mission. Aswad would have anticipated that. That would explain why she and the SEAL team were still alive, to be human shields from attacks from F/A-18s and cruise missiles. If all else failed, they could be used as hostages. Would anyone know that Fuller was a traitor, complicit in such a grand scheme? What about Jake? Once the *Bush* was struck, they would serve no further purpose and her death and the deaths of the SEALs would be only a minor footnote on the black day the jihad sank a nuclear aircraft carrier, killing thousands of men and women who served aboard.

Hamilton was also coming to terms with her impending death. She prayed it would be swift, although she was almost certain it would not be. These men would do what they wanted; and death, when it came, would be a welcome relief.

"Don't do it, Aswad," Hamilton said. "You know what happened to bin Laden. We will hunt you down and kill you, no matter how long it takes."

"Like you, I am not afraid to die for my cause. And although he is dead, Osama bin Laden remains an inspiration to Muslims and the jihad, just as I will someday."

"We'll find you. And like him, one day an American will look you in the eyes and kill you or will launch a missile that will disintegrate your body," Hamilton said with conviction. "You will not wear us down. There are not forty virgins waiting for you in paradise. You'll rot in hell for all eternity."

"Help me if you will, Commander Hamilton. After I destroy the presidential palace in Kabul, can I command Perseus to return to the carrier?"

"You have no coordinates to lock onto."

"I won't need them. I'll simply command the drone to return home. Once within the strike zone, the tracking dots will guide the missile to the *Bush*. How ironic that the strike will be against the *Bush*, named for President George H. W. Bush, who was responsible for the first Gulf War and who is the father of President George W. Bush, who ordered the attack on my homeland in October 2001."

"You sorry son of a bitch."

"That's enough!" Aswad shouted. He nodded to one of the men in the room. "Bring in their leader and butcher him in front of this bitch."

60

OWEN FULLER HEARD the faint sound of sirens in the distance and knew that Akbari had been successful—another martyr for the jihad. He reached to the table beside his desk, turned on the police scanner, and listened to the chatter for a few minutes. A multiple vehicle accident with fatalities had occurred. The tunnel would be blocked for hours, not only to Jake Palmer, but also to police and military vehicles coming from Virginia Beach, Norfolk, and Portsmouth. The emergency responders would need hours to clear the tunnel, more than enough time to accomplish his mission.

If the Navy had figured out what was happening, they would dispatch boats and helicopters, possibly with SEAL teams aboard, to his home. They could come by water or air, but he had made contingency plans for that. Fuller smiled to himself. He calculated it would take at least an hour to complete his tasks.

Fuller turned down the volume on the police scanner and returned his attention to his laptop and the controller to observe virtually what his father was doing. Fuller wanted to direct Perseus, but his father's orders had been clear that he had to control the drone. It was essential for the jihad, and it was his destiny. That was the least he could do for his father, a man he respected above all others. Fuller was there to follow through if there was any problem with the operation of the drone.

Perseus was approaching the first target Fuller had programmed into its navigation and targeting systems. Fuller's heart rate increased as he watched the screen. His father was directing the drone to the presidential palace in Kabul, Afghanistan. The latitude and longitude coordinates would move the drone into position and the physical characteristics recognition targeting system would identify and confirm the palace as the target. A green light on the bottom of the screen indicated it was within range. He watched the cross hairs steady over the target and hold for a few seconds until the building was confirmed to be the target and the light turned red. A huge silent explosion filled the screen. After the missile was fired, the Perseus drone turned, heading toward the next and final target, the USS *George H.W. Bush*, which would be in range in one hour and twelve minutes. If the military or the police charged the house before then, he had an exit strategy.

61

PALMER TOOK A deep breath, exhaled, and then stepped out, dropping straight toward the water. Death from cliff and bridge jumps most often results from hitting the water at an angle, smashing ribs that in turn puncture vital organs. He kept his body erect and pointed his toes down. He took another deep breath on the way down. The impact would rip the pistol case from his body and could break his arms. Seconds before he hit the surface, he pushed the case away from him and put his arms straight by his side. He hit hard and the impact was jarring, but he was unharmed. When his descent into the dark water stopped and the buoyancy of his oxygen-filled lungs caused him to begin to ascend, he exhaled slowly and followed his air bubbles to the surface. The boat idled over him, about fifty yards away. When he surfaced, he took a deep breath. He looked around and saw the case floating near him. He swam to it and grabbed it by the handle.

Green pulled the boat up beside him. Palmer handed her the gun case and climbed aboard. As soon as his feet hit the deck, she pushed the throttles, the outboards roared, and the boat's bow rose high in the water.

Palmer dried off with a towel she threw him when he got on board. He looked back at the bridge and saw the Bay Bridge policeman talking into his radio. A few curious drivers, who watched him jump, were applauding.

"I need to get to Cape Charles," Palmer said. "Somehow, I think you already know that."

Green kept her eyes forward and smiled.

Palmer looked around the boat and at her. On the seat behind her were his gun case, two Kevlar vests, and an assault rifle. She was wearing a shoulder-holstered 9mm pistol with a radio clipped to the strap of the holster. "Who the hell are you?" Palmer shouted to be heard over the noise of the outboards.

"Later. There's no time."

Was she rescuing him or was she going to kill him? Either way, he would be prepared. He took his Sig Sauer P226 9mm pistol from the gun case and examined it to ensure it wasn't damaged or wet. He slammed the full magazine into the pistol and shoved it in his belt. He put the extra magazines in his pocket. He had been stuck on the bridge with no way to get to Fuller's house and intervene in whatever plot was in progress. Why would she have come to his aid if she was part of it? Palmer remembered the note he found on the floor beside Wade Jansen's chair. He had written "spooky." Had Jansen sensed she worked for a government agency? Before closing the case, he got the map with the directions to Fuller's house and the satellite phone.

Green's radio squawked. "Status?" the voice on the radio asked.

"Rockfish aboard. ETA CPV twenty minutes."

Palmer followed the conversation. They were twenty minutes from Cape Charles. Green's entire demeanor had changed. She was not who she had previously appeared to be.

"Rockfish? Really?"

Green laughed. "That's all I could come up with on short notice. Do you know the exact location of Fuller's house?"

He spread out the map on the console in front of Green and put his finger on Fuller's house. "Here's where we're going. It's near Cape Charles. Keep on this course. When we get close, we'll leave the main channel. The water will get shallow quick, so go slow. We'll beach the boat and wade ashore."

"Gotcha."

Palmer picked up one of the Kevlar vests. On the back of the vest was FEDERAL AGENT. He held the vest up and looked at her, pointing at the words.

"I'm on your side. That's all you need to know. What's the target?"

"They don't know. The Navy's notified the countries and military in the region."

"If Fuller's seeking revenge for his father's death, he'll want to make a statement. It has to be a U.S. target and politically important—one that's personal."

"What if Aswad isn't dead?" Palmer asked. "The LTG team lost communication with the team. Something's happened."

"Aswad saw himself as bin Laden's successor. Coming back from the dead with a shot heard round the world just might do it."

"Shit!" Palmer shouted, looking skyward. "Why didn't I see it?"

"What?"

"It's not a Middle East country. It's not a military base. It's the *Bush*!"

Green snapped her head around. She looked at him. Her face told him he was right.

Palmer grabbed the satellite phone.

Schmidt answered, "The presidential palace in Afghanistan has been struck by a missile."

Palmer hesitated before replying, "That's a diversion. The primary target is the *Bush*."

"How do you know?"

"It has to be. The palace is political. He wants to strike America. It's the most significant American military target in the region."

"Whether you're right or not, I need to tell the captain."

"Don't rule out the possibility that Aswad is alive. Think about it. He fakes his death in a drone attack and plots a major terrorist attack with his son."

"Where are you?"

"In a boat en route to Fuller's house."

"A boat? Don't tell me. Stay in touch. I'll talk to the captain." Schmidt disconnected.

Green turned hard to skirt around a couple of fishing boats. She handled the boat like a pro.

"What's the plan?" Palmer asked.

"Plan? There is no plan. All we have is what we've gathered from monitoring your movements and telephone calls over the past few days and monitoring the Perseus field test. Enough to convince us something big is going down if we don't stop Fuller."

"He won't be much of a problem; however, he's going to have company, maybe lots of it. He's not going down without a fight."

"Backup's on the way," Green said. "We could wait."

"I'm not waiting. I'm going in."

"We're going in."

62

"SOUND GENERAL QUARTERS. This is not a drill," Captain Quateraro ordered after being handed a classified communication from Admiral Edwards regarding an explosion at the presidential palace in Kabul, Afghanistan. Based on the timing and description of the explosion and the preliminary damage and casualty reports, Quateraro believed a missile fired from the Perseus drone had caused it. Jake Palmer was right. Someone had seized control of the drone, and the SEAL team was either dead or in trouble. Schmidt told him that Palmer believed the *Bush* was the primary target. Because Perseus carried multiple missiles, maybe the palace was only the initial target and the *Bush* was next. The other ships in the carrier strike group were also going to general quarters. Their captains would put some distance between their ships and the *Bush*, widening the ring of protection around the carrier and reducing the risk to their ships and crew in the event the *Bush* was hit.

Quateraro gave orders in the stern, professional tone of a seasoned senior naval officer. The call to general quarters alerted the crew. Every one of the six thousand crewmen rushed to his or her battle station assignment. Quateraro was confident of the *Bush's* ability to defend itself, but also aware that the chink in the armor was that the Perseus drone was stealth and might not be picked up by their systems. If the *Bush* was the drone's primary target, he had to rely on the ability of the ship's systems to detect and destroy the missile after being launched by the drone, something that had never been put to the test. Within the combat direction center, the Aegis combat system integrated the ship's powerful radar system, capable of locating and tracking over one hundred targets within one hundred nautical miles, including other surface ships and submarines. Aegis could then lock onto multiple targets with the anti-ship multiple defense systems. An integral part of the defense systems was the Vulcan Phalanx 20-millimeter close-in weapons system. The unit, which resembled a combination of the R2-D2 droid from *Star Wars* and a Gatling gun, was capable of locking onto a target and firing up to four thousand rounds per minute, so fast that the output sounded like a roar rather than individual shots. The carrier was also armed with missile systems that provided short-range defense against various air-to-surface missiles. However, the truth was that since World War II, no one had attacked an American aircraft carrier. As technologically advanced as they were, the carrier's defense systems were untested against a stealth drone.

Quateraro ordered the launch of four more F/A-18 Super Hornets. They would fly a direct line to the presidential palace. If the drone was headed to the *Bush* from the palace, the pilots might find it. Also flying above the carrier strike group was an E-2C Hawkeye aircraft with its airborne surveillance radar.

"Status, Smitty," Quateraro said.

"Still unable to contact the SEAL team or locate Perseus, sir. LTG can't reach the Perseus project leader, Owen Fuller."

"Whether Palmer's right or wrong, I must assume we're a high priority target for a Perseus strike." Quateraro turned to his executive officer. "XO?"

"The two F/A-18s we launched earlier are en route to the SEAL team op site to assess the situation, ETA thirty minutes."

"Other than the Afghan presidential palace and us, has the Department of Defense identified other potential targets?"

"We have the list," the executive officer said. "There are hundreds, including the carrier group. The most likely are in

Israel, followed by government and military targets in Iraq and Afghanistan. The heads of state of all Middle Eastern countries have been notified and are on alert, as are military units in the region. All drones have been grounded or are returning to base."

"One more thing, sir," Schmidt said.

"Spit it out, Smitty,"

"Palmer's on his way to Fuller's home, where Fuller is supposed to be working today. The Navy's sending a team, but Palmer will arrive first."

"Do you have confirmation that Fuller is there?"

"No, sir."

63

PALMER STUDIED THE chart of the lower Chesapeake Bay that he found on the boat. They were passing west of Kiptopeke State Park. They needed to beach south of Cape Charles. At the present course and speed, they would be ashore in ten to fifteen minutes. As he suspected, the chart showed that the water became very shallow just outside the channel. Based on the size of the boat, he estimated it required a minimum of three or four feet of water. They would go in slow, eyes glued to the boat's depth gauge.

Palmer heard them before he saw them. Two Jet Skis came from behind, roaring toward them at full speed and closing in fast.

"Keep an eye on them," Palmer said.

Two men, one driving and one on the back, were on each of the Jet Skis. Green pushed the throttles all the way down. The Jet Skis were zooming by, close on the right side of the boat. As they did, the Jet Skis slowed briefly. The men looked at Palmer and Green, and then they accelerated. Once past the boat, one of the Jet Skis cut left in front of them, and the other cut to the right away from them. The Jet Skis passed by, far outside their course; then each made a sharp turn to come behind the boat.

Green looked at Palmer. "Hold on. Here we go."

Palmer looked at the pistol by his side. Other than target practice, he had never fired it. He hadn't shot anyone since he left the service. He had observed the men closely when they passed and slowed down. All four wore bathing suits and personal flotation devices, looking like any other Jet Skiers on an adrenaline rush of speed on the water. "Maybe we're being paranoid, and they're just coming over to jump our wake."

"Let's hope so."

As the Jet Skiers approached the boat from behind, they split off, one going to the port side of the boat, and the other, to the starboard side, each about fifty yards outside the boat's course. Just before overtaking the boat, the Jet Skis turned sharply and hit the boat's wake at the same time, crisscrossing behind the boat and going airborne before slamming back onto the water.

"False alarm," said Palmer, looking at Green, who had also been watching them. "Make full speed for Cape Charles."

"Aye, aye, captain," Green said.

Her words were still hanging in the air when sound-suppressed automatic weapon gunfire came from both sides of the boat. The Jet Skis had slowed to match the speed of the boat. The men on the rear of the Jet Skis had small Uzi-style automatic weapons. They remained slightly to the stern of the boat to avoid shooting each other in the crossfire.

Green once again pushed down on the twin throttles. Palmer squatted on the deck and grabbed the assault rifle.

"What are you waiting for?" Green shouted.

He had no option other than to fight or die. He fired two rifle shots toward the Jet Ski on the left side, hitting the shooter, who fell into the water. The driver turned the Jet Ski away from the boat.

When Palmer diverted his attention to the Jet Ski on the left side, the one on the right side raced closer and the man on the back began firing. Palmer ducked below the gunwale. When the shooting stopped, he raised to fire; but before he could shoot, the boat turned hard to starboard, cutting off the Jet Ski, forcing the driver to go behind the boat.

"Nice move," Palmer said, still looking back.

"I'm hit," she shouted.

Palmer spun around and saw Green lying on the deck of

the boat. The boat was going in a wide clockwise circle. Green reached for the wheel, but fell back. Palmer made his way to the center console, holding on to the gunwale to avoid being thrown overboard. He lunged for the wheel and grabbed it. Pulling himself up, he straightened the boat and glanced down at Green, who was holding her right side. Blood was running down her right arm.

Palmer backed off the throttles, and the Jet Ski rocketed behind them and turned to come back. The shooter brought up his weapon to fire. When the Jet Ski got closer, Jake cut in front of it. The shooter on the back fired before the driver jerked the Jet Ski away. The bullets struck the bow of the boat above the water line. Palmer pushed the throttles all the way forward and steered the boat behind the Jet Ski. The boat, however, was no match for the Jet Ski's speed and maneuverability. The Jet Ski turned sharply, coming toward the side of the boat. Palmer saw the shooter rise to fire.

Keeping a tight grip on the wheel, Palmer pulled the throttles all the way back and dropped to the deck of the boat. The bow dropped, and the boat coasted forward. He let go of the wheel and lay motionless beside Green.

"What the hell are you doing, Palmer?" Green asked.

"Quiet. Keep down."

Palmer heard the Jet Ski approach. Several more rounds hit the side of the boat and center console. He had his 9mm pistol in his right hand. The shooter would bring the Jet Ski close beside the boat and rise up to look inside and ensure that Palmer and Green were dead. Palmer listened to the engine, idling close by and getting closer. When the Jet Ski bumped the side of the boat, Palmer rose on one knee. With both hands on his pistol, he fired three rounds into the shooter, and then did the same with the driver. Both fell from the Jet Ski into the water. He looked for the other Jet Ski. It was on the shore near the marina. He knelt beside Green.

"Are you OK?"

"Does it look like I'm OK? I've been shot."

"Let's have a look." He examined the wounds. Her arm wound was bleeding profusely, but appeared to be a through-and-through. "Serious, but not fatal." He ripped off her tank top, revealing a black one-piece swimsuit, the same swimsuit she wore at the Outer Banks. He tore the tank top in two, using one half to tie around her arm to help stop the bleeding.

He examined her side. The bullet had grazed her, slicing through her swimsuit and opening a gash about five inches long. Jake grasped each side of the swimsuit where it had been split and tore it open to see the wound.

"Any other time, I might be aroused by you ripping off my clothes," Green said.

"You're not now?" He stuffed the other half of the tank top into the opening.

Green tensed up and groaned.

"You're lucky; it's just a graze. Put some pressure on it. You'll be OK until we can get you some medical attention."

"Don't worry about me. Beach the damn boat. Get Fuller."

Palmer opened the throttles and headed toward the shore with an eye on the depth gauge as he drew closer to the sandy beach. About fifty feet from shore he gunned the outboards, cut the throttles all the way back, and hit the switch, raising the outboards out of the water so they wouldn't drag the bottom and stop the boat too soon. The boat coasted fast until it came to a stop with half the keel on the sandy beach.

"Now get the hell outta here!" Green took the pistol from her holster and inserted a new magazine. "I'm fine. I'll call for help on the radio."

Palmer put on the Kevlar vest, grabbed the satellite phone, his pistol, and some extra magazines. He stuffed the satellite phone in one of the pockets of his pants and magazines in the pockets of the vest. The assault rifle would draw too much attention from anyone watching; he left it with Green. Palmer took one last look at her and jumped over the bow onto the beach.

64

PALMER'S FEET HIT the beach. Was he ready for this? Could he alone do what needed to be done, whatever that might be? His skills were nowhere near as sharp as they once were, if they existed at all. The self-questioning was rhetorical because the smell of gunpowder in his nostrils, the feel of the bulletproof vest pressing against his chest, and the weight of the gun in his hand were all as familiar to him as a briefcase and a cup of coffee were to a man walking into his office. This was more than bringing Wade's killers to justice. The lives of Lara, Mac, and the other team members were at stake and, most likely, many more. He had to stop Fuller, even if it cost him his life.

He thought through the approach and entry into the house. There was no opportunity for reconnaissance and planning. This would be an improvisational operation, relying on past training and instinct, assessing and acting on what he encountered.

Palmer assumed one of Fuller's team had crashed into the truck in the tunnel to block the approach from Virginia Beach. The four men on the Jet Skis were also Fuller's, sent to guard the approach by water. Both events caught him off-guard. That would not happen again. Behind him, Palmer heard Green talking on the radio. She reported she had been hit and that Rockfish was proceeding to the location without her. She requested medical attention and backup. He hated to leave her, but Alona Green was no run-of-the-mill skirt for hire. She knew what she was doing. He reflected on how she got the laptop from Fuller. That assignment took weeks of research and preparation. Then there was his initial meeting with her at One Fish-Two Fish. She monitored him for at least thirty minutes before she approached him. There was the leap from the stern of the boat when they were being chased, a picture perfect flat dive from a moving boat, followed by a nearly flawless swim stroke. And the body armor, guns, and her body—oh, yes, her body. She had not acquired that physique by going to the local gym and doing Zumba and Pilates three times a week. Alona Green was a highly trained, extremely fit operative. The pieces all fell into place. *How could I have missed it?*

Palmer surveyed the area to get his bearings. They had beached south of the town of Cape Charles and the harbor. No homes were in sight. He studied the map, finding the point at which he came ashore, and used his index finger to trace the route to Fuller's house. Heron Point Drive should be straight ahead. He walked through the brush until he saw a house in the distance. Several cars were parked on the road. When he was about a quarter mile away, one of the cars started and drove toward him. Palmer reached behind him and grasped his pistol; but when the emergency lights on top of the police car came on, he released the pistol and put his hands by his side. He had nowhere to hide.

65

MCKIERNAN WAITED UNTIL dark to leave his position. He was cautious to a fault, although getting inside the base was easier than he anticipated. The Taliban were overconfident, inexperienced, or just plain careless. He saw them scan the sky more often than they looked beyond the base perimeter. McKiernan assumed they perceived their greatest threat was from above, via a drone strike, F/A-18s launched from the *Bush*, or SEALs coming in on helicopters or by parachutes. They were not looking for a solitary soldier on foot. He had seen the Taliban move his teammates into one of the buildings and Lieutenant Commander Hamilton into another. His first priority was to assess the location and condition of his fellow SEALs.

McKiernan maneuvered to a position behind the building where they were being held. The small windows were open to provide some cross ventilation of the hot air through the building. He made his way to a window near the center of the exterior wall. Using a mirror similar to a dental mirror, he peered into the room. His teammate's body was on the floor. Lieutenant Nelson, his legs shackled, was caring for them using supplies from their blow out kit, the medical pack each SEAL carries with him. Two SEAL teammates were in restraints nearby. Three Taliban, each armed with an AK-47 automatic rifle, stood guard. Two were near the only door. The third was sitting on the floor, leaning against the wall on the opposite side of the room, his head nodding as he fought sleep. Battery-powered lanterns provided the only light. McKiernan quietly moved to the other windows on the backside of the building and using his mirror, looked through each. No one else was in the building.

McKiernan returned to the first window, resisting the urge to start shooting. He needed to observe the men and their routine prior to taking any action. While waiting, he attached the sound suppressor to his weapon. After about an hour, McKiernan used the mirror to check the position of the three men for a final time. They had not moved. He returned the mirror to his pocket and knelt facing the wall of the building. Slowly he rose, raising the leading tip of the rifle barrel until it was just below the window. He took a deep breath and then exhaled slowly, then took another. McKiernan rose in one swift motion, extending the barrel of the rifle through the window. In less than two seconds, he fired six shots, and three Taliban were down and dead.

He thought about using the door. The risk of being seen was too great. Without a sound, he climbed through the window and slid into the room.

Lieutenant Nelson pointed to the shackles on his ankles and then to one of the dead men. McKiernan handed his Sig Sauer P226 9mm pistol to Nelson, whose hands were free. He found the keys and unlocked the handcuffs and chains on his teammates. No words were spoken. Using hand signals to communicate, each man knew what he had to do. Three of them dragged the dead men out of sight and took their rifles. They stood on each side of the door and waited to see if anyone had heard the sound-suppressed shots or the men hitting the ground.

One of the men by the door signaled that someone was coming. They could hear two men talking, but there might be more. Their voices were getting louder.

Nelson, pretending to be bound, stayed by his wounded teammates in plain sight of anyone entering the room. The door opened. The men looked at Nelson and then to the empty room where the others had been restrained. Before they could react and bring their weapons up, McKiernan fired two sound-suppressed shots from his rifle. The men were each hit in the forehead and were dead before they hit the floor. He dragged the bodies away from the door and took their rifles.

"They have AJ. Your guns and ammunition are in the building with her," McKiernan whispered, pointing to a building on the other side of the compound.

"How many men did you see?" Nelson asked.

"Between eight and ten. They're scattered along the perimeter. I think they're expecting a team parachuting in or a retaliatory strike from F/A-18s. I had no trouble getting by them." McKiernan drew a diagram of the outpost and approximate locations of the Taliban. "They were moving around. They won't be in the same positions they were in an hour ago."

"We have to get AJ," Nelson said. "Take position on top of this building, and hold your fire until the firefight begins. We'll work our way around both sides of the base toward the building where she's being held. If either team is caught up in a firefight, the other will use that as a diversion and go to the building where she's being held. The priority is to stop them from whatever they're doing. The leader called her by name and knew about the controller. Something big is in the works. He's running a terrorist op using the Perseus drone. AJ won't cooperate without a fight."

Nelson motioned toward Parker's body. "They were probably coming for one of us to torture in front of her," he said.

Warren and Miller, wanting to join the fight, tried to get up. Nelson ordered them to stay and handed each of them an automatic rifle.

Nelson, McKiernan, and the two other SEALs climbed out the window. McKiernan got a boost onto the roof, and the three others moved out.

66

OWEN FULLER HAD heard Jet Ski engines revving up and down in the distance and then heard gunfire. When the noises stopped almost simultaneously, he hoped it meant Palmer was dead. However, after several minutes, when his men did not call, he knew Palmer was on the way. He needed only thirty more minutes to complete what he needed to do. After that, neither Palmer nor anyone else could prevent them from completing their mission.

He had dreamed of this day for a long time, beginning with the study of the Department of Defense public information on defense projects. When he saw that LTG had been awarded the Navy contract for the drone's navigation and targeting systems, he applied for a job and was hired. After that, everything he did was part of a well-executed plan to become the Perseus project leader. Fuller worked day and night to become the best and most capable person for the job. By the time the project was ready to move to the full development phase, he was a shoo-in for the project lead.

Fuller set the controller screen video feed to wide angle. His father was returning Perseus to the *Bush*. The fire control target acquisition was set for the DoSTA tracking dots that Fuller had concealed within the black lettering on all four sides of the equipment container. After the Perseus drone locked onto the DoSTA signal from the *Bush*, it would fly low to the surface of the water, undetected by radar. Flying at maximum speed, the drone would launch the first missile at the equipment container. Because the tracking dots would be destroyed in the explosion, it would then use the Physical Recognition Targeting Auto Find and Fire for the carrier itself and launch the remainder of its missiles. He had programmed an automatic function that would take it through the launch verification and confirmation sequence, a process requiring thirty minutes, during which he would make his escape.

67

NELSON MOVED BETWEEN buildings, a hundred yards from where Hassan Aswad was holding Hamilton. Their satellite phone was in the building with their guns and packs, the one where they had taken Hamilton. They needed to contact the carrier team and warn them. Nelson feared that after they lost contact with the carrier, F/A-18s were launched and on the way to their location with orders to do a flyover or worse—destroy the outpost in order to stop the drone attack. Sacrifice the few to save many.

Nelson was ready to move to the next building when he heard gunshots. He peeked around the corner of the building. A few Taliban were headed toward the far side of the base, blindly firing their weapons as they ran. One of them was hit and fell to the ground, then another, then a third. McKiernan was picking them off, one by one. Nelson feared once the gunfire started, Aswad would kill Hamilton.

Nelson sprinted to the next building and without stopping, moved toward the building where Aswad was holding Hamilton. Nelson heard a woman scream. Having no time to assess the building and locate the best point of entry, he rushed to the door, gun at the ready, and kicked it open.

Hamilton was face down on the floor, struggling to fight off the inevitable. Her pants and panties were on the floor beside her. A man was at her head, holding down her shoulders, while another man, his pants pulled down, was kneeling between her legs. Both lunged for their guns, which were on the floor.

Standing at the door, Nelson fired, killing the two men. He swept his weapon around the room, confirmed the room was clear, and rushed to Hamilton.

"Where's the leader?" Nelson asked, shoving the bodies away from Hamilton. He held out his hand and helped her to her knees. Blood trickled from the corner of her mouth. She was trembling and wiping tears from her eyes as she reached for her trousers and covered herself.

"It's Hassan Aswad. He's alive. When the two men he sent to bring one of you here to torture didn't return, he became suspicious. He told them to do what they desired with me and then kill me." She looked at the two dead men and pointed at one of them, the one who had been between her legs. "His name is Shadid. From what I could pick up from their Arabic conversation and their gestures, Aswad wanted Shadid to leave with him. Shadid refused, saying he would stay behind, kill me, and hold you off while Aswad escaped. After Aswad left, he freed me, and then he knocked me to the floor."

"The Perseus controller?"

"Aswad has it."

"Shit!"

Nelson saw movement in his peripheral vision and thought his teammate had returned. Before Nelson could turn his head, a gunshot broke the silence, and Nelson went down. Hamilton looked down the barrel of the insurgent's pistol. Every muscle in her body tensed. She closed her eyes involuntarily, as if not wanting to see her own death.

68

PALMER HELD HIS arms out to the side and walked toward the police car. The driver was on the radio. A patrolman opened the front passenger door and got out of the vehicle, staying behind the open door.

"Jake Palmer?"

His clothes were wet, and he was wearing a Kevlar vest. They knew who he was. He continued toward them without answering.

The patrolman drew his pistol and pointed it at him, holding it with both hands, his arms braced on the top of the car door.

"Stop. Are you Jake Palmer?"

Palmer turned his back to them and pointed to the back of the vest. "I'm a Federal Agent. I need to get to Owen Fuller's home. He's the leader of a terrorist cell launching a strike against America."

"And I'm Barack Obama. Put your hands behind your head and get on your knees."

Palmer did as the patrolman ordered. He looked toward the house. It had to be Fuller's. There were no other homes on this section of the road. Fuller had obviously chosen the house because it was isolated from the small town and nosy neighbors who monitored who came and went. If the police took him into custody, Palmer would be helpless to stop Fuller.

The other patrolman got out of the car. They walked toward him side by side with their pistols drawn.

"I told you, Billy. Aren't you glad we came back to the house after that wreck in the tunnel?" one of the patrolmen said.

"Shut up, Sam! Stay focused," the one called Billy said.

It was all Palmer could do not to shake his head at the mistake on their part. One should have remained behind the open car door.

Sam and Billy stopped five feet in front of him. Billy reached for his handcuffs. Mistake number two. With the handcuffs in his hand, Billy walked to Palmer's left side. Palmer could see Sam's hand shaking ever so slightly, his finger on the trigger. One nervous twitch and he would discharge his firearm.

Palmer reached out with his left hand, grabbed Billy's arm, and jerked. Billy fell hard to the ground. It had happened so fast, neither policeman had time to react. Palmer threw himself on top of Billy and rolled over. Sam aimed his pistol at them but did not shoot. As Palmer rolled over, he drew the pistol from behind him. From the prone position, he rose back to a kneeling position with Billy between him and Sam and with the barrel pressed against Billy's head.

"Drop your weapon, or I'll blow his head off," Palmer shouted in a firm, commanding voice.

Sam moved the pistol from side to side. He was looking for a shot, but there was not one.

"I said drop your weapon. You've got three seconds—one, two—"

"OK, OK," Sam said, his voice shaking. The young patrolman dropped his service pistol.

"Get on the ground, facedown, hands behind your head," Palmer commanded.

Sam slowly knelt and then laid facedown on the ground and interlocked his fingers behind his head. Palmer shoved Billy away from him and struck him in the head with the butt of his pistol, knocking him unconscious. Sam moved to get up. Palmer hit him in the temple with the pistol. Both officers were alive but would be out for a while. He took their pistols, shoved them in his belt, and dragged the men to an oak tree about twenty feet off the road. He leaned them against the tree on opposite sides, facing each other. Taking the handcuffs Billy had intended to use on him, he cuffed one's right arm to the other's left. Then he took the handcuffs from Sam's belt and cuffed their other hands together. Before leaving, he ripped the radios from their shoulders and threw one in the brush.

The patrol car was still running. Palmer jumped in, flipped off the emergency lights and headlights, and drove slowly to Fuller's house. The two-story, wood frame house with a front porch and attached two-car garage faced the road. The large lot was clear of trees, creating a wide expanse of open area to observe anyone who came onto the property. As he stopped beside another car in front of the closed garage door, he heard a window shatter and looked up. A rifle barrel was pointed at the car. He ducked below the dash, a moment before a bullet went through the windshield. The bullet struck the driver's headrest. Semi-automatic weapon fire erupted from the house. He pressed himself against the bottom of the dashboard. Another burst of gunfire penetrated the windshield and roof of the car.

Palmer held the steering wheel with one hand and jerked the gearshift into drive. Using his free hand, he pressed the accelerator to the floor. As the car surged forward, bullets ripped into the roof. The car crashed through the door and into the garage. Before Palmer could take his hand from the accelerator and press the brake, the car smashed into the back of the garage with such force, the rear of the car lifted off the ground. He sat up and tried to get out. The impact had crumpled the door; it was stuck.

Using his feet to push out the bullet-ridden windshield, he crawled onto the crushed hood. He had to move quickly. In three large strides, he was at the door to the interior of the house. Hesitating for a moment, he imagined what he would see when he entered. Garage doors usually opened into a small mudroom or kitchen. Considering the size of the house, there would be doors leading into a family room and a dining room. Palmer took a deep breath and exhaled before firing two rounds from the police pistol into the lock mechanism and hitting the door with his shoulder. The door flew open. Still wearing his Kevlar vest, Palmer entered the kitchen with his pistol extended in front of him in his right hand and the police pistol in his left; the other police pistol was in his belt in the small of his back. He panned the kitchen with the pistols.

69

THE MUZZLE FLASH was visible through Lara Hamilton's closed eyelids, and she heard the gunshot. She was alive. When she opened her eyes, the man who had shot Nelson was on the floor, the side of his head blown away.

Nelson looked up at her. "Mac."

She knew without asking what he meant, that McKiernan saw the man run to the door and shot him from wherever he had positioned himself. She turned her attention to Nelson, who had a gunshot wound in his side.

Nelson waved her off.

"Aswad told me that he fired a missile into the Afghan presidential palace. The *Bush* is the next target," Hamilton said.

"Get the sat phone. It's in our gear. Contact the carrier."

Hamilton rummaged through packs until she found the satellite phone. She punched in the number for Schmidt.

"Smitty, it's AJ. Hassan Aswad is alive and has the Perseus controller. He's going to blow up the *Bush*. You have fifteen minutes max before it's in position to fire." Hamilton's voice was almost drowned out by the noise of the jets flying over the base. She turned to Nelson. "Whether we can stop the attack on the *Bush* or not, we can't allow him to escape. We have to capture him."

^ ^ ^ ^

The two F/A-18s flew close together and low to the ground over the base.

"See that?" the lead plane pilot, call sign Wizard, said. "Looks like a firefight."

"Roger that," said his wingman, call sign Digger.

"Let's take it up and do a slow pass. I'll report home." Wizard reported to the *Bush* that a firefight was underway at the base. Distinguishing the good guys from the bad was impossible, so there was little they could do. The combat direction center aboard the carrier confirmed that the SEAL team was in a firefight with the Taliban and that Hassan Aswad, a senior Taliban commander, was attempting to make an escape. He was ordered to stay over the site and await orders.

The pilots took their Super Hornets up, made a tight turn, and flew over the base, observing the muzzle flashes of the firefight below them, helpless to do anything but watch.

70

OWEN FULLER HEARD the crash and felt the house shake. He wiped the beads of sweat from his brow. Fifteen minutes—that's all that was needed for his father to lock Perseus on the tracking dots and activate the firing mechanism. Fuller was monitoring his moves and would take control if a problem arose. Once Perseus was locked onto the *Bush* and his father had executed the fire command, the drone would spit out its payload of missiles until none remained and the carrier was ablaze and sunk. The six members of his cell, who were in the house, could hold off anyone for fifteen minutes, including Jake Palmer.

^^^^

Palmer had no idea how many men he faced or where in the house Fuller was, if he was there at all. One thing was certain: He was outmanned and outgunned. He stood still and listened to the footsteps upstairs—at least four sets, maybe more. Hugging the wall, he crept to the door leading to the dining room. When he got to the doorjamb, he took a quick look to be certain the room was clear before he went in. The floors creaked under his weight. His eyes took in what he could see of the lower level of the house. The dining room opened through a large arched passageway into a family room. To the left of the family room were the front door, foyer, and a flight of steps to the second floor. His arms moved in front of him, pistols ready, through the family room and into the foyer.

Out of the corner of his eye, he saw something move—an automatic rifle barrel at the top of the stairwell. He jumped behind a three-foot wide wall that separated the foyer from the family room. The plaster wall offered little protection, other than to keep him out of sight and away from the direct line of fire. A long burst of gunfire shattered a small wooden table by the door. The man was hidden from view and firing wildly, reminding Palmer that in a firefight, the bad guys often resort to spray and pray tactics—fire as many rounds as possible and hope to hit something. His instinct was imprinted after thousands of hours of training and experience: First, confirm there is a target; second, confirm it represents a threat; and third, fire with deadly accuracy—all done in a fraction of a second.

The instant the gunfire stopped, Palmer stepped from behind the wall and aimed his pistols at the top of the stairs. The shooter was descending. He saw the man's legs and the barrel of the rifle and fired both pistols. One bullet hit him just above the left ankle. The other struck him in his lower right leg. The man screamed and tumbled down the stairs. Before he hit the bottom, Palmer shot him again. The man lay motionless in the foyer, his automatic weapon beside him.

The first of the police pistols was empty. Palmer tossed it aside. Keeping his eyes on the top of the stairwell, he stooped to pick up the rifle. Behind him, the front door crashed open. Palmer swung his body around. His left hand, grasping his Sig Sauer 9mm pistol, followed the motion of his head. He saw the man with the shotgun in his peripheral vision. Before Palmer could bring the pistol in position to shoot, the man fired the shotgun.

^^^^

Fuller was in his office upstairs. On the large desk in front of him were his laptop, a Perseus controller, a desktop computer, and a satellite phone. Two men were in the room with him and three more in the hallway outside. He had heard a man scream earlier and then what sounded like someone crashing through a door followed by another burst of gunfire. He picked up the controller, pulled up the time to missile launch digital clock, and locked the screen so that no one could revert to the menu screen without the password. The display showed fifteen minutes, thirty-one seconds, and was counting down. He set the controller upright on his desk and facing the door. Fuller would rather Palmer was dead. But if Palmer made it into the room, Fuller wanted him to watch the final seconds tick off.

^ ^ ^ ^

Palmer heard the simultaneous firing of an automatic rifle and the shotgun. The shotgun blasted away a portion of the ceiling. Plaster rained down onto him and the foyer floor as the man fell forward inside the house, landing on top of the other man's body.

Palmer had dropped to the floor and rolled to his right. Still on the floor, he grabbed the first man's rifle, crawled to the doorframe, and peered outside. He exhaled and smiled. Alona Green was walking toward the house with the stock of an assault rifle pressed against her shoulder, pointing it back and forth at the windows on the front of the house. Green had shot the man the moment he smashed through the door. The impact of the bullets slamming into his back caused him to jerk the shotgun barrel upward and pull both triggers as his body tensed. Palmer rushed outside. He turned and aimed his pistols at the upstairs windows, covering Green while she limped the short distance to the house. They leaned against the doorframe on the porch, out of sight of the stairwell and the line of fire.

Palmer got his first good look at her. She had a rag tied around her arm and was wearing her Kevlar vest. The bottom of the vest and her khaki shorts were red with blood.

"Looks like you needed my help after all. I heard the shots from the boat. I couldn't wait there any longer," she whispered.

"You OK?"

"OK enough to save your sorry ass."

"Another one's down inside. The rest are upstairs. I assume

Fuller's there too. Cover the door and ground floor. I'm going up."

"They're not going anywhere. Backup's on the way. Wait here with me," Green pleaded.

"I can't. I don't know how much time the *Bush* has."

Palmer stuck the pistol in his belt beside the second police pistol and shouldered the rifle. He crouched to see up the stairwell and moved back inside.

"I'm going to kill you, Jake Palmer," a man shouted from upstairs. "Just like I did that piece of shit friend of yours."

71

BEFORE ASWAD FLED the outpost, he had located the carrier strike group's position and locked Perseus onto the signal coming from the tracking dots on the container on the carrier deck of the *Bush*. After firing a missile, the drone was now programmed to switch to Physical Recognition Targeting/PRT, and it would fire the remaining missiles into the carrier. Victory was his. The carrier would be destroyed, and the Americans aboard it would be dead.

Aswad jerked the camouflage tarp from the truck and drove off, still hearing gunshots at the base, although the shots were less frequent and more sporadic. His men stood no chance against the SEALs, who now had the upper hand, but they would keep them busy long enough for him to escape. A few minutes later, the jets screamed by as he drove away from the base on the path to the road into Pakistan. Even with the truck's lights off, he knew that the pilots, using their F/A-18s' night vision imaging capability, could spot him. Regardless, he had to put some distance between himself and the base before ditching the truck and hiking off the path. He slowed to navigate the rutted mountain path in the dark. After spending months here during the offensive against the Marine base, he was very familiar with the path and the overall landscape. The jets made another pass over him. Just a little farther.

The F/A-18 lead pilot radioed the *Bush*, "This is Wizard. I have a lone vehicle on a road less than five klicks from the SEAL op site. Request permission to fire."

"Negative, Wizard," came the reply from the *Bush's* combat direction center. "Target is being pursued on ground. Stay over target area until choppers arrive."

∧ ∧ ∧ ∧

Nelson lay on the floor as he spoke to Quateraro on the satellite phone. "The bad guys have surrendered. At last count I had three men to keep them corralled. I can only spare one to pursue Aswad." Nelson looked at McKiernan, who was poking his chest hard with his finger, indicating his desire to pursue Aswad.

Hamilton interrupted. "I'll go with him."

Nelson grimaced and looked at McKiernan.

McKiernan said, "We'll get him. If we can't catch him, I'll send up a flare; the fly boys can take him out."

After Nelson relayed that information, Quateraro gave the order to capture Aswad. He added that, to all of the world, Aswad was already dead, so while capturing him was preferable, letting the terrorist elude them again would be a grave mistake.

McKiernan and Hamilton were out the door before Nelson could finish giving them the OK to proceed. McKiernan was familiar with the area, having studied it from his position on the hilltop. They left the outpost and headed northwest, the direction Aswad would also have taken to get to the path. Several hundred yards from the base, they came across the tarp, partially covering a small, rusted-out Toyota truck. McKiernan looked inside. The keys were in the ignition. He cranked it, and the engine sputtered and coughed to life. Before Hamilton could get settled in the passenger seat, McKiernan floored the accelerator. The wheels kicked up a mini-sandstorm behind them. Hamilton held on for dear life as the truck bounced along. In less than a mile, they saw a vehicle stopped in a curve. The front of the vehicle was smashed into a large boulder. Steam poured from under the hood. McKiernan stopped the truck a hundred yards behind it. He climbed in the truck bed and looked through his rifle's night vision scope at the vehicle and the surrounding area.

"I see him. He's moving toward the rocky crest to our right," he whispered. "Stay twenty yards behind me."

Hamilton nodded in acknowledgment. She watched McKiernan move away from the truck and marveled at how quickly and silently he walked. From time to time, she saw him stop, his head moving from side to side. He would then look through the scope before proceeding. When they reached Aswad's vehicle, McKiernan pointed to a location on the hill and then to himself. He then pointed to her and at the ground behind the vehicle. She nodded.

Within moments, McKiernan was out of sight, and Hamilton was on her own. She patted her holstered 9mm pistol and pressed the butt of the M4 rifle into her shoulder, keeping the barrel pointed at the ground in the general direction McKiernan headed. She heard the distant rattling of brush and suspected it was Aswad. The next fifteen minutes seemed like an eternity. Hamilton was enveloped by the eerie quiet of the Afghanistan night. *Why didn't I go with him? What good am I waiting here?* She became angry with herself for being afraid. She took deep breaths, holding them in before exhaling. Her mouth was dry as she whispered the words, "Stay calm, dammit, stay calm," but nothing could keep the barrel of her rifle from shaking. She heard a noise nearby, like pebbles rolling down the hill toward her. She stepped from behind the vehicle and squinted to see through the darkness.

They say you don't hear the shot that kills you, the bullet arriving well ahead of the sound from the weapon. All she felt was a horrific thump in the center of her chest. She fell straight onto her back and into semiconsciousness, as she fought to breathe. The last thing she remembered was that her face felt wet. She rubbed it and looked at her hand. Even in the dark, she knew the warm liquid was blood.

∧∧∧∧

McKiernan had lost Aswad and was coming down the hill toward the truck when he saw the muzzle flash. He raised his rifle and looked through the scope at the area where the flash had appeared. He saw Aswad moving fast toward Hamilton, who was on the ground. There was too much distance for McKiernan to cover. He would not make it down the hill before Aswad got to Hamilton. He steadied his rifle and followed Aswad until he stopped over Hamilton and pointed his gun at her. His orders were to bring him in alive, but under no circumstances to let him escape. In the instant before McKiernan pulled the trigger, he weighed the options of wounding Aswad to stop him from killing her, if she were still alive, or going for a kill shot to the head.

∧∧∧∧

Hamilton heard someone calling her, "AJ, AJ." The man's voice seemed to echo in the distance. She gasped for air and rose to a sitting position. Someone was holding her. It took a moment for her vision to clear enough to see that it was McKiernan.

He eased her back onto the ground. "You're fine."

"The blood?"

"It's his. Aswad's AK-47 bullet hit you square in the middle of your body armor. Damn good shot for a Taliban. He came in and stood over you, ready to finish you off. I had no choice."

Hamilton turned her head and saw Aswad lying face down beside the truck.

By the time they arrived at the base, Hamilton was alert. The center of her chest between her breasts was sore, like someone was pressing against it. McKiernan had plucked the flattened bullet from her body armor and gave it to her, telling her she could have it made into a necklace or wait until she was shot again and have earrings made. She said she would rather not be reminded of the experience, and that displaying a bullet that had not actually wounded you elicited no more than feigned interest in the special warfare community.

Nelson told them an Army special operations team and paramedics were minutes away, inbound on Black Hawk helicopters.

72

PALMER BACKED OUT of the front door, the rifle stock pressed against his shoulder. Green was still sitting on the porch, leaning against the wall of the house. He moved away from the open door and knelt beside her again.

"Change your mind?"

"No—my strategy. I need a distraction. Can you go to the back of the house and fire a few rounds into the upstairs windows?"

"Do I have to do everything?" Green groaned.

Palmer helped her up. She winced and grabbed at her side.

"Put a couple of rounds into each window. After you fire, get against the side of the house and stay there."

Palmer motioned to the right of the house, using his middle and index fingers. After Green left, he reached around and took his pistol from his belt, inserted a new magazine, and shoved it back where it had been. He checked the police pistol. It was fully loaded. He tucked it in his belt beside his pistol. Once inside the house, he stood near the foot of the stairs with the dead man's rifle, which was now set to semi-automatic.

Palmer looked at the rifle and set it down. In close quarters, the long-barreled rifle would not be as effective as the pistols. He took them out of his belt and waited until he heard gunfire coming from the back of the house. With the gunfire, crashing glass, and shouting providing the distraction he needed, he took a deep breath and charged up the steps, his pistol extended to the right and the police pistol extended to the left. The men were at both ends of the hallway firing wildly at him. He jerked his head back and forth, pinpointing the location of each of the men before he fired. He felt a sting in his arm and another in his thigh. Another bullet struck him in the side of his body armor and knocked him against the wall.

Palmer kept firing until both pistols were empty and the men were dead. He studied the hallway: five doors—two against the back of the house, two on the front, plus one on the right at the end of the hall. All were closed except the one at the end of the hall. He threw down the police pistol and put a fresh magazine into his. He rushed into the open room, jumping over the bodies of the men he had shot. It was the bathroom—empty. He reentered the hallway and went to the room on his left. He stood to the side, turned the doorknob, and pushed opened the door. As he did so, he moved into the doorway, his 9mm pointed ahead of him. It was a bedroom. No one was inside. He felt the warm wetness of blood on his thigh and side. No time for that now.

An electronic crackle came from the room to his right, probably a police scanner or VHF radio. He rushed to the door, drew his right leg up, and kicked his foot near the latch. The hollow placement interior door flew open. A man with a sawed-off shotgun pointed at the door was crouched behind a desk to Palmer's right. Palmer dove away. The shotgun blast splintered the doorjamb. Palmer immediately lunged low into the doorway and fired twice. One shot struck the man in the throat, and the other hit him in the head.

Palmer got up and looked at him. He was not Owen Fuller. The Perseus controller was on the desk along with a VHF radio, police scanner, and a desktop computer. The Perseus controller's digital timer displayed the countdown to missile firing. He had to make a choice between clearing the other rooms and stopping the drone. There was not enough time for both.

He tried to remember the simulator Smitty had shown him. He pressed the menu button and discovered it was jammed. He snatched the satellite phone from the pocket of his vest. With

the phone to his ear, he walked to an open window to improve
the satellite signal. An emergency fire escape ladder hung from
the windowsill to the ground. He stuck his head out and looked
for Fuller, but instead saw Alona Green facedown on the ground
below. He heard an engine start and saw a jet boat pull away
from a dock in the distance, out of range of his pistol. From his
vantage point, he could see that the creek led to the Chesapeake
Bay. The engine roared as the boat sped off.

Palmer heard the floor creak behind him. Before he could
turn around, he was struck in the head and went down. His
handgun and the satellite phone fell to the floor beside him. He
was conscious, but dazed.

An Arab man kicked the pistol away and stood over him, his
gun pointed at his head. "I'm Ragheb Ata' Allah Nazari, the last
person you will ever see. I killed Jansen, and now I'm going to
kill you."

Palmer's eyes locked onto Nazari's. They glared at each
other.

"You can't," Palmer groaned.

"And why's that?" Nazari asked, laughing as he said the
words.

A voice on the VHF radio on the table said, "Ragheb, are you
there?"

Nazari's head didn't move, but his eyes glanced toward the
radio for a fraction of a second. It was all Palmer needed. Palmer
grasped his hands around Nazari's hand that held the pistol,
moving the barrel of the gun upward and away from him. Nazari
brought his free hand up to the pistol over Palmer's hands. Both
men pushed with all their strength. Even with all of Nazari's
weight behind him as he pushed downward, the pistol inched
back until it was pointed at Nazari's head.

"Because I'm going to kill you."

Nazari's finger was still on the trigger. Palmer tensed his
hands and held the gun in place for a moment to allow Nazari
time to process the inevitable. Nazari's eyes widened, and he
opened his mouth to say something. Palmer was not going to
allow him to have a final word. He squeezed Nazari's finger. The
bullet hit Nazari in the throat and blew off the back of his head.
His body dropped onto Palmer's chest.

"Ragheb, are you there?" said the voice on the VHF radio.

Palmer shoved the body off him, got up, and pushed in the talk button. "Is that you, Fuller? Nazari's dead, and I'm coming for you."

73

PALMER PICKED UP the satellite phone. Before he could go after Fuller, he had to phone Smitty.

"I'm at Fuller's house. There's been a firefight here. Several men are down. Fuller escaped on his boat. The Perseus controller shows five minutes to launch."

"I'll put you on speaker. The SEAL team contacted us. Hassan Aswad has their controller and has escaped."

"Abort the launch," shouted Schmidt.

"I can't. He's locked it on a countdown function."

"That's the countdown to when Perseus is within range to launch the missiles," Schmidt said.

"If it is the *Bush*, Fuller must have placed tracking dots on something you have on board, something that would have been taken on board with the drone where the signal wouldn't be blocked by the steel hull of the ship. Either that or he is using the physical recognition targeting function."

"Physical recognition would require the drone come in high with a better structural view of the ships. It has to be DoSTA, but where?"

"You have less than five minutes," Palmer said.

"The equipment container. That has to be it. It's on the flight deck."

"Push the damn thing overboard along with anything taken from the container that is out in the open."

"We'd better be right. That's millions of dollars' worth of equipment."

Palmer could hear Smitty speaking, followed by shouting. He looked at the countdown clock—four minutes to go. Palmer, holding the phone in one hand, bowed his head into his other hand. He was not a churchgoing Christian, but his faith was strong. "Please, God, let me be right. Save those men and women," he prayed aloud.

Three minutes to missile launch. "Talk to me, Smitty," he pleaded. No response. He heard more frantic shouts in the background. *Under two minutes to go. What the hell is going on?*

There was absolute silence. The countdown clock displayed all zeros, and a message: "Missiles Fired" appeared on the controller screen. Palmer's heart pounded in his chest. He heard a muffled explosion followed by people yelling.

"No, no, no," Palmer said. He dropped to the floor by the open window and put his head in his hands.

∧∧∧∧

Owen Fuller glanced at his watch. A laugh grew low and silent in his chest before it burst out loud. He threw his head back and let go of the steering wheel of the boat long enough to shake both fists above his head. He'd done it. The missiles were launched. The *Bush* had been struck and was sinking—now for the perfect getaway. After pulling away from the dock behind his house, he was in the Chesapeake Bay, headed south. The boat was small and fast, with a top speed of sixty-five miles per hour. In less than thirty minutes, he would disappear. A front was approaching, and although the skies were clear, the wind had increased, and the swells in the bay were about two feet with whitecaps—not enough to put off an experienced boater, but enough to make Fuller uncomfortable. The boat was skimming the crests of the swells, at times flying out of the water before slamming into the troughs.

74

PALMER SAT ON the floor, staring at the ceiling. He pictured the men and women aboard the *Bush*, some killed instantly, some injured and in the sea, awaiting rescue by the other ships in the strike group. He had failed, and Fuller had escaped. He was thinking through what he should have done differently when he heard a voice coming from the satellite phone on the floor and picked it up.

"The missiles struck the container seconds after it went overboard," Schmidt said. "The container was in the water just aft of the ship. We sustained some damage to the fantail and some injuries, but we're OK. As soon as the missile was launched, we locked onto the approximate location of the drone. The strike group ships fired everything they had—hundreds of thousands of rounds—into the area and hit it."

Palmer looked to the ceiling of the room and said, "Thank you, God," then remembered Green. He ran down the stairs and to the back of the house. She was unconscious, the back of her head covered with blood. He sat on the ground beside her and pulled her hair back enough to see the wound. She had a nasty cut on her head that was bleeding profusely. He carefully rolled her over.

"Alona! Alona!" He looked into her eyes for signs of life.

"What happened?" Green whispered. Her eyes opened ever so slightly. "I must have passed out."

Palmer examined her wound. "Fuller knocked you out. You're lucky he didn't kill you." He looked around. Her rifle was missing. Fuller would have shot her if not for the risk of attracting his attention.

"The *Bush*? Did you stop him in time?"

"Yes, thanks to you. The carrier has only minor damage, and Perseus was destroyed."

Palmer looked up to see two gray Navy helicopters descending fast onto the property, along with a black helicopter with no military markings. The three helicopters landed in the clearing adjacent to Fuller's property. As soon as the wheels of the choppers touched down, teams of Navy men jumped out and ran toward the house. A Navy lieutenant and three men, including a paramedic, rushed to Palmer. The paramedics went immediately to Green and assessed her condition.

"Are you Jake Palmer?" the lieutenant asked.

"Yes, sir."

"Anyone in the house?"

"No one who's alive."

"Including Fuller?"

"He escaped in a jet boat."

"Our men will sweep the house to make sure. I'm going after Fuller."

"I'm going with you. I can ID the boat, and I know what he looks like."

"Ordinarily, I'd say no. But given the circumstances, I'll allow it."

Before Palmer left, he told Green, "I'm going after Fuller. You OK?"

"I'll be fine."

"You don't look fine."

"And you look like crap too. Now go!"

Before he could leave, one of the paramedics examined Palmer's wounds. A bullet had entered and exited his left thigh, leaving a deep open wound. The other bullet had grazed his upper arm on the right side. Both required medical attention. Palmer told him he was not going anywhere in an ambulance.

The paramedic sprayed some disinfectant on the wounds and slapped on sterile bandages, telling Palmer he needed to be seen by a doctor soon.

Palmer caught up with the lieutenant and the two men with him and jumped aboard one of the helicopters that immediately lifted off. He put on earphones with a communicator and went into the cockpit. He described the boat to the pilot and told him Fuller would probably head south and east toward open water rather than north up the Chesapeake Bay.

^ ^ ^ ^

Fuller went under the Bay Bridge-Tunnel and made a straight line to the cargo ships anchored in the Lynnhaven Anchorage between the Bridge-Tunnel and the mouth of the bay at Cape Henry. Most were coalers waiting their turn to be filled with West Virginia coal at Lamberts Point, the largest coal exporting facility in the Northern Hemisphere.

An intermediary had paid the Dutch captain of an Egyptian ship fifty thousand dollars to provide Fuller passage to the Middle East. The arrangements had been made weeks earlier to coincide with the pre-arranged date for the Perseus field test and the ship's arrival in Hampton Roads.

Because the ships looked alike, Fuller had taken his boat to the anchorage the week before to confirm the ship's precise location. Within minutes, he would disappear without a trace. As he neared the ship, he saw the ladder had been lowered from the side to the water. Once he was aboard, the ship's cranes would lift the boat from the water and lower it into a compartment.

75

THE HELICOPTER FLEW low and fast. The Bay Bridge-Tunnel lights were on, as were those on the ships in anchorage. Palmer looked to the north and west, in case his guess at the direction Fuller took was wrong, and saw no sign of the boat. Ahead on the bridge near the entrance to the tunnel, Palmer saw the blue and red lights of emergency vehicles. Wreckage from the earlier crash was still being cleared. It was late in the day, and not many boats were on the water. Looking south, he spotted a boat in the distance, traveling at high speed. He tapped the pilot on the shoulder and pointed. The pilot nodded his affirmation and banked the helicopter. Palmer looked to the rear of the chopper. The men were positioned to fire. He wanted Fuller alive. He was the only one who could answer his questions.

^^^^

Owen Fuller drove the boat along the starboard side of the coaler. The massive ship, over eight hundred feet long and one hundred and fifty feet wide, was empty and riding high in the water. He slowed the boat and moved toward the ladder hanging down from the main deck for him to climb. He had purchased the boat for the sole purpose of having a means to escape. When he did, he made a point of going out when the seas were calm. He was not accustomed to coming alongside a ship with the waves and wind pushing the boat around. Over the noise of the boat's engine, he heard a helicopter and looked over his shoulder. Military helicopters were a common sight over the bay, but this one was flying straight toward him. He'd been spotted. He turned and looked at the ship. The crewmen were hauling up the ladder.

"You spineless assholes!" Fuller yelled at the men pulling up the ladder. He drove the boat around the bow of the ship to the other side and out of view of the helicopter. He looked for another way of getting aboard. There was none. Several crewmen were at the rail, watching. The helicopter circled the ship, hovered above him, and descended. Fuller pushed the throttles and headed for the shoreline at First Landing State Park.

"Take him out," the lieutenant ordered. The men brought their rifles up and prepared to fire.

"No!" Palmer shouted, rushing toward them. "We need him alive."

The lieutenant looked at him, then at his men. "You're right. Take out the boat," he ordered.

The men each fired several shots.

Fuller heard gunshots and the thud of the bullets hitting the boat. He picked up the rifle he had taken from Green and fired at the helicopter, which began to rise and make an evasive maneuver. He continued firing until he ran out of bullets. Smoke rose from the boat's engine compartment. He pushed the throttles to the maximum. The engine sputtered and coughed, then burst into flames. The boat was going to explode.

The helicopter was coming back, fast and low to the surface. Fuller stuffed his pistol in his belt, kicked off his shoes, and jumped from the boat. He was an average recreational swimmer and did not think he needed a life jacket for what looked like a short swim. But he was not accustomed to swimming in open water, and the current and swells quickly took their toll. He tired and began to panic. The helicopter was hovering a couple of hundred feet overhead. Ahead of him, a long row of posts extended in a line toward the shore. His strength was fading fast. He had to make it to the nearest post. He was struggling and starting to go under. He was going to drown.

The lieutenant looked at his men. "Who's going in?"

"I am," Palmer said as he stripped off his Kevlar vest.

"You've done your job, Palmer. We'll do ours."

The helicopter lowered into position over Fuller. One of the men prepared to be lowered into the water. If Fuller were captured, Palmer would lose his only opportunity to question him.

"Sorry, lieutenant. I'll see you on the beach with Fuller, dead or alive.

Before the lieutenant could respond, Palmer threw off his shoes and jumped out the open door of the chopper, dropping toward the water. His clothes were still damp from his earlier jump into the Chesapeake. He took a deep breath before he hit the water and for the second time today, his momentum took him deep into the dark water of the bay. When he surfaced, he looked around for Fuller. At first, the swells and prop wash from the helicopter hindered his vision. But after the helicopter pulled up, he saw Fuller, a hundred feet away. Palmer swam hard in the rough water. *You're not going die yet, asshole,* Palmer thought. When Palmer got close, he heard a gunshot. He stopped and treaded water. Fuller was firing a pistol at him. Another shot rang out. Palmer dove underwater and swam toward him. When he got close enough to see Fuller's legs in the dark water, he surfaced near him. Fuller was flailing his arms in a state of panic and going under when the swells washed over him. He still had the pistol in his hand. Water rescue had been drilled into Palmer. Drowning men will drag down a potential rescuer. Palmer took a few strong strokes toward him. Fuller saw him and extended the arm with the pistol. Palmer reached out with his left hand and jerked the pistol from Fuller's hand. Before Fuller could grab him, Palmer drew back and struck him twice in the jaw with his right fist, not hard enough to knock him out, but hard enough to get his attention.

"Palmer, you're insane!" Fuller shouted.

Palmer let Fuller sink below the surface and held him under with his legs. Fuller came up spitting and coughing.

"Tell me the truth, or you'll drown. No one will blame me. It will look like an accident."

"Why Jansen?" Palmer let him sink again.

"They were following Alona Green," Fuller said, gasping for air. "She was returning my laptop." Fuller coughed and took a deep breath. "It had information and applications imbedded in it that I needed for the Perseus test. Jansen called me and said he needed to see me immediately. I let Nazari and Akbari in the side entrance and had them wait outside his office while I went inside."

Palmer held Fuller above water and let him catch his breath. "Go on."

"Jansen started questioning me. I demanded he give me my laptop. He said no. He was going to go through every kilobyte. I called Akbari and Nazari to come in. Nazari shot Wade in his chair before he could move."

"You bastard."

"None of it matters. My father and I have achieved a great victory for the jihad."

"Screw you and your jihad. I know about your father and his plan to blow up the *Bush*. It failed, you son of a bitch."

Fuller laughed. "You're wrong. The missiles were set to launch when I left the house. No one could change it."

"The crew pushed the launch platform off the deck. The missile struck it as it was going into the water. Then they threw everything at the drone and destroyed it. The *Bush* suffered only minor damage. No one was killed."

Fuller was working hard to catch his breath.

"Why did you kill Huntington?" Palmer asked, assuming he had killed her.

"I didn't."

Palmer pushed Fuller away. Fuller had regained some of his strength and swam toward shore. Palmer dove under the water, grabbed Fuller's legs, and pulled him under. He swam down several feet and held him for about thirty seconds.

When he surfaced, Fuller gasped and took several deep breaths.

"Talk, or this time, I'll hold you under until you're dead." Palmer started to dive.

Fuller flailed his arms. "OK! OK! I killed her." He gasped for air before continuing, "She suspected something was going on." He took in several breaths of air. "She had issued that damn report. She was going to make too much noise. I couldn't let her."

Palmer swam under the water, holding Fuller's mouth and nose. He wanted to hold him under and look into his eyes until he took his last breath. He was responsible for Wade Jansen's death, not to mention Huntington's and the two men in Conshohocken. Fuller struggled and then became still. Palmer kicked to the surface and released his hand from Fuller's face.

"The only thing that has stopped me from killing you to avenge Wade's murder is that it would make me no better than you."

76

PALMER WAS UP before dawn. He took the elevator to the hotel lobby and returned to his room with a large coffee, the local Virginia Beach newspaper, and *The New York Times.* Sipping his coffee, he flipped back and forth between CNN and the local television stations.

The lead story in the national and local news concerned a raid on a possible terrorist cell on Virginia's Eastern Shore, reporting that all the suspected terrorists were killed in the ensuing shoot-out. A Homeland Security agent gave credit to the Cape Charles Police Department for their assistance and involvement with federal agencies. The reporter interviewed two Cape Charles policemen, Sam Giddens and Billy Turner, who had bandages on their heads, playing the modest heroes. The reporters said that the authorities were still investigating a possible connection between the terrorist cell and a multi-vehicle accident in one of the tunnels on the Chesapeake Bay Bridge-Tunnel that took hours to clear. The driver of the vehicle responsible for the crash was identified as a Middle Eastern man.

CNN reported that the Norfolk-based carrier, USS *George H.W. Bush,* sustained minor damage during flight operations in the Persian Gulf. Several crewmen were injured, none seriously.

On one of the local stations, a female reporter on location

outside Lynnhaven Technology Group said that the police had arrested LTG employee Owen Fuller for the murders of Wade Jansen and Angela Huntington. She said those close to the case speculated that he and Huntington were having an affair that went sour and he poisoned her. The station cut to an interview with Virginia Beach Police Lieutenant Mike Hawkins, who said that when Wade Jansen, LTG's head of security, confronted Fuller about the poisoning, they got into an argument and Fuller shot and killed him. Hawkins stated that Fuller confessed to the murders after he was arrested.

The New York Times reported that the Navy had conducted a test of the first of a new class of drones, built to take off and land on aircraft carriers. A Navy captain was quoted as saying the test was successful, although based on the results, some alterations would be made to the navigation and target acquisition/tracking systems. No mention was made of the death of Virginia Beach-based SEAL Lieutenant Junior Grade Steve Parker. Palmer knew death of a service member is usually not announced for a few days to allow time for next of kin to be notified.

Also leading the news was a report that the presidential palace in Afghanistan had been damaged in an apparent mortar attack. The number of deaths and injuries was unknown. Witnesses reported seeing a missile, but military sources downplayed the likelihood of a missile attack. Government and military officials assigned responsibility to insurgents who were opposed to peace negotiations with the Taliban or to the Taliban itself in retribution for Hassan Aswad's death the previous December. A spokesman from the State Department said the attack would not alter the plans for withdrawal of American combat forces.

Palmer was relieved his name was not mentioned in any of the television news reports or newspaper articles. He left the hotel and headed for the Naval hospital, located across the Elizabeth River from Norfolk, glad that he remembered to retrieve his rental car from the Bay Bridge-Tunnel police late the previous night. The rush hour traffic doubled the time it should have taken to make the trip to Portsmouth. He had been told that Alona Green would be registered as Jane Doe.

When he arrived at Jane Doe's room, two men in suits, wearing communicators in their ears, were standing outside.

"Photo ID," demanded one of the men, extending his hand, palm up.

Palmer took his driver's license from his wallet and placed it in the man's hand. "Are you protecting her or keeping her from escaping?"

Without acknowledging the question, the man studied the photo, then looked at Palmer, and then again at the photo. He returned the license and told him to put his arms out to the side and spread his legs. Palmer knew the drill. The man patted him down and nodded to his partner.

"You missed my crotch."

"Unless you want a body cavity search, you'll mind your manners." He nodded his head toward the door, indicating for him to go in. "Make it short."

"If she's asleep, can you wait until she wakes up to start the clock?" Palmer asked with a smirk.

Green was lying in the bed, half-awake. She had an intravenous line in her arm and an oxygen tube in her nostrils. The monitor beside the bed displayed her vital signs. When she saw him, she smiled and said, "Jake." Her voice was weak. She cleared her throat and reached for her cup of ice water on the tray at her bedside. Palmer moved closer to help her take a drink.

"I'm glad you've come." She pushed a button on the bed controls, raising the head of the bed almost to a sitting position and extended her hand toward his arm.

Palmer slid a chair close to the bed. She grasped his hand and squeezed it.

"I would have come sooner. I was told you weren't allowed visitors."

"I was pretty much out of it until this morning.

"You look great," Jake said.

"Liar."

"Seriously, how are you doing?"

"I've been better. I lost a lot of blood. They tell me I'll be here for a couple of days for observation."

"You're going to have a couple of nice bullet wound scars to show off."

"For men, that's a badge of honor; for women, not so much. I heard you got Fuller."

"Yeah, I should have killed the bastard."

"No, you shouldn't have. He'll give up a lot of information before he sees a courtroom, if he ever does. Men like Fuller don't stand up well to interrogation or prison."

"I hope they ship his ass to Gitmo for an extended visit."

Green laughed and started to cough. "Yeah, too bad they're not accepting any more guests." She took another drink of water.

"Thanks for coming for me on the bridge and at the house. You saved my ass back there. Are those guys cops?" Palmer asked, motioning toward the door with his thumb.

"Sort of."

"Are you under arrest?"

Green shrugged without replying.

"Who the hell are you? Alona Green—is that even your real name?"

She didn't respond. Palmer sensed she was contemplating whether to tell the truth and, if so, how much.

"Well, is it?"

"Alona is my real name. I was named after my father, Alonzo. He wanted a boy."

"Green?"

"My name's Alona Kolvalyova."

"Kolvalyova? Russian?"

"Ukrainian."

"Got tired of spelling your last name for everyone?"

She tried to laugh, but coughed again. She cleared her throat. "That was a good reason to, but no. It's complicated."

"You work for the CIA?"

"I'm an independent contractor with the Defense Intelligence Agency."

"Why would the Defense Intelligence Agency contract with a Ukrainian?"

"My father was a member of the Soviet Committee for State Security. He—"

"The KGB? Now I'm confused, yet intrigued."

"I said it was complicated." Green told him that her father was disenchanted with the Communist Party and became a double agent, providing the U.S. with information through the early '80s. When the KGB became suspicious of his activities, he and her mother defected. The State Department moved them to Washington, D.C., where he worked with the CIA. Because of the anti-Soviet sentiment at the time, they were given new identities and names. Her father picked Green as their last name based on Green Ukraine or the Ukrainian Republic of the Far East, a country planned in the early 1900s that never came about. She was born in Washington, while her parents were living there. Her mother and father were dead now. He died of cancer, and she died of a stroke.

Palmer wasn't sure she was telling the truth about her parents or anything else for that matter. Perhaps her parents were still in the witness protection program.

"I don't know what to say."

"Jake Palmer at a loss for words?"

"Why would the DIA recruit the daughter of a former spy?"

The door opened, and a nurse came into the room. While she checked the IV line and vital sign monitor, Palmer and Green made small talk. When the nurse left, Green continued. She said she had no idea they were interested in recruiting her after she received her degree in computer science from MIT. She assumed they knew her because of her father, and perhaps they needed someone who spoke Ukrainian. Her first assignments were bland and uninteresting, but the money was too good to turn down. After her fourth or fifth assignment, her contact—a man she had only talked to on the phone—met her at a D.C. restaurant. A week later, she was at Camp Peary for six months of intensive training."

"The Farm, near Williamsburg? That's CIA."

"What did I know?"

"So how did you get involved in this case?"

"It's a long story."

"And my time is about up. The goons at the door will be coming to get me."

"Screw the guards." She went on to explain that the DIA had been investigating corporate espionage within the defense contractor industry. Companies working on unmanned aerial vehicles, or drones, were under scrutiny. For the most part, competing companies were the ones running ops; but in some cases, it was foreign countries. The DIA had a solid lead that another company was after LTG's navigation and target acquisition/tracking technology that was crucial to the U.S. defense strategy. She was brought in to run a sting operation and provided contact information for a man with the code name of "Zeus." She spoke with Zeus on the phone several times, but they never met. He wanted Owen Fuller's laptop, ID, and password and didn't care how he got it as long as his team had a couple of days to use it without LTG's knowledge. The money she received went into a numbered Swiss account established by the DIA to be used as evidence in the case. The DIA was set to grab Shaun and Graham as soon as she let her DIA contact know they were finished and the remaining money was in her account. They believed Shaun and Graham would lead them to Zeus.

"Why didn't the DIA simply contact LTG and work with them on the sting?"

"They wanted me to keep it real. The DIA trusts no one. For all they knew, someone at LTG was involved."

"When they were killed and you made off with the laptop, your assignment was over. Right?"

"That's what I thought. I called my DIA contact and told him what had happened and that I had the laptop. He said he would call me back with instructions. When he called, he told me to follow the trail, to take the laptop to LTG and see where it led. We both believed that once I gave it to Jansen that would be the end of it. No one knew or even expected Fuller was involved in a terrorist plot or that Jansen would be killed. And I never expected to meet you," she said, squeezing his hand.

"How'd you know I was on the Chesapeake Bay Bridge-Tunnel?"

"The DIA was monitoring your cell phone, both your calls and your location. They had told me you were on the way to Fuller's home in Cape Charles. I was in my car on my way there when I got a call saying a wreck in the tunnel had closed the CBBT to all traffic. According to the CBBT police chatter, the car that crashed into the truck had come from the Eastern Shore. They pinpointed your cell phone to the bridge, just short of the third island, near the entrance to the second tunnel."

"So how did the two Arabs, who I assume were members of the cell working with Fuller, find you and the laptop at the house in Conshohocken?"

"We think Fuller had installed custom tracking software, similar to LoJack, on the laptop," Green said. "It would have been almost impossible for Shaun and Graham to detect it. Fuller couldn't pinpoint the location until he got back to the office and accessed the programs on his desktop computer."

"But then he discovered LTG had locked him out," Palmer said. "He didn't get a new ID and password until Monday morning after Jansen interrogated him. That's the first time Fuller could have used the program to locate his laptop. Fuller didn't tell Jansen about the tracking software on the laptop because he wanted to eliminate whoever had it—you."

"And he didn't want Jansen and his team to examine the laptop, as they would have done, before returning it to him," Green said.

"I believe Shaun and Graham had already placed a tracking device on your car. When the Arab men arrived, they planted ones on both cars in the driveway. Once you left Conshohocken, they could have tracked you with either the device they had planted or since you then had the laptop, through information Fuller was providing them about its exact location. You and the laptop eventually led them to Jansen. They killed him, retrieved the laptop, and then came after you, using the tracking device they placed on your car. That's how they followed you to One Fish-Two Fish. Unfortunately, the device you destroyed on the way to Virginia Beach was the one Shaun and Graham placed on your car."

"What's happened to Fuller?" Green asked, her voice weakening.

"He's in custody, being held without bail, and his father, Hassan Aswad, was once again killed." Palmer wanted to stay longer but thought Green looked tired. He got up, bent over her, and kissed her lightly on the forehead. "Take care of yourself, Alona Kolvalyova. Get some rest. I'll stop by tomorrow morning on the way to Wade's funeral."

Alona smiled and whispered, "Promise?"

"I promise."

77

PALMER GLANCED AT the digital clock on the dashboard as he drove away from the hotel the next morning. He had time for a short visit with Alona at Naval Medical Center Portsmouth before Wade Jansen's memorial service, scheduled for eleven o'clock in Virginia Beach. He was looking forward to seeing her. Yesterday, for the first time since they met, she seemed unguarded and open. She answered many of the questions he had about her, but there was much more he wanted to know. He did not even know where she lived or how to contact her. He stepped off the elevator and glanced at his watch. He had thirty minutes, forty-five max, before he needed to leave for the church. When he looked up from his watch, the first thing he noticed was that the guards were gone from in front of her room. His first thought was that he had gotten off on the wrong floor. He looked at the elevator doors. The floor number was correct. He picked up his pace. The door to the room was open. An elderly man was in the bed. A woman, who Palmer assumed was the man's wife, was sitting in a chair by the bed, the same chair he had sat in, talking to Alona.

"I'm sorry," Palmer said. "I must have the wrong room."

She looked at him with a blank face.

Palmer stepped outside the room and looked at the room

number. He was certain it was Alona's room.

He went back in and asked. "Have you been in this room long?"

"My husband was admitted this morning," she said.

Palmer apologized and went to the nurses' station. "I'm looking for Alona Green. She was admitted as Jane Doe. Someone else is in her room. She said yesterday she would be here for a couple of more days. She must have been moved."

"That happens sometimes. Let me check." The nurse typed in some information and studied the computer monitor. "When was she admitted?"

"A couple of days ago."

She entered some additional information and again studied the results on the screen, which was hidden from his view.

"I'm sorry. We have no record of a Jane Doe or Alona Green."

"Check Alona Kolvalyova, that's K-o-l-v-a-l-y-o-v-a.

The nurse entered the name and looked at the monitor. "No. Are you sure that's the correct spelling?"

"Not really. Is there anyone with a name even close to that?"

"No. Sorry."

He left the hospital without going to the admissions office to see if they had a record of her admission or discharge. He knew no record of an Alona Kolvalyova being admitted to Naval Medical Center Portsmouth would exist.

78

THE LOWER LEVEL of the theatre-style auditorium at the church on North Great Neck Road was filled to capacity for Wade Jansen's memorial service. He would be laid to rest later at Arlington National Cemetery. His family, neighbors, and friends from church, Lynnhaven Technology Group, and Broad Bay Country Club were present. A large contingent from Naval Special Warfare Group Two, including those who didn't know him well, but who were present to honor his service, were also there.

Palmer listened as the pastor spoke of Jansen's faith and service to the church and of God's promise of everlasting life to those who believed in Jesus Christ. Thought by everyone to be fearless, Palmer had been known to break out in a sweat at the mere mention of speaking in front of a large crowd. When the pastor finished, he introduced Palmer, simply saying that he had served with Jansen in the Navy and was a close friend.

Palmer stepped to the podium, took a deep breath, and began his eulogy for Wade Cody Jansen. He started with an excerpt from the Navy SEAL Creed. His voice was strong and confident. Without referring to text in his hands, he slowly scanned across the auditorium as he quoted it, as if speaking to each individual.

"My loyalty to Country and Team is beyond reproach. I

humbly serve as a guardian to my fellow Americans, always ready to defend those who are unable to defend themselves. I do not advertise the nature of my work, nor seek recognition for my actions. I voluntarily accept the inherent hazards of my profession, placing the welfare and security of others before my own. I serve with honor on and off the battlefield. The ability to control my emotions and my actions, regardless of circumstance, sets me apart from other men. Uncompromising integrity is my standard. My character and honor are steadfast. My word is my bond."

Before Palmer continued, he stopped to compose himself and to wipe his eyes and nose with his handkerchief. He had not recited those words in over ten years, yet he realized they meant more to him now than ever. A few days earlier, when he flew into Norfolk and looked down at the Naval Special Warfare facility at Little Creek, he had thought he was glad he was no longer a part of it; and although it was true he was no longer an active member of this group of men of valor, he had and would continue to live his life by their creed, just as Jansen had done.

Palmer acknowledged in his remarks that were it not for Jansen's bravery and courage, he would not be standing there today. In total disregard for his own safety, Jansen had returned under heavy fire to save him from certain death. At the end of the eulogy, Palmer paused and looked at Carol Jansen, who was sitting in the front row with her children. Speaking to her, he apologized for not being as close a friend to Wade as he should have been since they left the service ten years earlier. He said he had his reasons for allowing the connections to his past and his former teammates slip away, but the short time he had spent with Wade before his passing made him realize that had been a huge mistake. He looked to the audience in uniform and thanked them and the Naval Special Warfare community for their service to their country and for their friendship to and support of Wade and his family. In closing, he paraphrased Pericles, the ancient Greek politician, general, and statesman: "What you leave behind is not what is engraved on stone monuments, but what is woven into the lives of others. Because of that, Wade Jansen's spirit was part of the fabric of the lives of everyone present."

A quartet of the church's singers led the singing of the Navy

Hymn, "Eternal Father, Strong to Save" and the service closed with a lone bagpiper playing "Going Home." As Palmer was leaving the stage, he saw a woman wearing a black dress and large sunglasses get up from her seat in the back and exit the auditorium. *Alona?*

^^^^

Alona Green made a quick getaway. A car was waiting for her at the drop-off area at the main entrance to the church.

The driver got out and assisted her into the rear seat of the car. Before driving away, he turned around and said, "Where to now, Ms. Green?"

"Just drive," she responded, never looking back at the church. Jake Palmer was the only man she had felt this way about. *What is it about him? Is he the one?* She was saddened that she would never find out.

^^^^

After the service, Palmer stood in the lobby outside the auditorium. Lara Hamilton, Mac McKiernan, and Howard Schmidt, all in dress uniforms, came up to him.

"Well done, Jake," Hamilton said. "Your words honored the man and meant a great deal to everyone here. He was a good person, a man who exemplified God, country, and family. There wasn't a dry eye in the house."

"That was really tough. When did you guys get in?"

"Last night."

"I was worried about you."

"Four wounded and one fatality on the team, and only minor damage to the *Bush.* The test was postponed until changes recommended by Angela Huntington are completed and ground tested." Hamilton was not going to say anything more about the mission and what had happened. It was not the time. This was about Wade Jansen, not her or anyone else.

"Ed Taylor called and apologized for firing me. He has a laundry list of things regarding company security that he wants me to do. I thought about telling him to stick it, but I bit my tongue. I'll be here a few times over the next three months."

"The Navy's not too happy with LTG," Hamilton said. "You'll have to assure us the holes in their security have been plugged."

"They will be. I owe it to Wade to see it through."

"We've got some work to do," Schmidt said. "See ya soon, Jake."

Before they left, McKiernan stepped forward and bear hugged Palmer. "Let's get together for a beer before you leave," he said.

"You're on."

As they walked away, someone tapped him on the shoulder. "Just wanted to say thanks." It was Cora Donegan.

"If you hadn't given me Fuller's address and directions, it would not have ended well."

"Nice eulogy. Stop by before you leave town."

"I will. I want my consultant fee to go to the Navy SEAL Foundation in memory of Wade."

"I'll have the paperwork ready for you to sign tomorrow."

The last person he saw before driving to Jansen's house for visitation was Lieutenant Hawkins. "Hey, Palmer, where's Alona Green?"

"You never give up, do you?"

"Never."

"I honestly don't know where she is. The last I saw her was yesterday at Naval Medical Center Portsmouth. This morning, when I went back, she was gone, and there was no record she had even been there."

"I'm not surprised."

"You're not?"

"Yesterday, the chief called. Mind you, in all the years I've been on the force, he's never once called. He told me to cancel the arrest warrant on Green and delete any reference to her from my case files. Can you believe that?"

79

AFTER STAYING A socially acceptable length of time, Palmer left Carol Jansen's and drove to the Hilton. He went to his room, changed into something more comfortable, and went to the outdoor bar. He was almost through his second beer. He looked at his watch—three o'clock in the afternoon, eight o'clock at night in Sevenoaks Weald. He had procrastinated for as long as he could. He stared at his cell phone on the table—five missed calls from Fiona. He was going to get an earful of chin music. He picked up the phone and punched in her number. She answered on the first ring.

"Are you at home?" he asked when she answered.

"Thank heaven you called. What's going on? I haven't heard from you in two days. I looked at the Virginia Beach news online and saw a story about the arrest of Owen Fuller. The BBC is reporting about an attack on the presidential palace in Afghanistan. They said the attack might have been in retaliation for the death of Hassan Aswad in December."

She was talking a mile a minute as she tried to knit together various reports on related subjects. When she stopped to take a breath, Palmer replied, "Which of those do you want me to address first?"

"Are you all right?"

"I'm fine. Yes, Owen Fuller's under arrest. And, at least for now, that's all I'm at liberty to say."

"What? You asked me to do your dirty work, and now you can't say anything? I'm surprised I haven't heard from Deb Fuller yet. She has my business card. Why didn't you tell me what was going on?"

Palmer took a drink of his beer. He held up the glass, motioning to the waitress that he needed another. "I can't say anything over the phone other than the information you gave me saved thousands of lives."

"Are you sure you're OK? You were probably in the middle of the action. It would be just like you not to tell me you're hurt."

"Really, I'm fine. I'm in Virginia Beach. The action was elsewhere."

"What should I say when Deborah Fuller contacts me? The international press is camped out on her doorstep."

"Don't worry about that. Deborah Fuller has been picked up for questioning and will be in protective custody for a while. And you'll be briefed on what to say."

"I'll be briefed? What do you mean? By whom?"

The waitress came with his beer. He intercepted it before she could set it on the table and took a drink.

"I only did what you asked and met with Deborah Fuller."

"Finding out Fuller's father was Hassan Aswad was critical to everything. You should receive a call from the State Department or the U.S. Embassy tomorrow or the next day. Until then, don't say anything to anyone." Palmer decided not to tell her about Aswad. He would leave that to them. The less that she and Deborah Fuller knew about what had happened, the better.

"This is all too much. Is this what life with you would be like?"

Palmer didn't respond. That was a loaded question, one that struck home. *Is she thinking about a life with me? Does anyone deserve to be put through this kind of life? Maybe I should be like Alona Green and avoid getting involved with anyone ... No. I don't want to wind up like her.*

"Well?" Fiona asked after the long pause.

"I love you, Fiona."

Now there was silence on the other end.

"Are you there?" he asked.

"Bloody hell! Men. You are all alike. You turn a woman's world upside down, make her worry herself to death, then think saying 'I love you' will make everything all right."

"I told you once that I don't seek excitement or trouble—it has a way of finding me. What if, at some point in the future, I put your life in danger, like in London last year? If you can't cope with that or with me, we may not have a future."

"Might not."

"What?"

"We might not have a future," Fiona said.

"Is that what you think?"

"No silly, the correct English use in that context is *might*, not *may*."

Palmer smiled and shook his head. She was correcting his English again, and that was a good thing.

ACKNOWLEDGMENTS

Since moving to Virginia Beach in 2009, I have been inspired by the natural beauty and rich history of the Hampton Roads area, as well as the dedication and sacrifice of the thousands of Hampton Roads men and women who serve in the military and intelligence communities, and their families. I hope, in some small way, my writing has highlighted this.

A writer can write in isolation, but to be successful a writer must depend on many people. I am indebted to everyone who provided me with encouragement, support, and technical advice. Without them, this work would never have been published. Most of all, I thank my wife, Mildred, former director of medical education and training for GlaxoSmithKline and adjunct associate professor at the Campbell University School of Pharmacy, for her heartfelt encouragement and reading of every version of my manuscript.

Writing and publishing a book is a complex process. In my opinion, one of the most important steps is selecting a group of beta readers to read and provide constructive criticism on a late draft of the manuscript. My superb group of beta readers included Judy Armfield, Robert Armfield, Lori Camper, Barbara Colavito, Diane DeAngelis, Caren Glenn, and Jeff Glenn. Their contributions to the quality of the final work cannot be understated. Judy Armfield, my sister and a lifelong teacher of English and journalism, also served as a proofreader, a talent for which I have much appreciation and little ability.

Special thanks also to the beta readers who wished to remain anonymous. To one in particular, our breakfast meeting at Citrus was the most valuable hour and a half I spent on the book. Next time, breakfast is on me.